"We didn't have an Xbox, so Josh thinks he's gone to heaven," she said.

Nate grimaced. "Molly hasn't touched it since Sonja and I split up. If I were a good father, I'd have played with her, but do you know what her favorite one is?"

Anna had to laugh. "Let's see. Would it be *Just Dance Kids*?"

"Dear God, yes. I felt like an idiot when I danced in high school."

She laughed again, even though it was impossible to imagine this man graceless. She was immediately ashamed of herself. Kyle had only died three months ago, and Nate Kendrick had played a role in the tragedy. She'd agreed to work for him because she was desperate, and for Molly's sake. Becoming friends and confidantes wasn't happening. Given his tall, lean body, the saunter that spoke of complete confidence and features that might be too rough to be called handsome, he had to turn women's heads wherever he went.

I can't be one of them, she thought desperately.

Dear Reader,

I hope I'm not too predictable, but I know I've returned to some of the same themes repeatedly in my Harlequin Superromance novels. Always love, but also family, the people who are missing in our lives, and the aftereffects of trauma or loss. Without intending any such theme, I've managed to combine all of that in this, my last Superromance.

His daughter, her kids, his troubled ex-wife and the blame game. Is Nate really a man who breaks promises? The heroine wants to blame him for her husband's death—but is that fair? And what kind of relationship can they possibly have when Nate also turns out to be the support Anna so desperately needs when she finds her husband's death left her and their two children destitute? Imagine having to let yourself lean on the person you also want to hate—or, from his perspective, to fall in love with a woman whose devastation might be your fault.

Love never comes easily in my books!

Look for me next at Harlequin Intrigue. Different kinds of stories, but I feel sure you'll still see the forces that have always driven my characters.

Signing out,

Janice

USA TODAY Bestselling Author

JANICE KAY JOHNSON

In a Heartbeat

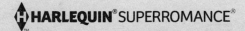

Recycling programs
for this product may
not exist in your area.

ISBN-13: 978-1-335-44918-4

In a Heartbeat

Copyright © 2018 by Janice Kay Johnson

Printed in U.S.A.

An author of more than ninety books for children and adults (more than seventy-five for Harlequin), **Janice Kay Johnson** writes about love and family—about the way generations connect and the power our earliest experiences have on us throughout life. A *USA TODAY* bestselling author and an eight-time finalist for a Romance Writers of America RITA® Award, she won a RITA® Award in 2008 for her Harlequin Superromance novel *Snowbound*. A former librarian, Janice raised two daughters in a small town north of Seattle, Washington.

Books by Janice Kay Johnson

HARLEQUIN SUPERROMANCE

Back Against the Wall
The Hero's Redemption
Her Amish Protectors
Plain Refuge
A Mother's Claim
Because of a Girl
The Baby Agenda
Bone Deep
Finding Her Dad
All That Remains
Making Her Way Home
No Matter What
A Hometown Boy
Anything for Her
Where It May Lead
From This Day On

One Frosty Night
More Than Neighbors
To Love a Cop

Brothers, Strangers

The Baby He Wanted
The Closer He Gets

Two Daughters

Yesterday's Gone
In Hope's Shadow

The Mysteries of Angel Butte

Bringing Maddie Home
Everywhere She Goes
All a Man Is
Cop by Her Side
This Good Man

Visit the Author Profile page at Harlequin.com for more titles.

I've been lucky to have worked with remarkably smart, strong, caring editors at Harlequin Superromance. To Victoria, Jane, Laura and Wanda: a huge thank-you. I wouldn't be the writer I am without you.

CHAPTER ONE

TRAFFIC WAS A BITCH, as always. Nate Kendrick ended one call when he was halfway across the I-90 bridge over Lake Washington and resigned himself to making the one he'd been putting off. Sonja would be pissed.

Nothing new about that.

She answered immediately, her tone suspicious. The minute she heard what he had to say, she screeched, "You always do this! What's your excuse this time?"

"I'm putting together a deal. It was supposed to be a go today, but one of the major investors got cold feet overnight. I have to find a replacement."

The silence unnerved him, since it was unlike her. Still quietly, she said, "Do you know how many thousand times I've heard that?"

"You knew what I did when you married me." Venture capitalism was high-risk, high-adrenaline and sometimes high-flying, like when a company in his portfolio went public in a big way or sold to an industry leader for a billion or more. You did not succeed in the business by taking a working day off to accompany a mob of six- and seven-year-olds to the beach. Or was it a river park? Nate couldn't remember.

"Some of us want an actual life." She sounded sad. Playing him. "I, for one, want my daughter to love me enough to come home for Christmas when she's an adult."

"Goddamn it, Sonja," he growled.

"We'll be fine without you."

Call ended.

Of course they would be. He loved his daughter, even as he knew she'd been slipping away from him since the divorce. But being one of two partners in a venture-capital firm meant demands that were never-ending. Who'd put Molly through college, if not him? Certainly not Sonja, who lived on her settlement from him. The settlement she wouldn't get if he crashed and burned.

Traffic opened up enough for him to merge onto I-5 for the short distance into downtown Seattle. By then he'd already taken the next call, obliging him to accept a no answer with outward amiability. But he and this guy would do business together again, so he ignored another incoming call to chat about the investor's son, excited about starting at Stanford this fall. Molly was ten years away from making any college decisions, thank God. Long practice let him think furiously as he talked.

What was his next best possibility? Stu Gribbin? He tended to like start-ups better than on-the-ground manufacturing, but it was worth a try.

Exiting from the freeway onto crowded streets hemmed in by tall buildings, Nate decided to wait to make the next call until he reached his office. He'd long since jettisoned his daughter's summer day camp field trip from his mind.

HONESTLY, THIS WASN'T the most exciting outing the camp director could have planned, but Melissa might have chosen the park without actually having visited it.

Anna Grainger wasn't complaining. Lounging on the picnic table bench with Kyle while the nearly forty kids ran off an excess of energy on the extensive mowed field was fine by her. From long habit, she kept an eye on her own two children—seven-year-old Josh and four-year-old Jenna—as well as the three additional kids she'd been assigned to supervise. All were buddies of Josh's, participating along with him in a crazy soccer game that didn't have any boundaries or rules she could see. Jenna had gravitated toward three or four other younger children also along for the field trip because their parents had volunteered to chaperone. Jenna didn't have a shy bone in her body.

Anna reached for her water bottle and took a

drink—tepid but wet. The coolers still held un-opened cans of soda and bottles of water on ice that couldn't have entirely melted, but she felt too lazy to get up.

"Couldn't they just have taken the kids to a local school?" her husband asked idly, not at all put out. With his hands clasped behind his head and his legs outstretched, he didn't look any more ambitious than she felt.

"You'd think so," she agreed. "Except Melissa did promise we'd go down to the riverbank after lunch. There's supposed to be a trail alongside."

"It's after lunch," he pointed out.

"Mmm-hmm." Wincing as Josh and another boy collided and crashed to the ground, she kept her eye on them until they jumped up, laughing and running back into the game.

"Some of the kids are heading that way," Kyle observed. "Is anyone paying attention?"

Anna straightened, seeing that he was right. And, no, Melissa was refereeing a dispute be-tween several quarrelsome boys, and Kimberly, one of the young assistants, had organized three-legged races that were winding up with most of the participants collapsed on the grass, giggling. Linda—no, she'd seen her escorting two girls to the bathroom facilities, such as they were.

"Maybe a parent," she began uncertainly.

"I don't see that little redhead." Kyle sat up. "The girl?"

"Molly? Her mother's here. She's probably with—"

But she wasn't. Anna spotted Molly's mother, Shana—no, Sonja, that was it—right away, sitting at another picnic table texting or playing a game on her phone, her head bent over it. Molly had been in Josh's class last year, and a couple times Anna had chatted casually with Sonja at special events.

Already on his feet, Kyle said, "I'll go on ahead, just to be on the safe side. I can catch any eager beavers." He set off at a trot across the field toward the band of trees along the Snoqualmie River.

For a second, she let her gaze linger on him. Unlike a lot of the other fathers, his body remained lean and athletic. By their mid- to late-thirties, so many men had started dressing to hide some softness around their waist, or had developed frown lines on their faces. Maybe stress did that; Kyle never seemed to feel a smidgen.

Disturbed by how acid that thought had been, Anna automatically checked on her daughter and the four boys. All were well.

A whistle shrilled and, like everyone else, she turned to the camp director. "Everyone, find your group leader! Time to head for the river, but stick with your adult."

Kids who had been spread across the field, including those who had been drifting toward the river trail, ran back to the adults. Just as the boys and Jenna reached her, Anna heard a woman say, "Anyone see Molly?"

She turned. Sonja was scanning the area.

"A couple of the girls went to the bathroom," another mother said.

"No, they're back," someone else said.

Anna stood. "Kyle thought some kids might have started toward the river, so he went ahead."

The whistle blew again. "Everybody, freeze!"

The kids became as still as statues, eyes wide. "Parents, is anyone from your group missing? Do you have an extra?"

Kids and parents sorted themselves out. Only one child was missing: Molly Kendrick, who, with that bright head of hair, would have stood out, anyway.

Hyperventilating, Sonja cried, "But I was watching! I just…"

Just let her attention stray. Which almost any parent did on occasion, although this was a poor time and place to take her eyes off not only her daughter, but also the other three children she was supposed to supervise.

Skin tight beside her eyes, the middle-aged director, a wiry, energetic woman, said, "Anna, can you take my group, too, while I make sure your husband has found Molly?"

"You bet." Smiling, she collected the additional three girls and said, "Okay, let's start that way, but stay together."

Melissa jogged ahead, disappearing into the trail through the trees. The rest of them followed in a clump.

Where was Kyle? If he'd located Molly, Anna thought he'd have ushered her back to join the group. On a tinge of fear, Anna glanced over her shoulder at the parking lot. Could Molly have wandered that way? Been lured into a car? The river wasn't the only frightening possibility.

Seeing that Jenna was lagging, Anna said, "How about a piggyback ride, kiddo?"

"I'm tired." She still napped and, really, had held out well today, considering.

Anna crouched to let her climb on, after which she walked faster. The older kids had no trouble keeping up. The nine of them reached the trail first, plunging into the cool, shadowy depths beneath the trees.

A minute later, José said, "Did you hear that?"

"No—" But then she did. It sounded like sobbing. She broke into a run, the kids thundering behind her.

She saw the river first, green and higher than it should have been in late June. All the rivers were, after the exceptionally rainy spring and early summer they'd had. Close to the shore, the water was clear enough for her to see rocks beneath the surface, which seemed placid, except…well, those ripples might be deceptive.

The supposed riverbank trail seemed to be partially overgrown with blackberries and other nuisances like salmonberries. But a small beach allowed passage along the water.

The screams reached a crescendo. Jenna bouncing on her back, Anna raced upstream toward Melissa, who crouched with her arms around the sobbing girl. Oh, dear heavens—Molly was soaked, head to toe. She'd gone into the water. Anna's next thought was overwhelming relief. They'd come so close to a tragedy.

Somebody brushed by her. Sonja. She raced to her daughter and dropped to her knees. "What were you *thinking*? You know the rules!"

Molly cast herself into her mother's arms and cried even harder.

Melissa straightened, her gaze going to Anna as she waited for her to approach.

Only then did Anna feel a faint drumbeat of apprehension. Where was Kyle? Shouldn't he be here, too? Unless, once he was sure Molly was safe, he'd gone looking for other strays…

But she knew. She knew, even before Melissa drew her away from the boys, who stared in fascination at the girl who would be in *so much* trouble.

"Molly says—" Melissa swallowed. "She says she was being swept away, but Josh's daddy went in the water after her. That he threw her toward the bank, but when she turned around he was being carried downstream. Then she couldn't see him at all. He's probably made it to shore somewhere, but I called 911 to be on the safe side."

Anna began to tremble. "Kyle can't swim."

NATE IGNORED THE first two calls from his ex. He was having an intense conversation with another of his "angel" investors, who was on the fence about taking this opportunity.

"Send me what your analysts have, and I'll take a look. But you know I'm leery of anything geared to the young twenties. Hell, I don't understand most of it. Or them."

Nate laughed. "Who does? But the money is in that market, whether we like to admit it or not."

"Yeah, yeah," John Reynolds grumbled, a note of humor in his voice. "Let me look, and I'll call you back."

"Good enough."

Just as he ended the call, Nate heard the beep of yet another call coming in.

And, yes, it was his ex-wife again. What, she needed to let him know what a good time they were having without him? Irritated, Nate answered nonetheless.

"Sonja?"

"Nate, you know we were visiting a river-side park." Her voice shook. "Molly sneaked away and waded out into the river. She…she got pulled out into the current. One of the fathers went in after her and managed to push her to a gravel bar. But Nate…he didn't make it out. This man I don't know *died* to save our daughter."

"Jesus," he whispered.

"And you couldn't even answer your phone!"

Sidestepping the accusation, he said, "Molly. Is she okay?"

"She's hysterical, how do you think she is?" Sonja's voice was thickened by what had likely been a storm of tears. "We're on our way to the hospital. She swallowed water and… I don't know. She wants her daddy," she said bitterly.

He seriously doubted Molly had expressed any such desire. Since the divorce, she'd grown increasingly shy with him. Each time he took her for a weekend, she acted as if she was being palmed off on a stranger.

He said simply, "Overlake Hospital?"

Background voices told him Sonja wasn't alone with their daughter, thank God. She came back. "Yes."

He strode out of the office. "I'm on my way. Wait for me there." Pausing only to tell his assistant that he had an emergency, he went down the hall to the elevator.

As it dropped to the parking garage, Nate saw

that he had missed texts, too. He'd felt the phone vibrating, but that was normal—texts piled up all day. This time, there were three from Sonja. The last one was all caps, multiple exclamation points.

MOLLY ALMOST DIED BECAUSE OF YOU!!! WHY WON'T YOU ANSWER YOUR PHONE????

Shit.

At least it was early enough that traffic should still flow. Tension riding him, he pushed the speed limit, weaving in and out, risking a ticket during this reverse commute to the Eastside of Lake Washington. *Molly almost died because of you!!!* What about the man who'd rescued his daughter? Had somebody really died, or had that been Sonja hyperbole?

Pain shot up his neck, wrapping around his temples and forehead. Fear, regret, guilt—they all churned in his belly.

He didn't make it out. This man I don't know died to save our daughter.

Overlake Hospital overlooked Highway 405 in Bellevue. Even so, after exiting the freeway Nate had to make several turns before he reached the parking garage beneath the hospital. Frustrated at each red light, he tapped his fingers on the steering wheel. In the garage, he took the first available open slot, ran for the elevator and rode up to the ground-floor emergency services.

A dozen people sat scattered throughout the waiting room, but Nate saw Sonja and Molly immediately, merged into one with his daughter on Sonja's lap, head on her shoulder.

Sinking into the chair beside them, he said huskily, "Kiddo. How are you?"

The distress in Molly's big eyes felt like a sucker punch to Nate's belly. Instead of answering, she buried her head against her mother's neck so she didn't have to see him. Maybe it hadn't been a punch. A knife twisting, instead.

Staring straight ahead, Sonja didn't want to look at him, either, but she said in a near monotone, "The doctor says she swallowed a lot of water, that's all. Mostly, she was petrified. I'd take her home, except I was too upset to drive. My car is still at the park. I'll have to take a taxi."

He ignored that. Of course he wouldn't let her take a taxi, and she knew it. "What about the man? Was he brought here, too?"

Very slowly her head turned. Her eyes blazed, her lip curled. "So they could bring him back from the dead?"

The air left his lungs in a whoosh. "He really died?"

"You think I just *said* that?"

"No. I hoped they'd pulled him out."

"They did. Dead."

A man had died rescuing Nate's daughter. *Because I wasn't there.*

"Who is—" Oh, hell. "Who *was* he?"

"Kyle Grainger. His son, Josh, was in Molly's class last year. *Both* of Josh's parents came today."

The searing words were bad enough, but the hatred in her eyes...

No wonder Molly had become so skittish around Nate. What had Sonja been telling his daughter about him?

"Is she here?" he managed to say. "Josh's mother?"

"How would I know?"

What would he have said, anyway? *I'll come to your husband's funeral in thanks for him saving my kid's life?*

"All right," he said. "We can go pick up your car if you feel up to driving. If not, I'll take you home. If you'll give me the keys, I'll have somebody bring it to your place."

"Mr. Fixit," she jeered. "But why not? Molly needs to go home, not drive all over the county."

She was right, of course. Maybe he did suck at being a parent. He loved his daughter, though, and he'd have sworn she loved him, too. He worked long hours, but he'd spent a great deal of his off time with Molly. The one who had been shorted was Sonja, but he'd expected her to understand. But, hey, probably his marriage had been over a lot longer than he'd known.

Standing, he reached out for Molly. "Let me carry her."

"No!" Shielding their little girl with her body, Sonja struggled to her feet. "She needs her mother. Just take us home. Then you can go back to work."

Aware that people were staring, he clenched his teeth and said nothing. He might go back to work. Clearly, Sonja wouldn't be inviting him in so he could talk to Molly about her terrifying experience. His beautiful house wasn't much anymore but a place where he slept. He'd have happily let Sonja have it, but she'd wanted only money.

"If I stayed in this house, I'd keep thinking *you* might walk in the door anytime." Her ringing endorsement of their marriage.

He walked beside his ex-wife and daughter down the corridor to the elevator. Molly clung to her mother and didn't once look at him.

They had the elevator to themselves until it stopped at the lobby level, where the doors opened. A lone woman waited, blond hair falling out of an elastic, strands straggling around her too-pale, fine-boned face. She looked drained, as if she couldn't summon the will to so much as step into the elevator even if she had pushed the button to call it.

Instinct drove Nate to take a step toward her. As he did, her vacant stare shifted from him to Sonja and Molly. Horror took over her face. Her eyes fastened on him, and she lurched back. The next thing he knew, she was hurrying away, walking faster and faster.

The elevator doors tried to close but bounced back open with him in the way. He didn't move. It tried again, and finally he stepped back.

Not looking at Sonja, he said, "That was her, wasn't it?"

"Yes."

An impassive expression was his default. Inside, he'd been shredded. His heart raced. He didn't think he'd ever forget the way the new widow had looked at him.

CHAPTER TWO

THE MIDDLE-AGED WOMAN gazed at Anna with unmistakable pity. "You weren't aware your husband cashed out his retirement fund?"

Given the past weeks, she'd grown increasingly numb, unable to feel much other than a crawling sense of fear. Pity couldn't touch her.

She didn't respond directly to the question. "When did he do that?"

"The week before..." She hesitated.

He died.

The matching fund wouldn't have been much, given the short time Kyle had worked here, but anything would have been better than nothing.

Somehow she managed to nod and even smile as she rose to her feet. Pride was a wonderful thing. "Thank you. I so wish he'd kept better records." Anna held on to her smile until she'd left the building and was making her way across the parking lot.

Better records? What she so wished was that her husband hadn't been a fool. She'd begun to realize that much over the past few years, but her attempts to talk sense into him hadn't made a dent. Learning how deceitful he'd been, *that* came as a surprise. He'd erased every bit of security she'd thought she had. And for what? She'd been so enraged to see the pittance he'd gotten when he cashed out his life insurance. It hadn't developed much value, since they'd only purchased it when she was pregnant with Josh, but it would have been paid out in full now that he'd died—$100,000.

"I want to be sure you and any kids we have are taken care of," Kyle had murmured in her ear after they'd left the insurance office. His smile had been so tender. "Even if something happens to me, you'll have this."

That shock had been the worst, if not the last. No insurance payout. No savings. No retirement funds. Over time, he had cashed out everything, often paying substantial penalties to do it. With what he'd gotten, he had made risky investments that all bombed, apparently certain each time that he'd make big money.

No, what she should wish was that *she* hadn't been such a fool. She'd asked about money and investments, but allowed him to get away with explanations that didn't quite make sense and reassurances that he had everything handled. Since he had been working and she hadn't, she'd felt a little funny about demanding an equal financial partnership.

And yet Anna had grown increasingly uneasy and frustrated with Kyle's inability to stick with a job. Early in their marriage, she had believed in him wholeheartedly, but by the time they started a family, she saw the pattern.

With each new job, he would start with great enthusiasm. Like clockwork, she'd watch that enthusiasm dim. He was bored. They weren't making use of his talents. He'd start looking around for something better. "Today was the last straw," he would finally declare, with great indignation. "I had to quit. But don't worry, I won't have any trouble finding a new job. A better one."

He hadn't, until the last time, two years ago. His inconstancy had begun to look bad on a résumé. It took two months before he was offered a position he grudgingly accepted. She'd cut every corner she could to get them through until a paycheck.

Kyle teased her for being a worrier. "Lucky you have me to provide balance." How many times had she heard him say that?

In her car now, Anna put the key in the ignition but didn't start the engine. She sat without moving, staring ahead blindly as her mind raced.

She'd have to take Josh out of day camp. One less bill. Except…then when she had to go out, she'd have to pay Mrs. Schaub more to watch both kids. He was happy with his friends at the camp. If she could find a job right away...

Waitressing? Being a receptionist? Day care? She could offer day care at home and not have to pay other people to watch her kids, but only if she could afford to keep the house, which she couldn't. Substitute teaching for the local school district, even if the work proved to be reasonably steady, wasn't an option. Given the area's cost of living, the pay was inadequate, and as a part-time employee, she wouldn't have benefits. Anyway—school didn't start for another six weeks.

Fear cramped in her again at the reminder that in less than two weeks, she and the kids would lose their health insurance.

What it came down to was that no job she was qualified to do would pay the basic bills, never mind justify the additional day care. Staying home with the kids, not working for so many years, had been a mistake of monstrous proportion. She'd trusted the man she loved, who had been *un*trustworthy.

A man who'd willingly sacrificed his own life to save a young girl he didn't even know.

How could she harbor feelings so bitter, so angry, for the funny, kind man who would do something like that?

How could she not?

She almost had to leave Josh at day camp

until she could finish painting the entire interior of their house and pack enough of their possessions to make it ready for prospective buyers to view, she concluded. At least Jenna took naps and was usually able to play quietly while Mommy scrubbed and painted and sorted. With his energy level, Josh couldn't be as patient.

Maybe there'd be a quick sale. But her panic didn't subside, and for good reason. Even if the house sold at full price, she wouldn't end up with all that much money. The market had sagged since they'd bought the modest rambler in Bellevue. They hadn't spent the money they should have to update it. Increasingly, people expected granite countertops, skylights, hardwood floors, not aluminum windows, ancient Formica, worn beige carpets.

The real estate agent had strongly advised new carpet, at least. Anna could put that on a credit card and pay it off once the house sold. Other improvements were out of reach.

She had no choice but to move away. The Seattle area was chasing San Francisco and New York City for the most expensive places in the country to live. Of course, salaries would be lower in Montana or eastern Oregon or wherever else she went, too. At the very least, she'd have to find a college town where she could take classes to refresh her teaching certificate or make herself employable doing something besides hoisting a heavily laden tray or answering phones.

When finally the tension eased enough to leave her limp, she started the car and saw the dashboard clock. She'd been chasing herself on the hamster wheel for twenty minutes. Twenty wasted minutes. Usually, she put off her frightened scrabbling in search of solutions until bedtime. Who needed sleep when you could lie rigid in the dark and try to figure out how to survive with two young children when you had next to no money?

Anna had never imagined being so close to having no home at all.

THE ONLY LIGHTS in the family room were one standing lamp and the ever-shifting colors of the TV. Through the window, Nate saw the glitter of lights across the lake in Seattle and a few sparkling on the mast of a boat gliding through the dark water.

Staying unnoticed in the doorway, he glanced at the TV to see what Molly was watching. *The Lego Movie.* Amusing, as he recalled.

He switched his attention to his daughter, who had curled into the smallest possible ball in the corner of the sofa. She clutched a throw pillow in her arms as if it was a flotation device—all that would keep her from drowning. He'd swear she hadn't blinked in at least a minute. She was either mesmerized by the movie or not seeing it at all.

At least she wasn't watching *Moana* again. That one, with the tense father/daughter thing going, made him uncomfortable.

All she'd wanted since he'd picked her up this morning was to watch a succession of DVDs. Having a waterfront home on Lake Washington used to be a plus. Today, she'd been careful to keep her back to the view of the lake. Okay, that was understandable, but she hadn't wanted to ride her bike, which he kept in his garage, either, or play a board game. He'd bought two skateboards a while back, one child-sized, one adult, along with pads for knees and elbows and helmets. Sonja didn't approve, of course, but skateboarding on the driveway was one of the few activities done with her father that had delighted Molly. Today? "No, thank you, Daddy."

After thanking him politely and refusing to go out to a pizza place they both liked, she nibbled at what he put in front of her for lunch and dinner. She hadn't talked any more than she absolutely had to.

Abruptly, he'd had enough.

He flicked on the overhead light and strode to the sofa, where he grabbed the remote and turned off both DVD player and television.

Molly sat up. "Daddy!"

"That's enough, honey. You haven't taken

your eyes off that TV all day. You and I need to talk." He sat on the middle cushion, within reach of his kid.

Her lower lip pooched out. "I was watching the movie!"

"How many times have you seen it?" Unsurprised that she didn't answer, he said, "Often enough to know how it ends."

She bent her head and stared at her lap.

He reached over and gently tipped up her chin. Her big eyes, a vivid green, finally met his.

"I know falling in the river scared you. But keeping everything you feel inside isn't healthy. You haven't told me yet what really did happen."

She mumbled something about her mother.

"I need you to talk to me, too."

Tears shimmered in her eyes. "Mr. Grainger is dead," she whispered. "Like Tuffet."

Tuffet had been her cat, named because he'd let her lie on him whenever she wanted. When Sonja had moved out, she'd taken the cat along with Molly. According to Molly, Tuffet got sick and died. Sonja had admitted to him that the cat had somehow slipped out and been hit by a car.

"I know," Nate said now, tugging Molly over to lean on him.

"Mommy says it's your fault, because it was hard to watch so many kids at the same time." Even her intonations parroted her mother's. "If you were there, you coulda watched *me*."

"That's true," he had to say, "but most of the kids only had one parent along, didn't they? And were assigned three other kids."

After a hesitation, her head bobbed against him.

His eyes stung from unfamiliar grief mixed with the rare joy at holding her in his arms. He'd loved his little carrottop with unexpected ferocity from the minute the doctor had handed over the beet-red, squalling newborn. If she'd drowned... Even as he shied away from an inner vision of her limp, lifeless, pallid body, his heart cramped painfully.

"Mommy said it's my fault, too, 'cuz I did something I wasn't s'posed to."

Sharp anger supplanted the pain. Molly was old enough to take responsibility for her actions, but not to confront that kind of guilt. What the hell was Sonja thinking?

"Okay." He shifted to allow him to see her face, wet with tears. "Here's the thing. Kids break rules all the time. They hide from their parents, or they run from them because it's fun to be chased. They sneak an extra cookie, or feed an icky food to the cat instead of eating it the way Mommy said they had to."

She'd quit blinking again, but she was listening.

"I broke my arm when I wasn't much older than you because I climbed a tree after my dad said I couldn't. My brother and I used to climb out a skylight to sit on the roof at night, too."

Her eyes widened. "Did you fall off?"

"No, and your grandma and grandad never caught us." Of course, there was the time Adam had jumped off, but that was another story.

Her forehead crinkled, and she gave a small nod.

Give your kid ideas, why don't you?

"The point is, kids don't always do what their parents or other adults say. Once in a while, they even hurt themselves, like I did when I broke my arm. But it would never have occurred to me that someone *else* might get hurt because of what I did. That's because it almost never happens. You didn't mean it to happen."

Nate was disconcerted to realize he couldn't tell what she was thinking. He forged on, anyway.

"Why did you sneak away?"

She didn't want to answer, but finally said, "I was bored. I was s'posed to stay with the other girls Mommy had to watch, but they didn't want to play with me. And anyway—" she began to sound indignant "—Melissa *said* we were going to the river, but instead there was this big, boring field, and I didn't want to play soccer or run dumb three-legged races or just sit there. Mommy wasn't any fun, 'cuz she was—"

She shrank from him in alarm at what she'd almost said.

Sonja was what? He decided not to press; asking Molly to betray her mother, if that was the case, would only do more damage.

"I would give anything to have been able to come with you that day," he said finally. "But I can't go back and make a different decision."

She nodded solemnly.

"I bet you feel the same."

Her face crumpled and she swallowed, but nodded again.

"Same deal. You can't go back. I'm more grateful than I can say to Mr. Grainger. I can't imagine losing you."

"But…Josh and his little sister lost their dad." Tears fell anew. "Because of *me*. And…and *I* can swim."

"Mr. Grainger knew that a girl your size couldn't possibly be a strong enough swimmer to get out of the current. It pulled you away from the bank, didn't it?"

Her head bobbed. "I was so scared, Daddy."

"I doubt he expected to die. He probably thought he'd be able to put his feet down, because rivers aren't deep like the lake, especially at this time of year. Or he hoped to reach a gravel bar or a snag he could grab. But because he wasn't a good swimmer, he must also have known that he might be giving his life to save yours. And you know what?"

She waited.

"Wherever he is, I don't think he regrets making that decision. Most adults would have made the same one."

"But you're a *good* swimmer," she argued.

"Sure, I probably could have battled my way out of the river. But something could happen another time." He groped for illustrations. "I might have to step out onto a ledge I know won't support my weight so I can throw a little girl to safety before it gives way. Run out into traffic on the freeway to save a child, even when the chances are good that the cars won't be able to stop and I'll be hit." He paused. "Do you understand?"

"Yes," she whispered. "Would Mommy do that, too?"

"Of course she would," he said, hugging Molly harder, even though he really didn't know. For Molly, yes—whatever Sonja's flaws, she loved her daughter. Otherwise? He hated that he even had to wonder.

"I wish…"

"I know, punkin, I know." He rested his cheek on the top of Molly's head. She'd talked to him. Thank God, for the first time in a long while she'd opened up.

Now he was left with that unfinished sentence. What *had* Sonja been doing while her daughter slipped away?

And what about the kids who'd lost their father? The woman who lost her husband? Every time he remembered that moment, her grief becoming horror when she realized who he was, the claws of guilt sank deeper into his flesh.

A MONTH LATER, Anna trotted down the sidewalk toward the nearest park. Wanting to stay aware of traffic, she hadn't yet turned on her iPod. There was a time she'd exercised when Kyle was home with the kids. Now, she had to pay Mrs. Schaub to watch Jenna for even this brief escape. Today she was killing two birds with one stone—awful saying that it was—because a real estate agent was showing her house. She knew he actually was, because she hadn't gone a block when she'd heard an engine and glanced back to see a gleaming silver sedan turning into her driveway.

If there wasn't an offer soon, she'd have to go to the bank that held the mortgage and explain why she couldn't make her payments. She prayed they'd give her some time although, of course, the unmade payments, and presumably a penalty, too, would then come out of the already too-skimpy proceeds when the house did sell.

Running was supposed to be a time when she could zone out, but no more.

At least the park lay just ahead. The trail was packed dirt, easier on her knees. Reaching the last crosswalk, she scanned automatically for traffic, seeing only parked cars.

She'd stepped off the curb when alarm zinged through her. There'd been an odd glint of light, as if… Was that a camera pointing at *her*? Continuing across the street, she looked.

A man sat in a black SUV, the driver's side window rolled down, and, yes, he was still pointing a camera with a huge lens at her.

The camera disappeared fast when he realized she'd seen him. When she broke into a run diagonally across the street toward the SUV, his window slid up. With the glass tinted, she couldn't make out his face.

Maneuvering out of the parking spot was taking him too long, though. Maybe this was stupid, but Anna harbored so much anger atop her fear these days, she didn't *care* if this was dangerous. She flung herself at the driver's door and hammered on the window, yelling "Stop!"

He edged forward. She leaped in front of his bumper, forcing him to brake or hit her. He braked. When she pulled her phone from the cuff on her upper arm, the window slid down.

She took a quick picture of the license plate before she confronted him. Taking courage from the presence of a couple across the street who'd started to get into their own car but were now gaping, instead, Anna glared. "Who are you, and why were you photographing me?"

Late thirties, early forties, the man was thin, pleasant-looking. Nondescript, really. "I'm a private investigator," he admitted. "Ah, your insurance claim…"

"I made no insurance claim. I want to see your license."

He produced it. His name was Darren Smith, and his employer was Moonrise Investigations.

"Smith? Really?" She handed it back.

Without a word, he tugged a wallet from his back pocket and flipped it open to show his driver's license.

"Fine," she snapped. And, crap, the couple were now getting into their car, believing the drama to be over. The busy playground was too far away for any of the parents to notice her. "I'm calling the police. You'll have to run me over to get away."

She tapped in 911. Before she could push Send, he swore and said, "Don't do that. I'll tell you."

Anna let her thumb hover over her phone. "Talk."

"I was hired by a Mr. Nathan Kendrick."

The name hit her like a sledgehammer.

"He wanted to know what's going on with you, that's all. Be sure you and the kids are okay."

Fury burned through her. "You've been taking pictures of my *children* without my permission?"

"Ah…"

"You son of a bitch," she said bitingly. "I bet your employer won't be thrilled when I file a lawsuit. With a little luck, you can kiss that license goodbye!"

Unable to look at him for another second, she ran up the street until she could easily dodge into the park. If she'd had the house to herself, she'd have gone straight home. Jogging held zero appeal, but she grimly started in on her laps through the park, anyway.

Once free to go home and shower, she would pay a visit to Nate Kendrick, the man whose own ex-wife blamed for Kyle's death.

CHAPTER THREE

DESPITE A FRACTURED ability to focus, Nate was doing his best to work through email when his desk intercom buzzed.

His assistant, Kim Pualani, said apologetically, "A woman is here to see you. She doesn't have an appointment, but says you'll know who she is."

He braced himself. "Her name?"

"Ah…Ms. Grainger. Anna Grainger."

Kim knew what had happened and must have guessed this visit had to do with the tragedy.

"Send her in," he agreed, although talking to Kyle Grainger's widow was the last thing he wanted to do after taking the call from the PI.

"She's on the warpath," Smith had warned.

But Nate didn't see an alternative to letting her lay into him. He couldn't guess whether she'd accept an apology or anything else from him, but he had to try.

The door swung open, allowing him a glimpse of the woman he'd seen so briefly that day in the hospital. He rose to his feet as she walked in and Kim closed the door behind her.

At least now, past the shock, Mrs. Grainger was vitally alive, if also furious. The red spots on her cheeks would have told him that much, even without the PI's warning.

Nate had the uncomfortable realization that he could be attracted to this woman, long and sleek, honey-blond hair captured smoothly in some arrangement he couldn't see, her dark blue eyes snapping with the same anger that accented high, perfectly honed cheekbones.

He didn't even want to imagine how she'd react if she guessed her effect on him.

"Mrs. Grainger," he said. "I'm glad you're here. I'd intended to stop soon at your house to speak to you. Please, have a seat."

She marched forward until his desk blocked her. Obviously, sitting down for a civil conversation wasn't on her agenda. "Once you'd compiled your photographic record of every step I've taken? Every step my *children* have taken?"

"I didn't ask—"

Anna Grainger talked right over him. "Do you have any idea how violated I feel? How enraged I am to discover someone has been spying on me? While he was at it, did your PI capture some suggestive pictures through a crack in my blinds? Or one of the kids undressing for bed? Which do you prefer, Mr. Kendrick, little girls or little boys?"

His own temper sparked, but with practiced

calm he said, "You must guess why I hired a PI firm to monitor how you're doing. I didn't ask for photographs, and I haven't seen any. All I've been given are verbal or written reports."

Vibrating with fury, she snapped, "Then please explain why I caught that…that *creep* photographing me when I went for a run? Did you need to know I was getting my exercise? Should I reassure you I'm taking my vitamins?"

This wasn't going anywhere good.

"Mrs. Grainger. All I wanted was to know how you and the kids were. Whether your husband had left you provided for."

Unfortunately, part of the initial report provided the disturbing answer. Anna Grainger was close to destitute. Her husband had apparently lost all their money and then some in ill-judged investments. He seemed to have had a genius for making terrible decisions. It was possible they'd shared that genius, except her name hadn't been on any of the paperwork Smith had been able to trace.

"That is none of your business," she said. "*I* am none of your business. Do you hear me?"

"I hear you, and I disagree. A series of circumstances led to your husband losing his life to save my child's life. That places me deeply in your debt."

She laughed, a caustic sound. "Then I absolve you. I do not want anything from you."

"I can't accept that."

Her head tipped. "What are you offering? Have you put a suitable price on Kyle's head?"

Nate winced. He had considered offering her money, which she needed as much or more than having her wastrel husband back. He hadn't thought of it that way, and now that he did, knew an offer would be ill-received. Still…

"If you sued me or my ex-wife, a court would determine a suitable settlement."

"Blood money."

He didn't say anything.

"That, Mr. Kendrick, is why I won't be suing you. When I caught your PI spying on me, I had every intention of suing his ass, and yours, too. But then everyone would think I was just trying to soak you for money in recompense."

"You care what everyone else thinks?"

She stiffened. "I care what *I* think of myself. Butt out, Mr. Kendrick. One more hint that you're stalking me and I'll call the cops."

Crap. He hadn't thought of what he was doing that way, either.

"Will you listen to my offer first?" Not money. He'd had one other, wild idea, which he'd go with.

"Oh, by all means."

"I'm guessing that you're applying for jobs."

Her shift of expression told him he was right.

"Let me offer you one. We have a large staff

at K & L Ventures. Large enough that there are nearly always openings."

"For a janitor, perhaps? Or do you run a day care down in some alcove in the garage? Well, probably not that, since you'd be depositing your own daughter in it, wouldn't you?"

He opened his mouth, but she didn't pause.

"What is it you think I can do, Mr. Kendrick? I have a teaching certificate, but my only class-room experience is student teaching. I'm not a whiz on a computer. Corporate finance? Well, no." She abandoned sarcasm. "I don't need your pity or charity. I don't want *anything* from you. Is that clear?"

"You're entitled to compensation for your loss."

Anna Grainger snorted and stormed out of his office.

HER REAL ESTATE agent cleared his throat. "The house has only been on the market for six weeks, Mrs. Grainger. That's not a long time."

Usually, Alan Lang glowed with energy and enthusiasm. However, he had the kind of mobile face that he could rearrange at will. Right now, he was projecting encouragement and understanding.

Unfortunately, he probably understood her situation all too well. In his business, he'd know desperation when he saw it.

They sat in her living room, freshly painted, decluttered and as clean as she could make it. She'd become a tyrant about making both kids put everything away the second they were done with it. With kids the ages of hers, it took constant vigilance to be sure the house was ready to show at any time of the day or night. Not a dirty cup was left in the sink, a toothpaste smear on a bathroom countertop, a bed unmade or the lawn a quarter of an inch too long.

She'd been astonished to discover how often the doorbell rang during the dinner hour. Invariably, she'd find an apologetic agent on the doorstep asking if she'd mind if potential buyers just took a quick look.

"Of course not," she'd say with a gracious smile. Like she could afford to say no.

She and her children were currently living an unreal life. A model family living in a model house, except she and the house both were unacceptably shabby.

This afternoon, Alan had stopped by ostensibly to pick up the business cards left by all the agents who'd showed the house. Anna knew he always followed up with a call to find out what the clients had thought. When he'd suggested they sit down and talk, a chill of apprehension had made her wish she had a sweater or sweatshirt at hand.

"When we bought this place, most houses

were snapped up within twenty-four hours of being listed." *We*. The very word gave Anna a pang that she had to shake off. "To buy one, you had to be in the right place at the right time."

"With even a slight downturn in prices, the market favors buyers. I'm sorry to say that's what we're facing right now."

"Okay," she said cautiously. "But people are looking."

"They are. Which I found encouraging at first." He cleared his throat. "But now… We haven't had so much as a nibble. The message I'm hearing from other agents is that the property is overpriced given the need for updates."

Anna's heart sank. He had set the price for her house higher than he'd liked in the first place at her insistence. She'd wanted to give herself room to negotiate. "You think we need to lower what we're asking."

"I suggest a twenty-thousand-dollar drop."

She closed her eyes. Twenty thousand dollars— and offers would likely come in ten to twenty thousand dollars lower yet.

A couple calming breaths later, Anna met his eyes. As with so much else these days, she had no choice. She had to get out from under the mortgage, even if she walked away with nothing.

"Go for it," she agreed, and saw his relief. He probably hadn't expected her to be sensible.

A minute later, as she was showing him out, he commented, "You've kept the place looking good despite, er…" His cheeks reddened.

"Having a four-year-old and a seven-year-old living here?" She knew he wasn't married and had no children yet. Even though he was probably close to her age, twenty-nine, Anna felt like a stodgy matron in comparison, their life experiences so vastly different. "You have no idea," she said ruefully.

"Well." He hovered briefly on the porch. "Let's keep our fingers crossed this week."

"Let's," she said, if somewhat drily.

After closing the door behind him, she stayed facing it as she battled panic. What if this drop in price wasn't enough? What if…?

"Mo-om!" Jenna called from the bedroom.

Anna squared her shoulders, turned and put her game face on. She hoped the kids attributed to grief most of the stress they had to sense in her. Whatever else she did, she had to protect Kyle in their eyes. That's what they needed—and what he'd earned with his sacrifice.

"CAN I STAY HOME?" Molly begged, sounding subdued. "I don't feel very good."

The minute Nate had seen who was calling, he'd known she or her mother would be making an excuse to keep her from spending the weekend with him. "Upset stomach?" he asked.

"Uh-huh."

Two weeks ago, a friend whose name he didn't recognize had asked her to a birthday party. Last minute, of course. He'd insisted on taking her out to dinner that Monday. She'd hardly met his gaze, nibbled at her pizza and mumbled a few words in response to his questions or remarks.

Phone conversations with her were useless. He kept having to say, "What?" or "I didn't hear what you said."

He'd learned that she hadn't gone back to day camp. She didn't know what teacher she'd have this year yet. When he asked if she was excited about school starting in less than two weeks, he got the verbal equivalent of a shrug.

The breakthrough he thought they'd made, talking honestly about the tragedy, had been a one-off. Molly didn't want to talk to him, didn't want to see him.

"You can be sick just as well here," he told her now. "I'll make you chicken-noodle soup, if you can keep it down, and rent some videos. I can give you hugs, too."

Silence.

Grimly determined, Nate said, "Go get your mom, Molly. I'd like to talk to her."

More silence. Waiting, he presumed she was doing as he asked.

"What?" his ex-wife snapped.

"What's up with Molly?"

"She doesn't want to go. What a surprise. Thash what happens when you let your daughter down nuff...*e*-nough times." If she thought the careful correction helped, she was wrong.

"You're drunk," he said flatly.

"I've had a cup...couple a glash...glasses of white wine. So what?"

She'd been drinking too much the last year of their marriage. He hadn't liked it then, and he liked it even less now that Molly was alone with her. Too often, when they spoke in the evening, he could tell she was plastered. If he thought she was drinking when she and Molly went out... But, so far, he had no indication that happened.

A lightning bolt struck. Had Sonja been taking nips from a bottle that day at the park? Was *that* what Mommy had been doing when Molly slipped away? Sickened, he wondered how he could find out.

"I'm on my way to pick up Molly," he said. "I'm legally entitled to have her, and considering your state, she'll be safer with me. I'll be there in fifteen minutes. Have her ready to go."

She was yelling at him when he cut her off. At least the other woman who had sliced and diced him recently hadn't raised her voice.

Nate sat for a minute in his car before he felt patient enough to join the crazy after-six-o'clock traffic in downtown Seattle, laid out with one-way north-south streets and steep east-west streets, all inadequate for the number of cars that poured out of parking garages at this time of day. Usually, he avoided the mess by staying late. Eight, even ten o'clock, although he could just as well answer emails and do his research on his laptop at home. Traffic, he knew, was only an excuse.

He heard Sonja's voice in his head. *Some of us want an actual life.*

That stung, because she was right. He didn't have a life outside work anymore. Why bother? He liked the highs and lows on the job better than he had living with Sonja's wildly swinging moods. Until another man died saving Nate's little girl, he hadn't seen any reason to change.

He shook his head and started the car. The one change he intended to make had to do with Molly. He wasn't prepared to lose his daughter because his ex-wife had turned her against him.

He was lucky enough to find a parking spot close to the thirty-floor tower where Sonja had bought a condo. When Sonja opened the door, he saw Molly on the sofa with a packed, pink bag beside her. His once bright, cheerful child sat with hunched shoulders, her hair hanging over her face.

Sonja called him a few vicious names before he could usher Molly out. Once she was in the hall, he turned back and said quietly, "Next time, I'll record you. You'd be smart to think twice before you use that kind of language in front of a seven-year-old child again."

The door slammed in his face.

He took the bag from Molly and squeezed her shoulder with his free hand. When she stole a look at him, he said, "Let's go home."

WEEKS LATER, ANNA still kept a sharp eye out whenever she left the house, with or without the kids. Catching the PI in the act had taught her a lesson. She'd never be so oblivious again when she went about her business. Mad as she was at Nate Kendrick, at least she didn't have to worry that he'd use what he had learned to hurt her or the kids.

Which didn't mean she wasn't humiliated all over again to find a message from him on her phone when she was waiting for her coffee to brew early Saturday morning.

"Doesn't look like your house has sold yet," he said tersely. "My offer is still open. Job or cash settlement. Is your pride more important than your kids?"

That was it. No "Hello," no "Goodbye." Her first, stupid thought was to wonder how he'd gotten her cell phone number. As if that mattered.

She stood there in her kitchen, barefoot but otherwise dressed, because she didn't have the luxury anymore of hanging around in her pajamas, not with the For Sale sign up at the foot of the driveway. Anger, humiliation, dented pride—yes, pride—and fear roiled inside her thanks to Nate Kendrick's terse message.

He was right. Dear God, he was right. But she'd meant it when she described his offer of a settlement as blood money. What if she had to explain to the kids someday that they'd been living on money from Molly's dad, paid to alleviate his guilt? She had no doubt that, once she cashed the check, he'd breathe a sigh of relief and go back to his workaholic ways, confident he'd done the right thing. Men like him never made time for their children. They were too addicted to adrenaline, to the pursuit of what Anna's grandfather had called "the almighty dollar."

But, with her stomach knotted, she had to face hard reality. If the bank evicted her and the kids, what would she do? Go to a shelter?

She'd give anything to have family to fall back on, but there wasn't anyone. After Mom died when Anna was eight, she had gone to live with Grandad. She was a sophomore in high school when he had his second stroke, after which she'd been placed in a foster home. His estate had put her through college. She'd been so sure she could take care of herself after that. If only she hadn't married so quickly, gotten pregnant almost immediately.

No, she couldn't regret that. Those decisions had given her Josh and Jenna. She couldn't un-wish them.

Anna poured herself a cup of coffee, adding more sugar and milk than usual in hopes of set-tling her stomach. She felt queasy even think-ing about eating.

"Mommy?" Still in her nightgown, Jenna wandered into the kitchen. "Josh told me to go away."

"Let me guess." Anna smiled at her daughter. "You tried to wake him up."

A miniature Anna, Jenna looked mutinous. "He didn't have to sound so *mean*."

"He also doesn't need to get up for another hour. You know he isn't a morning person."

"Like us," Jenna said with satisfaction, lean-ing against her mother.

Even as she felt the familiar sting of joy and fear, Anna bent down to hug her daughter. "That's right. So what's it going to be? Scram-bled eggs and toast, or cereal?"

"I want oatmeal," she declared.

Instant oatmeal, with lots of sugar, cinnamon and raisins, was a current favorite. Anna made herself have a small serving, too. Yesterday morning, she'd weighed herself before shower-ing to find she'd lost nine pounds. No wonder her face had begun to look gaunt.

After breakfast, she ran a bath for Jenna and

sat with her while her little girl pretended she was a mermaid, which involved splashing half the water in the tub onto Anna and the floor. Anna laughed and played along while keeping an ear cocked for the sound of the doorbell.

She had Jenna out of the bath and wrapped in a towel before she woke up her son. He chose oatmeal, too, and when she hustled both kids out to the car, he accepted the lunch she'd packed the night before. Normally Josh took the bus, but since she needed to do a few errands, she'd decided to let him sleep a little later and drive him, instead.

Once at the elementary school, she watched until he met with friends and went inside before starting for the parking lot exit. When her phone rang, Anna braked and grabbed it from the cubby between the front seats.

Alan Lang.

Her heart drummed. This was early for him to be calling. Could he have received an offer on the house?

Please, please, please.

CHAPTER FOUR

NATE HAD TAKEN to driving by Anna's house every few days. No Sold! banner had been tacked onto the For Sale sign planted in her yard.

Twice he saw her.

The first time, she was backing out of the garage, both kids with her. Probably on her way to drop her boy off at school. Nate was glad she didn't see him even as he fretted about her car, which had to be ten years old, at least. The PI had told him that the Graingers owned a second, much newer vehicle, a Kia crossover, the Sorento. The Kia wasn't in the garage. With her money tight, she'd been sensible to sell that one, even if it would have been more reliable. He wondered what else she'd had to sell.

The next time he caught a glimpse of her she was setting off on a run, wearing formfitting shorts and a tank top that didn't hide much of her long-legged slim body. She headed down the sidewalk the opposite way he was going. Unable to tear his eyes from the rearview mirror, Nate almost ran a stop sign at the corner.

He called once more, not surprised when she

didn't answer. After the beep, he said simply, "Let me help, Mrs. Grainger. We can make it a loan, if you'd accept that. Once you're on your feet again, you can pay me back."

When that time came, he wouldn't cash her checks, but he didn't say that.

`   She failed to return his call.

What he wanted to do was buy her damn mortgage so she and the kids could stay in the house. He might have done it if he hadn't felt sure that, given her pride, she'd pack up and move away, leaving him with a modest ranch house he didn't want and her without whatever pittance she'd get out of the sale. Then he'd have to sell the place himself and track her down to make her accept her equity. If there was any. After some of the sky-high surges in prices in the Seattle area, people found themselves having to sell houses for considerably less than what they'd paid for them only a year or two earlier.

Checking the website of the real estate company listing her house, he saw that she'd had to drop the price a second time.

Worry about Anna Grainger and her two kids might explain the burning in his stomach he had begun to suspect was an ulcer. Or maybe it was worrying about his own daughter that had him taking antacids like a chain-smoker reaching for his next cigarette before the last had burned down. Or was guilt doing the damage?

He'd gotten tough with Sonja, which infuriated her. Without fail, Nate had Molly every other weekend. He also took her out to dinner at least once a week. Spending more time with her, he still couldn't penetrate her shyness. Once in a while, they'd do okay talking about what kind of dog she wished she had or a movie or her new shoes. Anything touching on the accident, day camp and, especially, her mother shut her up fast.

One positive: at least Molly was no longer in the same school as Josh Grainger. After the divorce, Sonja had chauffeured Molly to Bellevue so she could finish the school year with her friends. This fall, Molly had started in a Seattle elementary school.

Of course, if that damn house ever sold, Josh would no longer go to Molly's old elementary school, anyway.

Nate called Molly several evenings a week, too, even if all he got were whispered responses. "Uh-uh." Or "uh-huh." Nate had to believe his persistence would eventually pay off. In his mind, persistence was an essential quality to achieve success in the business world. Brains helped—charm, too, and the ability to see the real motives of other people. But refusing to quit was number one.

In his darker moments, he had to admit that persuading an investor to trust him might not be analogous to earning a seven-year-old girl's trust, especially after he'd let her down in such a painful way. Had been letting her down since the divorce, he had come to see.

And then there was the fact that Molly's mother was undoubtedly bad-mouthing him.

This was one of his off weekends. Nate went into the office for half a day Saturday, but was too restless to concentrate. Finally, he drove down to the waterfront and walked onto the ferry going to Bainbridge Island. It was something he did every few months when he needed to think. This being the first week of October, he was fortunate for such good weather.

Today, he stood outside on the prow and turned his face into the cooling wind. Sunlight glinted off the water, and the Olympic Mountains reared crystal clear on the skyline. Not much snow on them, given the time of year, but they were jagged enough to be impressive, anyway.

When Molly was younger, he'd taken her on ferry rides a few times. If the weather held, maybe they could do that some night this week. The sun was still up in the early evening, and he bet she'd be happy with the food from the café on board.

For once, he tried not to think.

Winslow was as beautiful as ever, with spectacular rocky beaches and cliffs, the picturesque small town tucked in a cove. A couple sailboats were making their way in or out of the marina right by the ferry terminal. Seagulls dove, screeching, and pelicans sat atop pilings. On occasion he'd considered buying a house here, commuting on the ferry instead of in his car. Maybe this would be a good time. He could bring Molly along to look at houses with him so she felt included in his choice.

He actually did feel somewhat more relaxed by the time the ferry docked in Seattle and he walked to his car.

At home he decided not to look at emails. He scanned his missed calls and texts, but didn't return any of those, either. There was nothing that couldn't wait until Monday.

He'd have distracted himself by cooking something elaborate for dinner, but lately he hadn't done well stocking the kitchen. He ended up starting coals in the grill outside, and having a steak and baked potato for dinner. Then he turned on the TV, coasted through fifty channels or so and turned it off.

Mostly he read nonfiction because he never knew what knowledge would turn out to be useful in his job. Tonight he found a thriller he remembered buying and had never gotten to. It was gripping enough to keep his attention as the sun sank and shadows lengthened across the lake.

Dark had fallen when his phone vibrated on the end table. It was later than most people called. He picked up the phone to see Sonja's number. She might be just drunk enough to want to berate him.

Nate rolled his shoulders and answered, anyway.

"Daddy?" The voice was small and scared sounding.

"Molly? Shouldn't you be in bed?"

"I can't make Mommy wake up."

Oh, hell.

"Where is she, punkin?"

"She fell off the coach," Molly whispered.

"Did she hit her head?"

"I don't think so," his little girl said uncertainly. "She was sick on the floor."

"All right. I'm on my way. I'll call for an ambulance, too."

"I'm scared."

"I know you are," he said as gently as possible. "But I think your mom will be fine, and I'll be there in ten or fifteen minutes. Okay?"

Her answer was shaky.

He'd never made the drive this fast. On the way, he called 911, repeating what Molly told him. If Sonja had dragged herself up by the time he and an ambulance crew got there, she'd be hideously embarrassed, but he couldn't bring himself to care. Embarrassment was nothing compared to what she'd feel when he was done with her.

Rotating lights seen from a couple blocks away let him know the aid car had beaten him here. He was able to park right behind it. The two medics, carrying equipment and with a rolling gurney, were talking to the doorman, who from the sound of it didn't like taking responsibility for letting them into a condo without authorization from someone higher up in management. The doorman's relief was obvious when he recognized Nate, who joined the group and said, "I'm the one who called. I have a key."

A key he'd pried from a reluctant Sonja shortly after she purchased this condo. She'd finally conceded Molly might need him sometime. *Like tonight*, he thought grimly.

They rode the elevator up to her floor. The minute he opened the door, he saw Sonja sprawled, unmoving, on the shaggy white rug by the sofa, a cascade of flame-red curls covering her face. Leaving his ex-wife to the EMTs, he called, "Molly?"

Hair straggling from her braid, Molly appeared in the hall. Wearing only a nightgown, she was so pale that her freckles stood out. "Daddy?"

He crouched. With a sob, she flung herself at him. His own eyes stung as she cried, her body shaking.

Damn Sonja, he thought viciously. How could she do this to her child?

Molly wiped her wet face on his shoulder and pulled back enough to whisper, "Is Mommy dead?"

"I don't think so." Out of the corner of his eye, he saw the paramedics working over Sonja. "Tell you what, why don't you go get dressed and pack a bag. You're going home with me. I'll see how your mom is doing. Okay?"

She nodded, sniffled and retreated.

Nate returned to the living room just as the EMTs shifted Sonja onto the gurney.

"How is she?" he asked.

The woman glanced at him. "Still unconscious. Given the, er, odor, we took the liberty of checking the trash beneath the kitchen sink. It's half-full with hard-liquor bottles. She dropped a glass—" she nodded toward a side table "—that seems to have held gin."

He'd smelled it the minute he walked through the door. Sonja had loved martinis. Apparently, she'd quit bothering to add vermouth or an olive.

"As you can see, she vomited. It was lucky she was lying on her side. She could have choked on it."

The man said, "Her breathing is irregular and slow, and she's hypothermic. We need to take her in. She'll likely be kept under observation overnight." Expression sympathetic, he added,

"You may want to tell your daughter she might have saved her mother's life by calling you."

"Thanks." Nate looked at his unconscious ex-wife and shook his head. "I can't believe this."

Having a drinking problem was one thing, but boozing herself into a stupor when she was all Molly had? Had it ever occurred to her that she was scaring the shit out of her young daughter?

After watching the pair wheel Sonja out, Nate took the time to clean up the puke. Then he turned out lights, scooped Molly up and pulled her small suitcase with his free hand. He was past ready to take her home.

ANNA SAT AT the kitchen table, feeling numb. It was done. The house had finally sold—but for a price that would have left her still owing money on it if Alan hadn't told her, firmly, that he had reduced his commission by one percent. According to his calculations, that would allow her to pay off the mortgage in full.

She had wanted to argue, to tell him he didn't need to do that, but instead had said shakily, "Thank you. You've worked so hard to sell my house, it's not fair."

"I'm glad to do it," he'd said kindly, before gathering up his papers and departing.

Since the couple had been preapproved for a loan, Alan didn't foresee any problems.

Alone now, Anna couldn't even feel relief. Now she had to face all her other problems.

This past week, she had spent hours on the internet, applying for positions as a paraeducator, or teacher's aide, at school districts in eastern Washington, Oregon and Idaho. Unfortunately, so far they all had a full roster, as she'd feared. A month into the school year had to be the worst time to apply. She'd had several responses, however, expressing interest in using her part-time or as a fill-in, and possibly as a substitute teacher, too.

She'd be rolling the dice when she chose where to go. The work could be steady—or not. There'd be no benefits. But she'd concluded this was her best route back to teaching. It would give her experience and references; with luck, she'd be liked enough to be hired as a teacher next fall in the same district. Somehow, she'd pick up other part-time work to put food on the table.

Possibilities so far included Moses Lake in eastern Washington, La Grande in eastern Oregon or Idaho Falls, Idaho. Idaho Falls sounded touristy enough to push rents up too high for her.

She didn't have to decide today. Soon, though. And maybe she'd get more responses this week. This was only Monday. If she was lucky, one of those many school districts she had contacted would have a full-time aide quit unexpectedly.

She really ought to go over to Mrs. Schaub's and fetch Jenna. Josh, of course, was in school. More than Jenna, he didn't want to move, and she couldn't blame him. If she could stay... But it was impossible. Rent anywhere on the Eastside would be far beyond her means, even if she found a similar patchwork of jobs here. She had faith he'd adjust. Josh had always been good at making friends.

Her phone rang, and she recognized the number immediately. The man just would not give up.

This time, she answered. "Mr. Kendrick, I've asked you to leave me alone."

"Please. Will you listen to me?"

Surprised at what might have been a note of desperation in his voice, she sighed. "Yes, if it doesn't take long. I need to get back to packing."

Well, start packing, but he didn't have to know that.

"You sold your house?"

"At last." Her effort to sound pleased fell flat to her ears.

"The timing might be good." Was he talking to himself?

"Mr. Kendrick?"

"I'm sorry. I, ah, have something of a problem." He hesitated. "I'll ask you not to repeat what I'm going to tell you."

Was this a subterfuge on his part to get his

way? She was curious enough, though, to say, "I promise." Not like she'd be here to gossip even if she wanted to.

"My ex-wife has become an alcoholic," he said bluntly. "I've been worried, but she seemed to drink primarily in the evening and didn't go out. Saturday night, though, Molly called me because she couldn't wake her mother up."

Anna exclaimed, "Oh, poor Molly!"

"She was petrified. Turned out, Sonja was in a drunken stupor. I had to call medics, and she spent the night in the hospital. I insisted she enter a treatment program to have any hope of maintaining custody of Molly."

"So Molly is with you?"

"That's right. It's been a challenge. I left late for work this morning, came home in time to meet her school bus. I should enroll her in that after-school program, but she begged me not to. She's…fragile right now."

"Couldn't you…well, take some vacation?"

"A monthlong one?" He sounded incredulous. "No."

"You could—" The words *hire someone* died. *Duh.* Why else had he called her? At last, he had a job to offer that fit her qualifications.

"I have an attached apartment meant for a housekeeper that has never been used," he continued. "Would you consider moving in, even if only temporarily, to take care of Molly when I can't be here?"

Of course, she should say, *I'm sorry. No.* Whether Sonja's attempt to blame him for Kyle's death was unfair or not—and Anna didn't know enough to judge—she should keep her distance from this man.

But another thought crept in. With a month's grace, Josh could finish the soccer season with his team. Have a little longer at school with his friends and a teacher Anna especially liked. Only…wouldn't it be better for all of them to get the move over with, not put it off?

A temporary job like this would give her some breathing room.

"I don't know," she heard herself say. "Where do you live?"

"Just south of Meydenbauer Bay."

Waterfront? She didn't ask.

"I'll pay you on top of providing housing," he added.

"Don't be ridiculous. The savings on not having to pay rent would be huge." Was she seriously discussing this? "And given that you only need part-time help—"

"The apartment isn't ideal," he said with a hint of apology. "There's only one bedroom, so it'll be a squeeze for three of you."

It will. Apparently, he had no doubt about her answer.

She'd have time to make the right decision about what they'd do next. And she felt for Molly, undergoing a second trauma on top of the first. Even before this happened, living with an alcoholic parent must have been scary.

Had kids talked after the disaster about how Mr. Kendrick was supposed to have been there, that if he had been, Josh's dad wouldn't have had to go in the water to save Molly? If so, Josh hadn't said so.

She was still angry at Nate Kendrick. Even so… Anna sighed, ashamed to be succumbing so easily, but also aware of relief pouring through her veins. "You don't even know me."

"Molly likes you. She says you used to help out in her classroom."

"I did, but is that enough of a reference?"

"The PI's report was thorough."

At the reminder, she came close to hanging up on the man. It was for Molly's sake she didn't—or so she told herself. "If I do this, will you be satisfied?" she asked. "Will you stop trying to give me money?"

"No," he said without hesitation. "I owe you too much. This isn't about what happened. Molly needs you. I need you." The growl in his voice told her that he didn't like needing her. Or anyone?

He could hire someone else, of course, but trusting a stranger with your child wasn't easy.

He and she…weren't quite strangers, even though she'd only met him face-to-face the once, if she didn't count his appearance in the hospital elevator.

"Don't you have family who can help?"

"My parents would come if I asked, but my father has health problems. I don't want to lean on them right now."

When she didn't answer immediately, he apparently read her hesitation as resistance. "Do you and the kids still have health insurance?" he asked.

Low blow. She bit her lip. "No." She hadn't been able to afford to extend their coverage, which meant living in terror that one of the kids might get hurt or sick.

"My company provides insurance to employees. I'll add the three of you on it while you're working for me."

He knew just how to undermine her stubbornness. It caved in. She might regret this, but she made the decision. "Okay. I'll do it, with the understanding that it's temporary."

"Thank you," he said huskily. He cleared his throat. "Can you come soon?"

"Is the apartment furnished?"

"No. I'll pay to have your furniture moved here. We can put the rest into storage."

A new bill, but she'd call all the nearby school districts right away in hopes one or several of

them could use her as a substitute teacher and/
or aide. And, thank goodness, living so close
by, she could continue to take Jenna to Mrs.
Schaub's.

Thinking it through, she said, "I could come
tomorrow with what we'll need right away, as
long as you don't mind renting a truck twice.
I'd have to come back here daytimes to pack everything that will go into storage."

"Movers can do that for you."

Oh, so tempting, but she needed to weed their
possessions. "No, I'd rather do it."

"Why don't Molly and I pick you up this evening?" he suggested. "We could all go out for
pizza, then we can show you the apartment so
you have a better idea what you'll need."

Go out for pizza with a man she wanted to
hate? It wasn't too late to change her mind.
Only…she remembered her first sight of a sop-
ping wet redheaded girl sobbing her heart out.

She could be polite for the one evening. They
wouldn't have to see much of each other after
this. She'd hand off childcare duties and retreat
to the apartment. She and Molly's father could
leave each other notes, or he could call to let her
know his schedule.

"Yes. Okay," she said, even as she wondered
why she felt as if she'd made a decision more
momentous than it seemed.

CHAPTER FIVE

SHARING A BOOTH at the pizza parlor with Anna Grainger and her two kids felt surreal. She remained wary, at the very least, where he was concerned. Her answering the phone at all had felt like a miracle.

There was definitely a strain. He was too damned aware of what a beautiful woman she was. She didn't want to meet his eyes, and did her best to keep the kids chattering to forestall any need to speak to him. On the other hand… she'd already accomplished another miracle. Molly was talking, too.

Although it might have been the four-year-old who'd engaged Molly. The girl was bold and determined nobody would hold out on *her*. When Molly hadn't responded to her initial conversational forays, Jenna would say, "Huh, Molly? That'd be fun, wouldn't it? Even Josh says it would. Right, Josh? Right, Molly?"

In fact, her high, sweet voice filled any silence, which was fine by Nate. Josh and Molly started shy with each other, but once Jenna broke the ice, they, too, argued about TV shows and movies and whether this pizza was as good as the pizza at Pagliacci. The more gourmet places were not on her kids' radar any more than they were on Molly's. She liked plain cheese. As it turned out, Jenna concurred. The three kids shared one pie, with pepperoni on half of it for Josh. Nate and Anna agreed on a slightly more sophisticated choice, with mozzarella, Asiago, fresh chopped basil, garlic and sliced tomatoes. They ate salads, too. She didn't bother asking her kids if they wanted one. When he did ask Molly, she said, "No, thank you, Daddy," in that irritatingly polite way she had of keeping him at a distance.

Josh grumbled that frozen pizzas were never this good. Then he said, "We haven't been here for a long time. Mom wouldn't—"

She cut in, her tone light. "Mom abused you with home-cooked meals. Is that what you're saying?"

"No, but—"

Somehow she diverted him, but Nate noticed her cheeks had warmed.

He had to grit his teeth to keep himself from saying something. He didn't like the reminder that she'd turned down help from him even as she had to worry about every penny. It also hadn't escaped his notice that she had lost weight.

"Pizza's good," he commented, waiting until she reluctantly glanced at him.

"Yes, it is. Thank you for suggesting this."

"Tell me about the house sale," he said, wanting to hold on to her attention now that he had it. "Do you have any idea when you can close?"

Josh pantomimed slamming something onto the table, and Molly and Jenna giggled. Hearing that giggle, Nate felt lighter. The pizza didn't seem to be aggravating his stomach problems, either.

"No. The buyers need financing, so even though they were preapproved, we have to wait while the loan request goes through. Alan—my agent—thought about a month."

"Are you ending up in the hole?"

She leveled a stare at him. "I can't believe you asked that."

"I'm a pushy guy." She didn't appear to see persistence as the virtue he did.

Her eyes narrowed. "What's so funny about that?"

"A private thought."

"You mean, you do understand the concept of privacy?"

He laughed. "Yeah, I do. I just figure it never hurts to ask."

"It doesn't hurt *you*," Anna said very quietly.

Sobering, he nodded. "You're right. I'm sorry."

Seeing the deliberate way she turned a shoulder to him and joined the kids' conversation again, he realized he'd stepped in it. Damn it, why had he thought she'd answer a question like that? He rarely surrendered to impulse.

He tuned in to hear Anna asking Molly about her teacher. Josh didn't seem to be reacting negatively to seeing Molly again, so enrolling her in her old school here in Bellevue shouldn't be a problem.

Or, hey, Josh and Molly might be as good at hiding what they were really thinking as the two adults were.

They boxed up what pizza was left and took it with them, returning to their two cars. Hers looked even shabbier beside his Lexus.

"Stick close," he reminded Anna, after being sure Molly was belted in properly.

She was still strapping her own wriggling daughter into the back seat. "With the address, I imagine I could find it."

He dragged his gaze from her shapely rear end. "It's tricky knowing which driveway is ours."

"Fine."

Pulling out of the parking lot, Nate kept an eye on the rearview mirror. It took him a few blocks to notice that Molly hadn't said a word.

"You like Josh and Jenna?" he asked.

Anna's old car was hanging close behind.

"Yes, only—" Molly screwed up her face.

"It's *my* fault their daddy is gone, so why aren't they mad?"

Hating the agony he heard in her voice, Nate said, "Maybe they know it's not your fault. We talked about this."

"Yes, but…" She bent her head, hiding her expression.

He waited, to no avail. "Anna doesn't blame you, either, or she wouldn't have agreed to come live with us until your mom is better and ready to take you back."

No comment. He hadn't a clue what Molly thought about her mother's absence. Living with an alcoholic parent couldn't be easy at any age. Was she relieved? Desperate for Mommy to take her home? Or justifiably afraid Mommy wouldn't be better, after all?

Nate made the turn onto Shoreland Drive, satisfied to see Anna still right behind. The private lane wasn't well marked. At the end, it split into three driveways, his being the right-hand one. The view of the lake opened, and he tapped the remote control to access the garage, driving straight in. Anna parked where she'd have room to make a tight U-turn when it came time to leave.

He got out, circling to help Molly if she needed it, which she didn't. Anna's kids huddled close to their mother as they stared at his house, eyes wide.

"Somehow I knew you'd have lakefront," Anna said drily, her hands resting on her children's shoulders in reassurance.

Feeling defensive, Nate said, "This isn't as luxurious as some of the waterfront homes in Medina or Hunts Point."

"You mean, your house isn't forty thousand square feet, like Bill Gates's supposedly is?"

"No, it definitely isn't." He tried for a little humor. "I don't want to get lost in the middle of the night trying to find the bathroom."

Nobody laughed. The funny part, Nate thought, was that, once upon a time, Sonja had wanted to move. Plenty of celebrities called Yarrow Point or Hunts Point home. She liked the idea of living next to a star pitcher for the Mariners or a big shot in the software world. "You could afford it," she used to complain. Yes, he could, but he liked where he lived, or had until he lost his family. It was just as well he hadn't let her wear him down, or he'd be rattling around in an even bigger house now.

"Ah…come on in. We'll give you the grand tour."

Her kids moved in step with her when they followed. His Mediterranean style house clearly intimidated them, even though he didn't consider it ostentatious. The cream-colored stucco exterior was accented by a red-tile roof. Broad, double doors in a dark, carved wood gave an aged feel. Inside, light poured through the vast windows looking out on Lake Washington. The decor was simple—hardwood floors, scattered rugs, leather and brocade upholstered furniture, wood furniture mostly cherry in a modified mission style with clean lines. He'd bought some art he liked for the walls, since Sonja had taken what she considered hers. He'd erased most of the fussier accents that had her stamp, too.

"This is…really nice," Anna said in a stifled voice.

"Thank you." He showed her the family room, which was nearest to the front door but having French doors that could be closed to contain noise, then led her to the kitchen, open to the living and dining areas. He didn't use the room designed to be a home office on this level, preferring one upstairs that had a lake view. There were empty bedrooms upstairs, too. He kept those doors closed to keep the house from feeling any lonelier than it already did.

The tour continued upstairs to Molly's bedroom. Anna's discomfiture hadn't abated, and neither had her kids'. Even Jenna had been struck silent, which he had the impression wasn't a natural state for her.

Nate's bedroom was just beyond Molly's, the door standing open. He saw Anna sneak a peek, and was glad she couldn't see much from this angle. He surely didn't want to picture her *in* his bedroom. Her presence in the house unsettled him enough already, in part because he hadn't managed to squelch images of her not only in his room, but also in his bed. However, most of his discomfiture was the result of him trying to see his home through her eyes. His guilt revved into a higher gear.

Did she feel like the beggar maid, brought to the palace by King Cophetua? Nice thought. If he'd made a different choice, Anna would still have a husband and her own house.

Assuming, of course, he had made a difference in the day's outcome instead of paying more attention to texts and emails coming in on his phone than he did to his daughter.

He and Sonja hadn't split because of his dedication to his job—but it had played a part. Remembering what she'd said about wanting a life still stung, even though he knew damn well she wouldn't have been happy if he'd decided he could cut back on work and brought home a lower income.

Jenna broke the silence. "I like your bedroom." Still in the hall, peering into Molly's room, she sounded wistful. "Can I play with your Barbie house?"

Nate wasn't sure Molly ever did.

His daughter hesitated. "It's okay if you're careful with my stuff."

"There's no reason Jenna would be playing in

here when she isn't with you," Anna said firmly. "Your dad said we'd have our own apartment."

Molly's eyes darted to Anna. "But we can play together when I get home from school, can't we?"

Anna smiled. "Sure."

"Speaking of the apartment..." he said, sounding like an overenthusiastic tour guide.

Jenna gave a final, lingering look into a pink-and-purple bedroom that was stocked with entirely too many toys. Many Molly had left behind when she moved out with Sonja. He doubted she'd ever touched a lot of the dolls and stuffed animals.

Had he satisfied himself with the notion that if he bought her everything a little girl could want, she wouldn't notice that Daddy was hardly ever around?

Only one of many uncomfortable realizations he'd been hit with since Molly had come so close to dying.

He wished now he didn't have to show the Graingers where they'd be staying. The contrast was too stark.

THE APARTMENT WASN'T BIG, but Anna had sighed in relief when she saw it. It felt...snug. Like a cocoon, a refuge.

Once home, she worked for hours that evening after tucking in Josh and Jenna. She moved room to room, deciding what they'd need and hastily packing it. She'd do the kids' bedrooms tomorrow morning after getting Josh off to school. Tonight she whizzed through the kitchen first, boxing up the necessities except for what they'd use for breakfast. She tagged bright pink sticky notes onto the furniture she thought would fit into the apartment over the three-car garage on Nate's estate. That's all she could think to call a home that should have been in a magazine.

The apartment could be accessed from the outside, but also had a staircase that opened in the main house by the kitchen. Servants stairs, only not as steep and narrow as she knew they'd been in eighteenth- and nineteenth-century homes. Same principle, though.

Currently working in the dining room, she tossed two sets of place mats into a box, but left everything else in the buffet to go to storage. Or get rid of. When had she last used the set of eight crystal goblets that had been a wedding gift?

Her bedroom didn't take long, either. Everything that had been on the closet shelf was already packed in totes piled in the garage. She retrieved suitcases from the garage and filled the big one with her clothes and shoes. The medium-sized suitcase should handle a basic wardrobe for Josh—his sports stuff could go in the duffel—and Jenna had her own small pink rolling suitcase.

Both of them would want some of their toys, games and books, but they wouldn't need all. Especially books—they'd visit the library more often.

In front of her dresser, she sank to her butt in sudden exhaustion and leaned against her bed. This was crazy. Why had she agreed to do it?

She looked around her bedroom, both familiar and, weirdly, not. Kyle's half of the closet was already empty, as was his dresser. During the sleepless night after her discovery that he'd cashed out the life-insurance policy, she'd grabbed garbage bags and gone through all his stuff. She'd dropped most of it at a thrift store the very next day. Part of her was grateful for the anger that had carried her through such a horrible task. She'd packed a single box of his things that she or one of the kids might someday want, including a few shirts that had evoked him so vividly she had pressed the soft fabric to her face and cried.

Her mood was odd tonight, maybe because she was so tired Anna wondered if Kyle would even know her now. She didn't *belong* in this bedroom anymore. The bed was going into storage; she'd decide later whether she wanted to replace it. Her dresser could go in the bedroom closet in the apartment. In fact, she'd take over the closet, since the kids didn't need to hang up any of their clothes. They'd share one dresser—

Josh's, since it was taller—and the coat closet was the perfect place for his sports equipment. She hoped Molly didn't mind hanging around the soccer field during his practices and games.

Still feeling strange, Anna told herself it was too late for second thoughts. Tomorrow night, she'd sleep on her sofa in that small, bare apartment. She'd work for a man who made her uncomfortable in a thousand ways, starting with his too-perceptive gray eyes and obvious wealth.

No, she reminded herself, she wouldn't see much of him, anyway. And why get worked up about what was really only going to be an interlude?

NATE'S CONCENTRATION WASN'T the best Tuesday.

He'd started the day by calling the elementary school in Seattle where Molly had spent only a few weeks to let them know he was withdrawing her. Then he'd driven her to the school she'd attended for kindergarten and first grade, explained the situation and enrolled her. Trying to put her at ease, the principal decided to fit her into Josh's class. Nate didn't comment, but wasn't so sure that would help. Surrounded by his crowd of buddies, Josh might not be willing to speak to a mere girl. Nate reminded himself that she'd probably know some of the other kids in the class.

He and the principal walked Molly to her new

second-grade classroom. Absolute silence fell as they entered. Every single student stared as the principal explained quietly to the teacher, a Mrs. Tate, that she had an addition to her class. Molly seemed to become smaller and smaller, looking at her feet as she gripped his hand so tightly he suspected she was cutting off his circulation.

Fortunately, Mrs. Tate was young and immediately friendly, beaming at Molly as she welcomed her and said, "Class, we have a new student. Some of you will remember Molly Kendrick from last year." Then she looked around her room. "Let's see. Where shall we put you?"

A girl's voice rang out. "Molly can sit with us! Put her here."

Molly sucked in a breath and raised her head. "Arianna?"

He bent to murmur, "Is she a friend?"

"She was one of my *bestest* friends last year." Molly dropped his hand, and Mrs. Tate escorted her to a square of four desks put together. One was empty, at least for today.

Grateful to see he was forgotten, Nate had returned to the office to revise the short list of people authorized to pick up his daughter. The list had remained in her file from last year. With Anna's name added, he'd finally headed for work, arriving only two hours later than usual.

Then, instead of accomplishing anything meaningful, Nate worried about whether yanking Molly out of class and dropping her into a new one several weeks into the year was the right thing to do. He had no trouble imagining what Sonja would have to say about it.

How much change was too much for his little girl? Given that she'd probably have to switch back to the other school four weeks from now, she might have been better off if he'd continued to drive her to the school in Seattle and pick her up. Sonja would accuse him of selfishness and might even be right—but he'd be restricted to six-hour workdays instead of his usual ten or more. He couldn't ask Anna to do all that driving, especially not in her old car. He could just imagine her response if he offered to buy her a new one. If he had to get Molly to school and pick her up when it let out, he could do some work from home while Anna kept an eye on Molly, but he couldn't meet with anyone or extend his day for drinks or working dinners. It just wasn't feasible.

Too late, anyway. Nate consoled himself that Molly hadn't seemed to like her previous teacher very much. Maybe when she had to return to that school, they'd agree to shift her to another class. Or maybe *that* would be one too many changes.

He groaned and scrubbed his scalp, glad he was currently alone.

He also called Anna several times, once to be

sure the moving truck had shown up, and then again to confirm she was at the house before the end of the school day. Had she remembered to contact the school to let them know which bus Josh was supposed to ride?

"Yes," she said, almost patiently, "I went by in person so they know our current address. I also picked up some groceries. I'll put dinner on for you and Molly. If she's hungry before you get home, she can eat with us and you can reheat your meal."

Nate opened his mouth to tell her she didn't have to cook for him—and shut it again. Damn, it would be good to walk in the door to a home-cooked meal. To know Molly would be taken care of if he ran late here at the office, although that was unlikely to happen today. He already itched to get home. So he said only, "Thank you. Josh didn't have practice today?"

"No, they're Mondays, Wednesdays and Fridays. Games Saturday."

"That's quite a schedule."

"He loves it." Her voice became quieter. "He was really mad at me when we thought we'd have to move before the end of the season."

"When's that?" Nate asked.

"November. Depending on the weather, those last games are miserable."

They were conversing. Even though a beep

told him he had a call coming in, he didn't want to end this one.

"Rain and snow, huh?"

"Frozen feet and muddy kid," she agreed. "Josh plays goalie a lot, and once the weather turns, there's always a mud hole right in front of the goal."

Nate grinned. "I played youth football when I wasn't much older than Josh. Same season. I loved mud."

She sighed. "So does he. I've learned to keep a ratty old towel in the car for him to sit on."

Nate laughed, but after the conversation ended, he didn't immediately check missed calls. Instead, he pondered why Molly hadn't played any sports. Swim lessons in the summer, essential when she'd lived on the lake, and that was it. Did any of her friends play soccer? He wondered if she'd like to try it next year. To his recollection, she'd never participated in any after-school youth activities. And *that* got him to wondering whether Sonja had had her first glass of white wine a lot earlier in the day than he'd realized, and had developed a problem with booze a lot longer ago than he'd realized, too. With the hours he worked, she could have hidden too much from him.

He called the treatment center only to be politely rebuffed. The first days were always difficult. Patient information was kept confidential.

The woman he spoke to wasn't moved by his explanation that Sonja's young daughter was scared for her.

Nate returned a few calls before thinking, *To hell with it*. This day was past resuscitation. He was ready to call it, start anew tomorrow.

CHAPTER SIX

HAVING TURNED OFF the lights, he was letting himself out of his office when he came face-to-face with his partner, John Li. John had obviously been about to knock on his door. The two men had been friends since their freshmen year in college, when they'd been paired as roommates.

John had a file in his hand. Looking astonished, he said, "You're leaving?"

With anyone else, Nate would have claimed to be meeting an investor for predinner drinks. Instead, he said, "Yeah. I told you I found a woman to be there when Molly gets home, and she did start today. But I'd like to make sure the arrangement is working. And, frankly, I've had so many distractions, I'm useless, anyway."

"I understand," his partner said. He probably did; he was married and had two kids. His wife was an orthopedic surgeon, and somehow they juggled responsibilities with astonishing success. That didn't mean it was easy or that there weren't days when their arrangements for the kids failed. "This—" he lifted the folder "—can wait until morning."

Usually Nate wouldn't have been able to walk away without knowing what *this* was, without turning and going back into his office. It was part of the drive that had taken K & L Ventures to the top of the pyramid. Right now, he said, "Thanks," and continued on his way.

He did remember during the drive home why he didn't usually cut and run at five o'clock. Traffic crawled. He sometimes used the express lanes, which at this time of day required drivers to pay a toll, but he couldn't see that it helped all that much. Funny, though, that he looked forward to getting home, something he couldn't recall feeling in a very long time.

It would be good to smell dinner cooking when he walked in the door, he told himself. And he wanted to hear how Molly's day had gone. But Nate didn't make a practice of lying to himself. And the truth was he liked knowing his house wasn't empty, that somebody might anticipate his arrival.

He didn't kid himself that Anna would be glad to see him beyond the fact that, with him home, she could retreat to the apartment. Still, if he was lucky they might have another real conversation, the kind not barbed with hostility.

Though he shouldn't count on that.

ANNA WASN'T USED to having to take more than two or three steps from refrigerator to sink or anywhere else in her kitchen. This one was vast and so elegant and well equipped that a professional chef would be delighted. The pantry was as large as the entire kitchen in the house she'd just sold. Anna didn't even know how to use all of the small appliances she found, and wasn't 100 percent sure what some of them did.

Fortunately, the kids were happily occupied playing Xbox games. Josh had wanted either a Nintendo or Xbox gaming system for a long time and always came home hyper after having a chance to play with one at a friend's house. He'd been gleeful when he spotted it in the family room.

Anna had heard snatches of some initial squabbling. Molly liked something called "Just Dance Kids." Jenna had wanted that one, too. Josh said no way, creating a tempest. Left to themselves, they'd settled on "Lego Marvel Super Hero." Anna had made herself unpopular by checking the rating. When she explored the pile of games, she didn't see one that wasn't rated Everyone, which allowed her to relax and return to the kitchen. Apparently, Nate didn't have a secret addiction to "Call of Duty" or "Assassin's Creed."

Smiling as she heard a hoot from Molly and a groan from Josh, she stirred the spaghetti sauce and lifted the lid of the large pan to see if the water was boiling yet. Yep. She'd already decided to cook enough to satisfy a man's appetite on top of what she and the kids would eat. Just as she was dumping the pasta into the pot, she heard the front door open.

Imposingly handsome in black slacks and a white shirt, a red tie hanging loose around his neck and his suit coat draped over his arm, Nate came in. He looked immediately toward the family room. And no wonder, with all the racket coming from it. Smiling, he disappeared in there but didn't stay long. Oh, heavens, that smile was lethal.

Shaking his head and still smiling, he walked toward her, laying his suit coat and tie over a sofa back and dropping the briefcase on the cushion. "They seem to be happy."

"We didn't have an Xbox, so Josh thinks he's gone to heaven," she said, feeling a pang because a gaming system was not in Josh's foreseeable future. Having access to one for a month might end with him feeling entitled and thus more resentful.

Nate grimaced. "Molly hasn't touched it since Sonja and I split up. If I were a good father, I'd have played with her, but do you know what her favorite one is?"

Anna had to laugh. "Let's see. Would it be 'Just Dance Kids'?"

Humor in his gray eyes, he said, "Dear God, yes. I felt like an idiot when I danced in high school. I was an athlete, but friends told me that on the dance floor I looked like I was having a seizure."

She laughed again even though it was impossible to imagine this man graceless. She was immediately ashamed of herself. Kyle had only died three months ago, and Nate Kendrick had played a role in the tragedy. She'd agreed to work for him because she was desperate, and for Molly's sake. Becoming friends and confidants wasn't happening. She was appalled to have felt a startled moment of physical awareness. Given his tall, lean body, the saunter that spoke of complete confidence and features that might be too rough to be called handsome, he had to turn women's heads wherever he went.

I can't be one of them, she thought desperately.

She was glad to have an excuse to present him with her back as she turned on a burner. "I hope you like broccoli." Absurdly, the stove had six burners on a glass stove top that looked like polished black marble. Along with double ovens, the built-in microwave was big enough to cook a turkey.

"*I* do," he said, sitting on a stool across the eating bar from her.

"Oh, no." Anna whirled to face him. "I didn't think to ask her."

"Don't worry. She's dubious about most vegetables right now. I cook 'em and put 'em on her plate. I haven't been insisting she actually eat them, because she was only here every other weekend. I figured her mother was fighting that battle."

"I hope not," Anna said. "Turning it into a war makes kids less willing to surrender." *Right. Lecture him on parenting, why don't you?*

"Yeah?" He sounded wry. "Well, then, either my instincts were right, or I was being a typical noncustodial father trying to persuade his kid that it's *fun* to visit daddy because he's never mean enough to make her do anything she doesn't want to."

Curiosity overcame Anna. "Is that what you've been doing?"

Another twist of his mouth. "I don't think so. Truthfully, she's gotten increasingly shy with me, which limited our activities and conversation."

"Divorce has to be hard for kids." And wasn't that the understatement of the world? In her frustration with Kyle, she'd seriously considered leaving him, but had known it wouldn't be best for the kids. He annoyed her sometimes when he allowed or even encouraged them to break rules she'd set, but he was otherwise a good father who had spent a lot of time with Jenna and Josh. Kyle had loved his kids. Divorce would have devastated them. And then there'd been the financial considerations. Always money.

Now there was even less money, and they'd lost their father, anyway.

Lowering his voice, Nate said, "I told you I've been worrying about Sonja's drinking. I suspect Molly was scared, but determined not to betray her mother, which kept her wary with me."

"That sounds right." The timer went off, and she lifted the pot to dump the spaghetti into the colander she'd already set in the sink. "I'll dish up for you and Molly, and take enough for the three of us back to the apartment. I hope you don't mind me cooking for all of us at the same time."

He stared at her in apparent astonishment. "Don't be ridiculous. Can't we sit down and eat together? The kids are obviously getting along."

Anna hesitated. She wanted to escape... and she didn't. It would look odd if she divvied up dinner and escorted her children to eat at the small table in the rather bare apartment. "Okay," she agreed, "but just tonight. You and Molly shouldn't have to sit down to dinner with a bunch of other people."

"A bunch of other—"

She talked right over him. "There should be

plenty left over for the two of you tomorrow night. You can reheat it in the microwave."

"Anna—"

She shook her head at him without quite meeting his eyes. She couldn't afford to spend too much time with him, to succumb to his charm or his obvious love for his daughter, which she hadn't expected, given what his ex-wife had said.

"I'm here to provide day care. That's all. Well, except for some cooking, and why not, when I have to do that, anyway."

He frowned, but kept his mouth shut this time.

"Will you tell them to turn off the game and go wash their hands?" she asked.

"I can do that."

Within minutes, they were all seated at the large table in the dining alcove. There were eight chairs, so she put out place mats that clustered them at one end of the table. She suspected it could be extended to seat considerably more people. Did Nate often entertain? Or had he quit after he and Sonja separated?

"Spaghetti!" Jenna crowed, as Anna dished up for her. "That's my second-favorite dinner."

Nate raised an eyebrow at her. "What's your first favorite?"

"Macaroni and cheese. I like it from a box, but Mom's is good, too."

Smiling, Anna shook her head. "How kind of you to say so."

Nate, seated to her left, murmured, "Damned with faint praise."

He hadn't been quiet enough. Jenna's eyes widened. "Mommy says that's a bad word."

"You're right. It is. I apologize."

Josh said, "I know some bad words. Sometimes it's hard not saying them."

Anna rolled her eyes. "I won't ask where you've learned them."

"Jaden's stepfather swears *a lot*." He sounded impressed. "Even Coach forgets and does sometimes."

"Wonderful."

She heard the low chuckle from beside her.

"Do you say bad words a lot?" Jenna asked him, looking interested.

"Only sometimes, and I try not to around Molly. Some words are okay for adults, but not for kids."

"Why?"

"Ah…" He glanced at Anna in a silent plea for help.

"Because if you used those words, you'd shock other kids and their parents and even teachers. Anyway, there is almost always a better way to express yourself. You're at an age when your language skills should be developing, and swearing is a way of cheating when you could think of more descriptive words."

Her always-inquiring daughter kept asking questions that Josh seconded. Anna couldn't help noticing that Molly stayed quiet and looked alarmed. Would she have been shut down if she asked too many questions, or the wrong ones? Anna hoped not. She didn't see any indication that Nate minded, though, or thought her kids' directness was inappropriate.

Jenna didn't quite finish even the small portion Anna had given her. At routine medical checkups, she was above the eightieth percentile in height, but averaged only the twentieth in weight. Fine-boned and skinny, she was perpetually in motion—although her mouth got the biggest workout.

To Anna's gratification, Molly ate every bite of spaghetti, and Josh and Nate both had seconds. Jenna ate only half of one of the snickerdoodles Anna had baked earlier, but Molly and Josh scarfed down a couple, and Nate had at least four.

Then Josh slid off his chair. "Can we go back to our game?"

"For a few minutes," she said, using a firm tone he understood. "Once I have the kitchen clean, we'll go to our apartment and let Molly and her dad have some time to themselves."

"But there's nothing to *do* there," he whined.

She raised her eyebrows. "No homework?"

He sneaked a glance at Molly, who scrunched up her face. "Hardly any," he mumbled.

"Uh-huh."

They raced off before she could ask them to carry their own plates to the sink. Maybe it was just as well; the dishes were nicer than anything she used for everyday and would shatter if the kids were careless.

Nate stood at the same time she did, picking up his own plate and silverware, as well as Molly's. Her broccoli remained untouched. "I saw her watching your two eating the evil stuff," he said with amusement, "but she wasn't persuaded."

Anna wrinkled her nose. "To tell you the truth, I'm not that crazy about it, either. I'd never admit that in my kids' hearing, though. It's healthy."

"It's not my favorite, either. For future reference, Molly will eat green beans. Salads, with a bunch of vegetables mixed up together, are a big no."

"Asparagus?" Carrying more plates, she followed him to the kitchen.

"Not a chance."

"Well, then, I won't worry about her likes and dislikes." She set down her load of dishes beside the sink. "I'd like to know your tastes, though."

She hesitated. "That is, if you want me to cook for the two of you on weeknights."

He leaned a hip against the counter and looked searchingly at her, a faint frown showing in the lines between his eyebrows. "Anna, I don't want to take advantage of you."

"You wouldn't be. If it's a help, I don't mind doing it. If not, that's okay, too. You've given me a chance to…regroup. I'm grateful, even if I haven't said so."

His mouth quirked. "I think you have. You just don't want to be grateful."

"No, I let myself—" Whoa! Had she been about to admit to Nate Kendrick, of all people, how much of her independence she had surrendered to Kyle?

"You let yourself?"

She shook her head. "I don't like needing help."

Those disconcerting eyes gave the impression of seeing deeper than she liked. "I have noticed that," he said. "And, if it'll make you feel better, I'd be thrilled if you'd have dinner ready, at least some nights. On my own, I've gotten in the habit of grabbing a meal downtown before I head home, or having something simple. I guess you noticed how bare the cupboards were."

"I did stock them," she admitted.

"You saved the receipt?"

"I did." She nodded toward the built-in desk that was part of the kitchen. "It's over there."

"I'll write you a check before you go."

"There's no hurry." Trying to indicate that they were done, she opened the dishwasher.

His big hand settled on her shoulder. Anna jumped, a ripple of reaction skittering down her spine. What was he—?

"You cooked, I'll clean." Ending the physical contact, he unbuttoned his cuffs and began to roll them up. "No argument."

"But—"

Nate raised dark eyebrows.

"Can I put away the leftovers?"

"Sure." He went to the table for more dirty dishes. "Take some with you, if you're determined not to eat with us tomorrow."

"Okay. Um, shouldn't you change shirts before you do this?"

He didn't hide his amusement. "Afraid I'll get spaghetti sauce on my white shirt?"

Probably blushing, she said, "It does stain. And I'm betting you didn't buy that shirt off the shelf at a department store. It would be a shame to ruin it."

"You're right." He was grinning. "I'll run upstairs and change before I finish, if that'll make you feel better."

She didn't respond, wanting to send the message that nothing he did or didn't do could affect her state of mind—even if it was a lie. Hunting for plastic storage containers gave her an excuse not to look at him.

If she really hustled, maybe she could be ready to usher her kids out—well, up the connecting staircase—by the time he returned.

CHAPTER SEVEN

ANNA AWOKE TO find she'd jerked up to a sitting position on the sofa, the sound of a broken sob in her ears. Alarm pulsed through her. Was it one of the kids? They'd both had nightmares in the first weeks after Kyle's death.

But the apartment was dark, and not a sound came from the bedroom. Even so, she untangled herself from her comforter and slipped quietly to the bedroom door, where she could see a lump in each of the twin beds. The smaller one remained beneath the covers. The larger—Josh—had thrown them partially off, as he usually did. An arm dangled off the side of the bed, and a pajama-clad leg was visible in the dim lighting filtering between blinds.

Anna retreated as silently as she'd come. Her heart was still pounding hard. She'd have liked to turn on a light, but didn't want to risk waking either of the kids. She went back to the sofa, where she could see the digital clock on the end table—4:33 a.m.

Sinking down, she clutched her bedding around herself, chilled even though the apartment was at a comfortable temperature. She'd been dreaming, she knew that. Vivid, real dreams. Dampness seeped from her eyes even as she closed them, seeing Kyle's lopsided grin. He'd been teasing her, as he so often did, until she couldn't resist him.

Pain wrapped around her rib cage. She was the serious one, the worrier, but he'd always been able to make her laugh. Even making love wasn't serious to him; in his eyes, it ought to be fun.

Everything was fun to him, she thought, but didn't feel the usual irritation or even exasperation. Tonight's dream had been evocative, almost a slap in the face, and she knew why. Nate was so compelling, the sexual pull so powerful, he already threatened to loom too large in her life, overshadowing her husband.

She'd needed this reminder that, however flawed, Kyle had also been a good man. A loving one. It wasn't only the kids he'd loved, she knew. He'd always been perplexed at her frustration with him. He'd believed they were happy, up to the very end. And maybe that was because he hadn't really listened to what she was saying, was often blind to what other people thought. But a person who could take life so blithely was also disarming.

She accepted a truth she'd blocked out: she had still loved him, however diminished her faith in him had been. Despite everything, it wasn't only for the kids that she'd stuck to her marriage. Even at her angriest, she had shied from picturing Kyle's face if she said those brutal words, *I want a divorce*. How could she do that to him?

Drawing her legs up so she could wrap her arms around them and rest her forehead on the bony caps of her knees, Anna cried. Her mouth opened in a silent wail. The comforter soaked up the tears.

I was so mad at you, but I loved you. I did.

If only he could hear her. Could know.

Gradually the grief released her into numbness. No, not that—exhausted peace. She remembered him sitting beside her at that picnic table, his pose one of complete relaxation. No, no, his boss thought it was great that he was so involved with his kids, didn't leave their raising to his wife. She'd wondered then and still wondered whether that had been true. Had the boss said any such thing? Or had Kyle just called in sick? He was incapable of guilt.

She wiped her wet cheeks. Why wonder about something that no longer mattered? What *did* matter was that Kyle had been utterly contented. The day was sunny, he hadn't had to work, his beautiful wife—he often said that—was equally contented beside him, and his kids were having a great time.

Before he plunged into that river, he'd been a happy man. All was well in his world. Anna had no doubt at all that he'd been placidly certain she loved him.

He hadn't needed her reassurances. And she couldn't imagine that any part of Kyle lingered. He'd been a carefree soul who let other people's annoyance brush by without sticking to him.

Her lips trembled in a smile. She had to keep his memory alive for the kids. Thank goodness, she had some short videos and lots of pictures on her phone and computer. In one of those plastic totes destined for storage, she'd kept love letters he'd written when they were separated for a year after he graduated from college ahead of her. They were silly, like he so often was, and sweet, too. When Josh and Jenna were old enough, she'd excise anything sexual and let them read the letters.

It was past time she got over her anger at Kyle and truly grieved.

Now she had to pee, so she tiptoed to the bathroom, closing the door before she turned on the light. She thought she might be able to sleep again.

Once she lay down, though, she kept thinking about him and about her current circumstances. Maybe she'd been able to remember what was good about Kyle because she felt almost safe, however temporary that state was. That would be better than the alternative—that the dreams had come because she had felt an unsettling attraction to Nate Kendrick.

She'd tried hard to be fair to Nate. Maybe tried too hard, and she knew why. Kyle had taken the day off work because he didn't care all that much about his job. He'd volunteered to go with her on the field trip. "We deserve to have a fun day," he'd said. So often, she'd been angry because he'd never really committed himself to any job. Nate *was* committed. Anna had overheard Sonja calling him a workaholic as if that was a bad thing. She'd actually felt envy. The surprise was that he had agreed to come along on the outing in the first place.

And yet, apparently, he had, and then broken his promise. If Sonja was to be believed, he often did. Lying here in the dark, memories of Kyle close, Anna knew she did blame Nate. She didn't *have* to be fair. If he'd gone on the outing like he'd *promised*, Molly would never have been able to slip away on her own. Kyle would not be dead. Those were truths, the ones that counted to her.

Anna didn't blame herself for accepting Nate's offer. Kyle had sacrificed himself to save Molly, and Molly needed Anna now. But she needed to keep Nate at a distance, quit pretending they were in this together, could even be friends.

And, most of all, she had to prevent herself from responding sexually to the tall, dark man whose brooding intensity parted like storm clouds to reveal a sense of humor and dedication to his daughter.

An uneasy thought stirred. Unlike Kyle, Nate Kendrick *was* capable of feeling guilt. In her anger, she'd rejoiced knowing that. Now…it was undeniably disturbing to know that ability said something positive about him.

So what? If only for the memory of the man she'd loved, she couldn't forgive or forget.

WEDNESDAY, THE MINUTE Nate walked in the door at home, he felt the chill, as if he'd entered a refrigerated compartment. It emanated from Anna, who stepped out of the family room to meet him with a cool nod, her blue eyes guarded.

"I've labeled the leftovers with instructions for reheating, and made a salad for you. There's also French bread and cookies on the counter. Now, if you'll excuse me…"

"Did everything go smoothly today?" He couldn't imagine she was annoyed to have him coming home so late, almost seven o'clock. She knew his hours were variable and had calmly, without comment, taken his quick call letting her know.

"Yes. Molly didn't seem to mind going to Josh's practice. She's eaten, needless to say."

"Thank you."

"That's what I'm here for." She went back into the family room, where the kids sat around the coffee table. They seemed to be in the midst of a game of Chinese checkers, which he'd forgotten they even owned. "Time to put that away," she said.

Her announcement was met with predictable groans and complaints. She only shook her head. "We'll set it on the counter, and we can continue the game tomorrow after school."

Standing in the doorway, Nate glanced at the wooden board to see that there were four players, although Anna was likely helping Jenna, too.

"But, Mo-om!" Josh said, looking rebellious.

"You have homework. Which means you do, too, Molly. I should have insisted you both do it before we started a game."

"I *hate* homework," her son grumbled.

Molly chimed in, "Me, too."

"Tough," Anna said unsympathetically. "I'll bet it won't take either of you half an hour."

"But why can't we finish—" Josh said again.

"Because."

They knew when to quit arguing. Nate had to step aside to let them pass, Anna not even acknowledging him. In no time, she'd ushered her children through the kitchen, and he heard a door open and close.

Not even a "Good night."

He and Molly were left looking at each other.

"How come they had to go, Daddy?"

"It is after seven," he said, in fairness. "And she's right about the homework. Why don't you do it at the table so I have company while I eat?"

Her "I guess" lacked enthusiasm, for which he didn't blame her. What kid did enjoy homework?

While his plate of spaghetti warmed in the microwave, he dribbled dressing on his salad and carried it to the table. He studied the work sheets Molly had taken from the book bag and grimaced, although he was careful that she not see him. Yeah, those looked deadly dull.

Once he sat down with the spaghetti, a couple slices of French bread and a glass of milk, he said, "Mrs. Grainger didn't seem to be in a very good mood."

Molly looked up. "She was fun. She kicked a soccer ball with Jenna and me 'stead of watching Josh practice. And she played Chinese checkers, too." She added matter-of-factly, "She's beating us."

So the chill was reserved for him.

Nate couldn't deny Anna had reason not to like him, but he did wonder why the change from yesterday. Or maybe he was imagining that. She'd given him enough hints last night that she didn't plan to make a practice of dining with him. Probably she had only been ensuring the kids all felt comfortable.

Maybe his parents would have been grateful to be needed. In fact, when he called to tell them what was going on, his mother had sounded a little hurt that he hadn't let them know right away.

At the very least, he surely could have found someone who didn't not-so-secretly loathe him. Thinking of Anna the minute he realized he needed help had been natural; she'd been at the back of his mind since he saw her at the hospital that day. The strange thing was he hadn't immediately thought, *Now I can help her.* In fact, he'd been surprised when she'd asked him if that was why he'd offered her the temporary job.

His answer had been all too true. *Molly needs you. I need you.*

Being a part-time dad—both when he was married and parenting his daughter for two days out of fourteen since the divorce—hadn't prepared him for being solely responsible for her well-being. Reconciling work with her needs hadn't been his only problem. He'd panicked and instantly latched onto the idea of co-opting the warm woman Molly had described helping her in the classroom, the one he also knew was capable of being fierce in defense of her kids and herself.

And it appeared she was good to Molly. Good

for her. His daughter had opened up amazingly in only two days. It made him realize how lonely being an only child was. Nate and his brother, Adam, had maintained a fierce competition for much of their childhoods. Nate sometimes thought he owed Adam for the competitive streak, the drive that had made him a success in business. The next time they talked, he might ask Adam if he felt the same. Adam was young to be a lieutenant colonel in the army. Nate smiled wryly. Growing up, neither had ever had a chance to be lonely.

Molly asked a question about a problem on her math work sheet. He found he enjoyed helping her. When she said, "Mommy always says if I don't understand something, I should ask the teacher," he basked in the comparison. Evidently, all it took was a crumb to make him feel like a success as a parent.

He cringed to think he'd descended to trying to show up Sonja. *I'm a better parent.* Yeah, that was mature.

ANNA LEAPED UP from her lawn chair when the action moved toward the goal Josh guarded.

Parents on both sides of the field yelled as two opposing players broke free. A tall, lanky boy kicked it ahead to his teammate. In front of the goal, Josh half crouched on the balls of his feet, ready to leap any direction, his eyes never leaving the ball. She had a flash of seeing his father in him.

"You've got it, Josh!" Nate called.

A quick sidelong pass and the tall boy drew his foot back for a hard kick. The ball shot for the goal…and Josh flung himself right in front of it. He tumbled to the ground with the ball in his hands.

The parents on the other side of the field groaned. The parents on this side cheered and called, "Great stop!" to Josh, who jumped up and kicked the ball darn near the length of the field.

Nate flashed a grin at Anna. "He's good."

She felt a burst of maternal pride. "He is, isn't he? The coach says he's fearless."

He looked over his shoulder, automatically checking on his daughter and Jenna. "I wonder if Molly would like to play."

"It's a great sport for kids their age." Anna felt a sense of unreality. Why had he wanted to come along today? She'd half hoped he'd offer to keep Jenna so she didn't have to come to the game. Jenna usually found other kids to play with, but Anna made her stay close and she got bored. With multiple soccer fields, other games were going on to each side of this field. Every time a game ended, parents and kids streamed away, while the participants in the next game replaced them. Misplacing one little girl would be all too easy.

Earlier, just as she'd been herding her kids to the car and asking Josh if he was *sure* he had his shin guards and shoes, which he hadn't put on yet, Nate had opened the front door of the house.

"Can Molly and I come?" he'd asked. In a plain gray T-shirt and khaki chinos that hung low on his lean hips, he was obviously ready for the occasion.

Anna had stopped. "You're kidding."

"No, I want to see Josh play."

She'd stolen a glance at her son, to see him looking pleased. She didn't have much choice. "If you can be ready to go in about two minutes. Or you could follow us." And maybe never find the right field, she thought hopefully. Oh, that was mean, but she'd done really well avoiding him since Tuesday, and now what had he done but put her on the spot.

Somehow, they'd ended up in his Lexus instead of her aging Toyota. Given that this was Bellevue, the Lexus looked more at home in the parking lot at the athletic facility than her car ever did. One more small sting.

After popping the trunk, Nate had insisted on carrying her lawn chair and the small cooler with drinks and snacks she'd brought. Once she knew Nate and Molly were coming, too, she'd raced up to the apartment for extras.

Anna had been very conscious of curious glances from other parents, who knew about Kyle's death. Here she was, not even four months later, appearing with another man in tow. They'd look like a family to anyone who didn't know better. And who wouldn't look, given that this new man was gorgeous even in everyday clothes?

Nate stayed near her on the sidelines, too, keeping an eye on the girls as much as she did and clearly enjoying the game. He sounded so wistful when he wondered whether Molly would want to play. Anna would have guessed he'd been an athlete even if he hadn't mentioned playing some kind of peewee football. From the way he moved and the lean muscles bared by the short-sleeved T-shirt, he must stay active despite the hours he worked.

He paced a few feet along the sideline, calling encouragement to Josh's teammate who was moving the ball. Her cheeks felt hot as she eyed his body speculatively. He had to be an inch or two over six feet, broad-shouldered, muscles taut but not overdeveloped like a weight lifter's. Given his working schedule, whatever he did to stay in shape almost had to be at a health club. Maybe the elliptical or a treadmill or racquetball. Tennis? He didn't have a deep tan. In well-worn athletic shoes, he was light on his feet. Probably itching to be out on the field himself.

He might be less intimidating today than when he was wearing one of his obviously expensive custom suits, but he was no less sexy.

Suddenly, she realized he'd turned and caught her watching him. They stared at each other, she with her face burning, him with an inscrutable expression, and Anna knew how wrong she'd been. He was just as daunting like this. Even with his dark hair disheveled, Nate Kendrick had an air of command.

She started when all the parents on the sidelines leaped to their feet yelling. It gave her an excuse to look away from Nate's penetrating gray eyes. She was just in time to see a ball sail over Josh's fingertips and into the goal. She called, "Good try, Josh," but doubted he'd heard her amid the other voices.

He was dejected when the game ended with a 1-0 score. His teammates slapped him on the back and said things like, "Not your fault. We didn't score." The coach spoke quietly to him, and he shrugged and dragged his oversize feet as he walked to the car.

The minute all the doors were shut so nobody else would hear, he said, "I blew it."

Ready to back up, Nate braked instead, and turned in the seat to look over his shoulder at her son. "No, you let one ball go by. You can't stop them all. You know that. That's why you have teammates."

"Yeah, but we'd have won if I could've—"

"You wouldn't have won, because your team didn't score. They were seriously outmatched today. Most of the action took place in front of your goal. Do you know how many stops you made?"

"Um…a bunch," Josh mumbled.

"Way more than the other team's goalie. What I saw today was you saving your team from being embarrassed. You were dynamite."

At his matter-of-fact words, Josh straightened from the defeated slouch, pride replacing dejection. Feeling both annoyance and gratitude, Anna knew *she* could have said the same thing and Josh wouldn't have believed it. But how could she mind when Nate had given her son what he needed?

She tried to remember if Kyle had had the same gift for boosting a boy's self-esteem and couldn't remember any particular speech. No, she was being silly; Kyle must have. He'd been proud of Josh, and Josh had preened with his father's attention. Seeing him react the same to Nate's comments made her sad. A boy needed his father. As much as she wanted to tell Nate to butt out of their lives, she knew she couldn't, however much it grated to see him, of all people, giving Josh what he needed. Wherever they went from here, Anna resolved, she'd find ways for Josh to have male role models in his life.

Just…not *this* man.

CHAPTER EIGHT

THURSDAY THE NEXT WEEK, Nate came home early to share a hasty dinner with Molly—placed at the front in the refrigerator with the usual note telling him how many minutes it would need to reheat in the microwave. He'd barely set foot in the front door when Anna hustled her kids out through the kitchen. She'd been like that since the game Saturday. Or maybe he should say since Sunday, when he'd gotten out the skateboards and bikes. While Molly and Josh skateboarded, he'd held Jenna up so she could pedal Molly's old bike in circles around the paved area. She was a few years from being ready to ride on her own. She had one with training wheels, she'd assured him, but Mommy had said it had to go to storage.

Nate had every intention of suggesting they go get it. Of course, talking to Anna would be easier if he could get her to pause and look at him for more than a fleeting, evasive moment. And, damn, but her attitude was getting under his skin.

He gobbled his dinner and saw that Molly

was picking at hers. "Don't dawdle if you want to see your mom."

She didn't even look up, perplexing him. Didn't she *want* to see her mother? Yes, Sonja had scared her when she fell into a drunken stupor; maybe she had already been scaring her with alcohol-fueled scenes. But he'd have sworn Molly adored her mother, too.

Either way, he thought she needed to see Sonja. He wondered if she might believe he'd been lying to her and her mother was really dead.

"Okay, that's it," he finally said, tugging gently at her braid. "Find your shoes, and let's go."

She didn't protest, just moved slowly. Nate wasn't thrilled about having to drive over the bridge to Seattle for a second time today, but this was important. After checking Molly's seat belt, he cast a glance up at the apartment. Damn, he wished Anna was coming, too. She understood his daughter better than he did. The only person he saw in the window was Jenna, though. He waved, and she grinned and did the same. She looked astonishingly like what Anna must have at that age, but was a whole lot more cheerful.

Yeah, why would that be?

Mouth twisted, he accelerated up the long driveway.

On the way, he asked about Molly's day at school and got monosyllables in return. Once, he glanced in the rearview mirror to see her sucking on the tip of her braid, a habit he thought she'd dropped when she was four or so. Certainly before she started school. Under the circumstances, regression wouldn't be a surprise, but he wondered when she'd started up this habit again. After the divorce? Since he'd brought her home from her mother's apartment? Or today, because she dreaded seeing Sonja?

He didn't ask.

Nate held her hand walking into the treatment center. After signing in, the bearded man behind the counter encouraged—told them—to keep the visit to no more than half an hour. Then he directed them to a sitting room where a woman waited.

Nate glanced in, wondered where Sonja was…and felt a jolt. Good God, that was her.

He should have known immediately from her distinctive hair color, but… She wouldn't usually be caught dead in a plain and not very flattering crew-neck T-shirt, jeans and flip-flops. Her red hair was pulled severely into a ponytail. Instead of bobbing, it hung lank and lifeless. The only times he'd seen her without makeup were first thing in the morning, and then she hadn't had dark, swollen bruises beneath her eyes or sallow skin. She'd aged a decade, at least.

Molly shrank against him. He laid a hand on her shoulder and gave a subtle squeeze.

"Sonja."

Even her hazel eyes were apathetic. Her gaze moved slowly from Molly to him. Only then did some anger show on her face.

"I'd like to visit my daughter alone."

Nate hesitated. The request wasn't unreasonable, but he didn't want to desert Molly, either.

He bent to kiss the top of her head, murmuring, "Why don't you go sit with your mom, punkin. I'll be right outside, I promise."

She cast him a single, frightened look, then straightened and trudged to her mother, who enveloped her stiff little figure in a hug.

Finding it hard to watch, Nate retreated to the hall. He wanted to eavesdrop, but knew that crossed a line. Hearing a television, he strolled to the large opening across the hall into what was clearly a communal space with a large-screen television. A playoff baseball game was on. No Mariners, of course. Still, watching idly from the doorway was as good a distraction as any.

A couple men seemed engaged. The other half-a-dozen people sitting in the scattered chairs or on the sofas looked as blank as Sonja had. Presumably, they felt like crap. Drying out had to be hell. It was taking a toll on Sonja, a beautiful, usually vivacious woman with emotions that bubbled and seethed.

What was she saying to Molly? Wondering

had tension crawling up his neck. Did she have the sense to see that Molly needed reassurance instead of excuses or accusations? Gentleness?

He kept sneaking glances at his watch. Scanned incoming emails and texts on his phone while verifying that his watch was accurate.

At twenty-eight minutes after they'd signed in, he returned to the small room. Sonja had her arm around Molly and was murmuring into her ear. Molly had rounded her shoulders, giving her a hunched posture he'd seen so often when she'd been unhappy but wouldn't tell him why.

"Hey, kiddo. Time to say goodbye to your mom."

Sonja shot him a look of intense dislike, then kissed Molly on top of her head and said something he thought was "Remember." Remember what?

Molly stared at her feet as she came to his side. He nodded and said, "I'm glad to see you past the worst, Sonja. You may not think so, but I'm rooting for you."

"Sure you are."

His mouth tightened, but he nodded again, said good-night and steered Molly out of the room. He signed them out and they walked to the car. Dusk turned the sky purple, and the air felt pleasantly cool after an unexpectedly hot day. He'd have felt more relief at having this over with if he hadn't feared they'd have to visit several more times before Sonja completed treat-ment. And then what? Could he trust that she was recovered? How could he monitor her? He was damn well not going to turn Molly over to her until she'd demonstrated sobriety for a few weeks, at least. He made a mental note to talk to Anna about staying those extra weeks.

Driving from the parking lot, ready to wend his way through city streets to the freeway, he glanced in the rearview mirror. "Did you have a good visit?" he asked at last.

She shrugged.

Maybe this was none of his business, but he asked, anyway. "What did your mom mean when she asked you to remember?"

This look was distinctly fearful. "I don't know," she mumbled.

Startled, even shocked, Nate realized his seven-year-old daughter had just lied to him. He had a really bad feeling he knew what Sonja had urged Molly to remember.

DESPITE HER DETERMINATION to avoid Nate, Anna loitered the next evening while he greeted the kids. This had been one of his long days. For Molly's sake, she had to talk to him. She could be strong and ignore the shimmer of anticipa-tion at having an excuse to spend even a few minutes with him.

He backed out of the family room and saw

her hovering in the living room. "Hey," he said, strolling toward her and dropping suit coat and briefcase on the sofa as he did every day when he got home. "Is something wrong?"

"I did want to talk to you for a minute. In the kitchen?"

Obviously understanding that she didn't want the kids to overhear, he suggested, "Why don't we step outside?"

It was another beautiful evening, the sky vivid orange, Lake Washington in dark shadow. Glad he hadn't turned on porch lights, Anna drew in a deep breath and let herself enjoy the spectacular view. She could hear more than see a boat passing, the sound of the motor muted. Tiny waves splashed against the dock and shore.

"What is it?" Nate asked, his voice deep, quiet.

"I wondered how the visit went yesterday. Molly has been really withdrawn. She told Josh she didn't want to play, and sat at the table to do her homework all by herself, instead."

He gazed out at the lake for a minute before responding. "Sonja asked me to leave her alone with Molly. I didn't see how I could say no. We were limited to half an hour, so I waited out in the hall."

"Did she tell you what she and her mom talked about?"

The sound he made could have been a laugh

if it had held any amusement at all. "She locks down when she's scared or worried or even just feels uncertain. Turns inward. When she came out of the room, she was…changed. Not in a good way." He hesitated, then said with clear irony, "The last thing Sonja said was 'Remember.'"

"Oh."

"*You* have a right to be angry. What I don't understand is why *she's* so goddamn set on hating me for canceling on one outing."

"One?" Anna wished she could see his face better. "I used to hear her grumbling about how you were always breaking promises."

He said a word he *definitely* shouldn't use within the kids' hearing and swung away.

Feeling uncertain, she studied his back, an unrevealing sight. She swallowed, her essentially nice core overcoming her. "I'm sorry. I shouldn't have told you that. Or…or necessarily believed her. I mean, people tend to say ugly things about each other after a divorce."

Nate blew out a long breath, rolled his head as if to ease tight muscles and faced her again. Only a hint of color remained in the sky, but light from the kitchen and the one lamp on in the living room let them see each other.

"I'm not proud of how often I let Molly down. My only excuse is that my job is exceptionally demanding and stressful. I still believe that if

Sonja had understood, Molly would have, too. Sonja liked the money I made, but seemed to think I should still be able to cut out at five o'clock every day and never go into the office on Saturdays or Sundays. I don't know why I even deluded myself that I could take that particular day off. I will say that I never agreed to anything like that without warning her I might not be able to make it."

Anna felt worse about repeating Sonja's complaints and ashamed that she'd believed every word of them.

"As our marriage deteriorated—" the usually smooth voice had become ragged "—I made more excuses. I let my frustration with Sonja impact Molly. I can't forgive myself for that."

Anna's fingernails bit into her palms. "I know why she's set on hating you for canceling that day."

He went so still she thought he had even quit breathing.

"She feels guilty. It's…hard to live with thinking it might be her fault a man died. If she can blame you…" Anna couldn't believe she was saying this. There she went, determined to be fair again.

She also couldn't believe she was telling him anything he hadn't already guessed.

After a minute, he said, "I wondered."

"Well." She backed away. "I'll try to give

Molly some extra attention. Maybe she'll talk to me. Right now, I need to get my kids heading for bed."

"Wait. I need to ask you something."

Wary, she heard him out and couldn't argue with his reasoning. The original month they'd agreed upon wasn't long enough. Both of them should have realized sooner that he couldn't return Molly to her mother the minute she walked out of treatment.

"I don't see that a few more weeks makes any difference," she said.

He thanked her and she said something noncommittal, then retreated into the house, very aware of his quizzical gaze. She only hoped she hadn't given away her relief at having the reprieve extended.

ANNA'S EYES POPPED open to a dark room. There was the moment of disorientation she hadn't gotten past; the windows leaking faint light weren't in the right place, and neither was her clock.

Sofa. Apartment. Muffled sobs.

Josh.

She jumped up and rushed into the bedroom to see him curled away from her, his body shaking. Jenna, thank goodness, still slept. Anna sat on the edge of Josh's bed and touched his shoulder.

"Nightmare?" she murmured.

She thought he nodded amid the snuffles.

"Come on out to the living room," she whispered.

He didn't say anything, but he swiped his face with a corner of his sheet and, when she stood, slipped out of bed. She pulled the bedroom door almost closed behind them, then turned on a lamp in the living room. Anna detoured only long enough to grab several paper towels from the kitchen before sitting on the sofa and holding out an arm. Rarely willing to put up with hugs from his mom anymore, tonight Josh snuggled against her. She bundled the comforter around both of them.

"Here. Blow," she said, tucking one of the paper towels in his hand.

He mopped himself up, then leaned trustingly against her.

"Did you dream about your dad?" she asked after a minute.

He nodded, his thin face splotched with red and his eyes puffy. So often now she looked at him and saw the teenager he'd be in the blink of an eye. Tonight, he was very much her little boy.

"Do you remember it?"

"Not really," he said uncertainly. "But... I miss him." A shudder passed through his thin frame, and he pressed his face to her side. "Why did he have to die?" he begged.

Anna had to blink back tears of her own.

"Because he was the kind of man who couldn't watch a little girl die."

"I hate her!" he cried. His body vibrated with outrage. "Daddy would still *be* here if she hadn't been so stupid!"

"I understand," she whispered, resting her cheek on top of his head. "But I hope you'll get past blaming Molly. *All* kids do stupid things sometimes."

"I don't—"

She managed something close to a laugh. "Do you remember when Austin kicked the ball over your head and you ran out into the street to get it?" It had been one of the worst moments of her life. She'd been looking out the window, unable to do a single thing to prevent her son being hit and killed by a pickup approaching on the street. The driver had slammed on the brakes, almost too late. His bumper had tapped Josh, knocking him down. He'd been frightened, unhurt except for skinning both knees and the palms of his hands.

Now he peered up at her in chagrin. "That was kind of stupid."

"Kind of?" Her voice broke.

He scrunched up his face. Anna let the silence draw out, waiting for him to tell her what he was thinking.

"I guess it is kind of the same."

"Yes, it is. All Molly wanted to do was wade.

She had no idea the current was strong enough to knock her down. Even if she'd been to a river before, usually she could have safely waded in early summer."

"But Dad couldn't swim! He shouldn't have gone in."

She repeated a lot of what they'd talked about before, knowing Josh needed to hear it over and over. Anna had no doubt Kyle had been his usual heedless self. There wouldn't have been a question in his mind that he could pull Molly out without plunging in over his head. But she felt equally certain he would have made the same choice even if he'd been afraid. She wanted Josh to believe his father hadn't willingly left him—but also that, in the end, Kyle had died a hero.

Josh cried some more, and so did she. Even though his soccer game was an early one tomorrow, meaning they couldn't sleep in, she didn't suggest he go back to bed. Instead, she told him a few other stories about his dad, reminding him of times they'd all been together, talking softly, until she knew he was asleep.

Then she carried him to bed.

After turning out the light, she couldn't settle down as readily as he had. As she squirmed in an attempt to get comfortable on the couch, her emotions roiled. Kyle wouldn't be at tomorrow's soccer game to cheer on Josh—but Nate would. Nate, who should have been at the park that day…except she understood why he hadn't. Miserable and confused, it took her ages to fall asleep.

NATE WAS DAMN glad to reach the middle school where today's game was being played. This morning, neither Josh nor Molly were speaking. She hadn't wanted to come, and he'd almost decided to give her her way. But if he had, she'd have stared at whatever movie she put in the DVD player, and instead of being able to concentrate on work, he'd have felt restless and wondered how the game was going and what Molly was thinking.

Squeezed in the middle of the back seat, Jenna had given up on the other two and resorted to playing an irritating, handheld game that flashed lights and trumpeted loudly whenever she beat it. Beside him, Anna looked strained, too. Even once he found a parking place and they started for the field, he and she wouldn't have a chance to talk. Josh ran ahead to join teammates, but Molly and Jenna stuck close.

In an obvious attempt to prevent that talk, Anna planted her lawn chair beside another woman she knew. Eventually, both girls succumbed to the lure of playing with other kids, so Nate watched the game.

This week, Josh stopped every ball before it reached the goal in the first half. Because his team was ahead 3-0, the coach switched him to forward for the second half and put another boy in as goalie. The substitute let a couple balls by, but Josh slammed a hard kick past the opposing goalie to make the score 4-2, which held until the end of the game.

Sweaty and grinning as he came off the field, Josh was a different boy from the one he'd been earlier. "Did you see, Mom?" he demanded, detouring by her as another mother started distributing drinks and snacks.

She grinned at him. "I saw. You were awesome."

Nate held up a hand, and after only a brief hesitation, Josh gave him a high five. "Good game," Nate said sincerely. "You're a heck of a player, Josh. Your mom's going to be sorry when you're a little older and get picked for a select team."

She rolled her eyes in exaggerated dismay, and Josh chortled as he rejoined his teammates for the snacks and a huddle around the coach. Molly and Jenna showed up for the snacks and juice Anna had brought for them. When she offered him a juice box, Nate laughed. "I think I can wait until we get to the pizza parlor."

"Are we…?"

"Sure," he said in surprise. "Why not? Makes the kids happy, and then you don't have to cook."

Anna nodded, but something about his suggestion made her *not* happy. It was that bad, sitting at a table and eating with him? She hadn't seemed to mind last week. Did she dislike the fact that he had insisted on paying last week, and would again today?

Maybe. For good reason, money was a sensitive issue for her. If they kept this up, he'd have to let her pick up the check sometimes whether he liked it or not.

But all three kids cheered when he made the suggestion as they walked back to the car. Anna was watching, and he saw her lips twist in resignation and some other emotion he couldn't read.

He didn't like knowing he'd dropped some notches once again in her regard, but this wasn't the first time it had happened, and it wouldn't be the last. He ought to be counting the days until he didn't need her anymore, and she'd moved on with her life and out with her kids. Life would be a hell of a lot more peaceful.

If he felt something closer to dread than anticipation, Nate tried to convince himself it was only because when that day came, it would mean Molly had gone back to live with her mother.

CHAPTER NINE

"WHAT?" STUNNED, NATE leaned back in his desk chair, aware of his assistant's startled stare at his reaction to this phone call. At his signal, she left, closing the door softly behind her.

"Since Ms. Kendrick's participation in our program was voluntary, we couldn't prevent her decision to leave." The assistant director of the treatment facility was in defense mode.

"Are you able to tell me *when* she went?" he asked, unable to entirely rein in the sarcasm.

"Ah…I don't see any harm in that. She left Saturday morning."

"Saturday," he repeated. Sonja had walked out four days ago. She hadn't been in touch with him, and the treatment center hadn't felt any obligation to let him know even if he was paying the bills and caring for the daughter he and Sonja shared.

"I'm sorry." At last the woman sounded regretful. "We always hope for a better outcome, but this…didn't come entirely as a surprise to us. Ms. Kendrick's attitude wasn't the best. Counselors remarked that she didn't seem committed to success. She may just not have been ready."

Not even for Molly's sake?

"I understand," he forced himself to say. "I'm principally concerned that she hasn't been in touch."

"That is a worry," she conceded.

Probably brusque, he cut her off and called Sonja's cell phone. No answer. After the beep, he said, "Call me." Then he tried to decide what to do. He assumed she'd gone home. Why go anywhere else when she owned the condo outright, part of her divorce settlement. Should he drive over there now? Wait until he left work?

But, once again, she'd demolished his ability to concentrate, which meant he should go now, get any confrontation over with.

He stuck his head in John's office to explain what was going on and apologize for his lack of productivity. John snorted. "Don't be ridiculous. Go."

Sonja's condo was on Queen Anne, built to take advantage of a spectacular view of Elliott Bay and the ferry and shipping lanes. In another mood, he might have walked and taken pleasure in a sunny, warm day. Rain and gray skies would be here soon enough. Instead, he drove, and when he got there had to circle several blocks before he found an empty parking spot. The doorman greeted him with friendly familiarity, and Nate used his key to ride the elevator to her floor.

He knocked on her door, waited and knocked again. He didn't hear a whisper of sound. She either wasn't here, had chosen to ignore him or was passed out. *Take your pick.* At least if he went in, he'd know whether she had returned home. If she was unconscious again…he could save her life.

Nate knocked one more time, then let himself in. The reek of alcohol met him. Had the carpet retained the odor, or…? No, Sonja sat on the white leather sofa, a martini glass on the black-enamel coffee table in front of her. She wore stylish slacks and a silk shirt, but her hair straggled from whatever she'd done this morning, and makeup didn't disguise that extra decade.

"You," she said with loathing.

At first sight, he couldn't tell if she was drunk, but she had to be on her way.

"I was concerned."

"Why? You haven't cared about me in a long time. If you ever did." Her eyes burned with fury. "You're here in hopes of catching me indulging in a drink. And—gasp!—I am. What a crime."

"A crime, no." All he felt was pity. "You've proved yourself unable to care for Molly, though. And that, I do care about."

"Oh, you're such a great father," she taunted

him. "Mr. Always-Something-More-Important-to-Do. And now you've hired the grieving widow who wouldn't *be* a widow if it wasn't for your latest broken promise."

Refusing to allow her to see that her dart had struck home, he added steel to his voice. "I'm here to say that until you deal with your problem, Molly will stay with me. Visits will be supervised until I'm satisfied you've stayed sober for a minimum of a month *after* leaving treatment. Do you understand?"

"Just try it. *I* have primary custody, remember?"

"That can be changed."

Sonja leaped to her feet, screaming. She snatched up the martini glass and threw it at him, missing by several feet. It smashed against the wall. The stench stung his nostrils.

He said calmly, "You're still Molly's mother. I'll help when you're ready to get your life back together." And then he backed out and closed the door.

ANNA SAT CROSS-LEGGED on the ground at the soccer field, her head bent until it almost touched Molly's as they both watched a beetle struggle over the short-cropped grass. Not far away, Jenna shrieked happily as she played tag with several other younger siblings. Molly hadn't wanted to join them.

"Can we pick him up and move him so he won't get stepped on?" she asked.

"That's a good idea," Anna said gently. "Do you want to pick him up, or shall I?"

"I will." Her rather crooked pigtails—her dad's achievement—fell forward over her shoulder as she cupped her hand and waited until the beetle toppled off a grass blade onto her palm. "I like bugs. Most girls are stupid about them."

"Yes, they are." Anna grinned, and Molly gave a small, shy smile in response.

Anna's phone buzzed as she rose with considerably less grace than Molly did. "Your dad is calling," she said, hiding her apprehension. "I'd better find out what he wants."

Molly headed toward the line of poplars that edged the field. Seeing a reassuring wave from another mother whose daughter was playing with Jenna, Anna followed even as she answered the phone.

"Nate?"

"Yeah. I just remembered Josh has practice today."

"That's where we are." Hearing tension in his voice, she stopped where she could watch Molly on her rescue mission without being overheard. "Is something wrong?"

"I just found out that Sonja walked out on treatment Saturday. Apparently, nobody felt an obligation to let me know."

"Oh, no." Poor Molly.

"I left work to check on her. She's home, martini glass in hand. Until she threw it at me," he added.

"But…why didn't she call? Didn't she want to see Molly?"

"I have no idea what she was thinking," he said tersely. "I told her I'd pay for treatment when she's ready to give it another try, and that in the meantime, she can see Molly, but only under supervision."

"That's when she threw the glass at you?"

"More or less." He was quiet for a minute. "I have to tell Molly."

"Yes."

"How is she?"

"Quiet." Anna told him about the bug rescue. "She has such a good heart."

"I know she does. She's just so restrained. I wish… I don't know. I'd like to see her explode with emotion. Yell at me, or fall down laughing."

"I don't think that's her nature," Anna said, watching now as Molly bent and carefully released the beetle. A moment later, she turned and started back toward Anna. "And you really don't want to see her falling apart. I did, and it was heartbreaking."

"Yeah." He cleared his throat. "You're right. She did sob on me when we talked about what happened. It…was upsetting."

"Seeing her mother last week hit her hard," Anna said gently. "Until then, she was giggling and playing with my two."

"And what will the latest news do to her?" He sounded harsh.

"She might be relieved."

"She should be," he shot back. "Except…hell, knowing her mother can't make the effort even for her sake?"

"I don't know."

He gusted a sigh. "Can we all have dinner together tonight? Molly is more ghost than little girl when we're alone together these days."

She didn't feel she could do anything but agree. "I had a kid dinner planned, anyway." She smiled at Molly, who was close enough to hear and looked inquiring. "Hamburgers and scalloped potatoes and green beans."

"Yay!" Molly exclaimed.

"I heard that," Nate said in her ear.

Anna laughed. "The way to a little girl's heart is her tummy." She rubbed Molly's. Somehow, in the tussle, the phone fell to the grass, but, given the little girl giggles, Anna doubted Nate minded being cut off.

NATE FIRED UP the grill for the hamburgers and carried them out on a plate, Molly trailing him.

"You won't make mine pink, will you, Daddy? I don't like them that way."

"I know you don't. As if I could forget." He smiled at her. "Were you bored today watching Josh's practice?"

"Uh-uh. I never watch, 'cuz that *would* be boring. Sometimes I play with the other kids, but today Anna and me tried to find a four-leaf clover, and we watched some ants and I saved a beetle from being squished when someone stepped on him."

"You sure it was a he?" Nate asked as he shifted hamburgers to the grill. They sizzled, and the immediate smell of cooking meat made his stomach growl.

"I guess it could've been a she," she said solemnly. "I don't know how to tell."

"I don't, either."

"I wish we studied bugs in school." Her expression brightened. "Maybe we will, 'cuz Mrs. Tate says *we* get to have the tarantula in *our* class after Christmas. Mr. Ewing's class has it right now."

Had she forgotten that the plan hadn't been for her to stay in the Bellevue school even until Thanksgiving, far less Christmas? Did she not *want* to return to her previous classroom…or to live with her mother?

He hid his disquiet. "Lucky you."

She stood quietly as he turned the burgers. He began to suspect she'd followed him out here for some reason besides reminding him that she liked her meat well-done.

Finally, she said, "Do we hafta—I mean, are we going to see Mommy tonight?"

"No. You won't be seeing her this week at all." He'd intended to wait until later in the evening to talk to her, but this was his best chance to tell her what was happening without making a production out of it. "I found out today that your mom left the alcohol treatment center Saturday. Our deal was that she complete the monthlong program and quit drinking before you went home with her. So you'll be staying here until she can do that. I told her she could visit, but probably here, when either Anna or I am around. I don't want you going overnight until I know your mom won't get drunk and scare you again."

"Oh."

He set down the turner and crouched in front of her. "You may think I'm being mean…"

Molly shook her head. "I don't like it when Mommy gets that way."

"I know." He cupped her cheek. "When you've been drinking as much alcohol as she has, it's hard to quit. You feel really sick. She needs to get well for you, though, and I really believe she will eventually. In the meantime, *I* like having you here with me."

She gave another of those serious little nods. "Daddy, one of your hamburgers is on fire."

He swore and leaped up.

"MOLLY, DID YOU TELL Josh and Jenna about the beetle?" Anna asked, as she passed the bowl of green beans along.

Molly shook her head. Had she spoken yet? Anna looked at Nate, who gave a barely perceptible nod. Yes, he'd told her about her mother? That was the only interpretation Anna could arrive at.

"Here, honey." Taking the bowl from her, he dished up green beans for himself and his daughter before passing them along. "Good scalloped potatoes."

"Thank you," Anna said, "but it doesn't take a gourmet chef to make them."

"You're supposed to say, 'Thank you for the compliment, Nate.'"

She suppressed a smile. "Thank you for the compliment, Nate."

Would he tell her after dinner how Molly had reacted to the news? She'd insist he did, Anna decided. She couldn't help if she didn't know what was going on with her.

"Coach says the team we're playing Saturday is really good." Returning to his favorite subject, Josh took another big bite of his cheeseburger and chewed with enthusiasm. The minute he swallowed, he added, "They haven't lost a game yet."

"Then it's about time they do," Nate said. "You're playing goalie again?"

"Uh-huh. Coach says I'll play goalie the whole game unless we get ahead."

"At your age, I wish he'd give all the boys a chance to try out every position." She liked the coach, but worried that he placed more emphasis on winning than he did in letting the kids have fun, and explore their strengths and weaknesses.

"You could be a darn good forward, too," Nate commented. "You're fast, and you have a strong kick."

Molly ate, but with her head down. Did she mind her father's rapture about Josh's athletic prowess?

"In practice, Coach moves us around to different positions," Josh said, "but I think some of the guys are sort of scared of the ball. You know, like, having it come right at their face. Mostly, it's me and Ian that don't mind."

Anna decided not to correct his grammar. She had seen other boys playing goalie during practices, and while she'd noticed they were tentative, she'd thought it was only inexperience. Now she realized Josh was right.

"Are you coming to the game?" Josh asked Nate. He sounded casual. Just curious, either way is okay.

Anna knew better. She tensed.

Nate flicked a glance at her before he said, "I'm planning to be there, although I'll give you my, uh, usual caution. Molly has heard this a few hundred times."

Nibbling at her cheeseburger, Molly didn't react.

A couple lines appeared on Nate's forehead, but he looked back at Josh. "I work long hours, and I can't always be sure when I'll have to go into the office or meet with someone. So I'll try, but I can't promise."

"Oh."

Nate smiled at her son. "I've really enjoyed watching your games. If I had more time, I might think about looking for an adult league."

"That'd be cool," Josh agreed. "Soccer is fun."

Jenna said loudly, "*I'm* going to play when I'm old enough."

"And when is that?" Nate asked.

"Oh, another year or two," Anna said, purposely vague, "depending on the rules wherever we're living."

Molly gave her an alarmed look, and Josh's dismay at the reminder was obvious. Jenna might not even understand that the *moving* her mommy talked about would mean not going to Mrs. Schaub's house or seeing her friends from there ever again. Nobody said a word, although Nate's frown deepened.

He might need her to stay longer, given the situation with Sonja. Would that be good or bad? She didn't want the kids to get too used to his luxurious home or to having a seemingly ready-made father—but making an ill-judged move to an unknown town when she didn't have a real job offer didn't seem smart, either.

If she knew they might stay until, say, Christmas break, she should start subbing locally to strengthen her résumé and fortify her confidence. If he asked her...well, then she'd make some calls.

A TIME-CONSUMING part of Nate's job was to play nursemaid to the start-ups and companies in his portfolio. Venture capitalists didn't hand over substantial funds, then sit back waiting for the business to boom until they could rake in the vast profits. Instead, they provided steady guidance to protect their investments.

Nate did everything from helping adjust business plans to introducing suitable executives to entrepreneurs K & L had "seeded." He held regular meetings with people at every company in his portfolio, analyzing personalities, progress, how smoothly operations were going, how the capital he'd help provide was being spent. He'd intensify his attention depending on what stage the company was at. He looked hard at product development and initial marketing, at expansion or changes in management.

And he had to step in when sales, management or anything else went amiss.

He'd been trying to reach Andy Mayernik for several days, and grown increasingly uneasy when his calls weren't returned. Mayernik had been launching a software game company with an initial offering Nate had thought could be a big winner. He'd felt good about the investment until three months before launch when Mayernik abruptly fired the CEO and hired a new one without consulting Nate. His instinct was that the new guy didn't understand the target audience. Instead of building on the original marketing campaign, which he didn't think was exciting enough, the new CEO convinced Mayernik to throw it out and start afresh. Even if the new campaign had been fabulous—and it wasn't—Nate worried it wouldn't catch on so late, and the panicky phone call he was taking late Friday afternoon confirmed his instincts.

"I screwed up," Mayernik said gloomily. "Orders just aren't happening. We can't compete with the sales forces from the big guys."

Or this new player in the market had neglected to build a solid sales-and-distribution pipeline. This was why Nate put so much emphasis on the executive brought in to run any new enterprise. Mayernik had created a brilliant product, but had had no idea how to run the company needed to bring that product to market. He hadn't had the money, either, which was why K & L had put together several million dollars in funding.

Nate pointed out, "This isn't a stodgy industry, Andy. Gamers are always looking for something with a fresh look or twist. You know that."

"Well, they haven't noticed that's what we're offering." He sounded next thing to suicidal. "What do we do?"

"We need to sit down and take a hard look at marketing materials and the numbers. Who haven't you reached? Why?" Nate said.

"Tonight?"

Now, or tomorrow? He couldn't let his decision rest on whether he might disappoint a seven-year-old boy. "It's five thirty now. I'm wiped out," he said. "I can't give you my best after spending the entire day in conference calls."

"Tomorrow?"

"Yeah, I can do that." If he couldn't figure out how to turn things around, the loss would be sizable but not cataclysmic. It happened; not every startup flew, and good ideas didn't always mature into appealing products packaged and priced right. His obligation was to do everything he could to make at least a modest success of every company he'd believed in enough to hand over K & L money, as well as that of other investors who trusted him.

Ending the call, he sat brooding.

Would Josh understand Nate's obligation? Maybe more important, would Anna? Or would she label this a broken promise?

CHAPTER TEN

JOSH KICKED THE back of Anna's seat. "I wish Dad was there."

"I know, honey." Easing to a stop at a red light, she said, "You know how much he loved watching you play."

Since the nightmare, Josh hadn't once mentioned Kyle. But how could he help thinking of his father on game days? Kyle had been one of the men pacing the sideline from the first whistle to the last, calling advice and encouragement. He'd even talked about signing up to coach, although it hadn't happened. Maybe it would have this fall...although Josh was already well established with his team and coach.

"I liked Nate coming to games," her son said discontentedly.

To lighten the mood, she made an exaggerated huffing sound. "What, I'm not good enough?"

He was quiet for a minute. "Moms are different."

As she'd feared, he had been thinking of Nate as a father fill-in. And why not? Nate had been acting like one. She hadn't done nearly as much as she should have to keep it from happening, either. She'd even been grateful, nursing the possibly mistaken belief that Nate's attention would be good for Josh. What if she'd been wrong, and all it would mean was another loss in his life?

And how was she supposed to know what was best? Parenting Jenna had been easier for her from the beginning. Josh might think moms were different, but from her perspective, boys were different, too.

"You can tell Nate all about the game," she said cheerfully.

He hunched. "It's not the same."

Even Jenna stayed quiet. The girls probably felt as if they were strapped in the back beside a wild animal.

When they got home, he wanted to skateboard and became sulky when she made him change to jeans and wear pads and a helmet.

"I was just gonna…"

"If I ever see you setting foot on that thing without the helmet and pads, I'll burn it," she said sternly. "Do you hear me?"

He gave her a defiant look. "It's Nate's, so you can't burn it."

"Try me."

"Fine!" He snatched the keys from her hand and galloped up the stairs.

Anna didn't move for a moment, and nor did either girl.

"How come he's mad?" Jenna asked.

She smiled at both girls and said, "I have no idea," although, of course, she did.

Nate made it home just in time to eat with them. The lasagna came out of the oven at six, and Anna had had no intention of making the kids wait. She'd heard the garage door, but blinked at her first sight of him. Exhaustion carved deep lines in his face. His shirt was wrinkled, the sleeves rolled up, his dark hair standing up in tufts as if he'd been tugging at it. He grimaced at her in place of a smile, then greeted the kids in the family room with what was probably a pretense at good humor.

"How'd the game go?" he asked, to her immense relief. She couldn't hear Josh's response, but Nate's voice was clear. "That's great. Once we sit down to eat, I want to hear all about it."

Then he was walking toward her. "God, that smells good," he said fervently. "You're a blessing, Anna. I think if I had to cook dinner right now, I'd kill myself."

"No, you'd order pizza."

His laugh reformed the lines in his face, making her think it was the first of the day.

"You okay?"

"Beat." He pulled out a stool and sat. "Dealing with idiots takes something out of me."

She smiled. "That bad, huh?"

"Even I can be fooled some of the time."

Anna let her eyebrows climb. "*Even* you?"

"Confidence is a prerequisite for my job. The decisions I make are multimillion-dollar ones." He kneaded the back of his neck. "Damn. We worked out some plans today, but I have no clue whether the guy will follow through, or get another bright idea and gallop after it instead."

Really, she should feed him and get out of here. So what did she do but open her mouth. "Do you want to talk about it?"

His surprise embarrassed her. Why would he want to talk to her? Like she knew anything about business or investments. Or even had the kind of relationship with him that would make it logical for him to use her as a sounding board.

"No, that's silly," she said lightly, bending to take the garlic bread from the oven. "Considering my investments are, hmm, nonexistent."

His gray eyes met hers when she straightened. "Actually, I would, if you mean it. But… after dinner. I'm starved. And, you know—" a faint smile curved his lips "—the way to a man's heart…"

Her heart threw in some extra beats even as she told herself that he was kidding.

"Then tell the kids dinner is ready," she said, sounding only a little breathless. While he did as she'd asked, it occurred to her that he must not be seeing a woman. Had he been flirting rather than teasing?

Predictably, dinner-table conversation was dominated by a blow-by-blow account of the soccer game. Josh's team had accomplished the miracle of not only beating the unbeaten team, but also trouncing them 3-1. Josh wished he could have scored one of the goals, but Coach had kept him in as goalie. Anna rolled her eyes a little as he bragged about his spectacular stops, but his play had been amazing, especially for a kid his age. Okay, she was a proud mama. But she also suspected Nate had been right that select soccer was in her future—assuming she and the kids settled somewhere that *had* a select program, and that she could afford the extra cost of travel.

She was finding it harder and harder to envision that future.

With no school tomorrow, once everyone was done eating, she and Nate let the kids race back to whatever game had had them hooting and gasping earlier. Her two had never had trouble including Molly. In fact…they were all behaving like siblings. That thought was another uneasy one. They *weren't* family. She couldn't let herself forget for a minute.

Nate helped her clear the table and load the dishwasher, a domestic dance they'd perfected on the occasions they'd eaten together. He poured coffee for both of them and said, "Why don't we sit outside?"

Only a hint of color remained over the dark hump of Seattle they could see across the lake. This time, Nate turned on the outside lights. Anna savored the cool air. She could smell meat grilling and hear voices from a couple houses away, and lighted boats passed.

"So, who's the idiot?" she asked.

He grunted. "Oh, there are a couple of them."

"Thing One and Thing Two?"

He laughed at the Dr. Seuss reference. "Wish I'd thought of that while I was dealing with them."

She listened in silence as he talked until he started to sound hoarse.

"So they ignored your advice, but now you're supposed to fix everything that went wrong," she said at last.

"That would be it." Nate sighed. "This guy has genius ideas. I've seen the second game he and his team are working on now. He'll need more money to get it into production, of course." He shook his head and gave a disbelieving laugh. "I need to convince him to fire the other idiot, hire an executive who can take a firm hold, and thereafter butt out where marketing, manufacturing and distribution are concerned."

"Is he refusing?"

"No, he's suitably scared right now. He sat there nodding for all he's worth, saying 'You're right, absolutely...sure, sure.'"

"Not in front of idiot number two?"

"No, I spent the morning with both of them, the afternoon alone with Andy Mayernik. I just don't think he grasps that he's no businessman and never will be, that he has to hire people who know what they're doing and trust them to do it unless and until they screw up."

Anna said, "Let me guess. You'll spend the next few months breathing down his neck."

"As if I don't have anything better to do." He slouched lower in his chair. "Was Josh upset that I couldn't make it today?"

"There's no reason he should be," she said carefully. "We have no claim on you." She gazed at the lake as if she didn't know he had turned his head to look at her.

"Does a kid think that way?" he said after a minute.

Anna sighed, letting down her guard. "Probably not. He was disappointed, but he's not too young to understand that the adults in his life can't always set aside their other obligations for his sake. It's not as if he didn't have transportation to the game and his own cheering section."

"You're trying to tell me Jenna and Molly actually watched?" Amusement changed the timbre of his voice.

"Well, okay, he had his mom there." For some reason, she kept going. "He doesn't talk about his dad a lot, but on the way home he did. He admitted having me there isn't the same. Moms are different."

"I'm assuming he didn't mean in the obvious way." This amusement was enriched by a hint of sexual play.

She refused to see what that looked like on his face.

After a pause, he said, "Molly would probably say dads are different."

"Fathers are important to little girls."

"If I'd had a sister, I might have a better idea what she needs from me."

Laying her hand on his arm wasn't something she could imagine consciously doing, but there it was. Beneath her fingertips and palm, she felt warm skin, taut muscle, tendons, the surprisingly soft texture of the hairs on his forearm. Anna was also very conscious that he had gone completely still, although he was watching her.

She snatched her hand back as if she'd foolishly reached into a dying fire for a coal, hurrying into speech at the same time. "I think you're giving her what she needs most right now. Stability, faith that she can always depend on you. I know she's…turned inward, which might feel like rejection to you, but she's dealing with the hurt of having her mother let her down in a big way. Parents aren't supposed to be fallible."

"And yet I was." He sounded grim.

She almost asked if he really had been neglecting Molly, but she kept her mouth shut. In fact, a panicky need to escape almost overcame her. Her emotions felt too much like the ball crashing between obstacles in an old-fashioned pinball machine, the whop of paddles representing all the outside forces battering her. No matter how well she'd gotten to know Nate, a small part of her still wanted to believe his cancellation that day had been part of a pattern of neglect. Because then…then she was entitled to be angry.

And she knew quite well why she needed to hold on to anger.

She jumped to her feet. "Sitting here talking is probably the last thing you want to do after a long day. I'd better corral my kids and get them ready for bed."

"You're wrong," he said to her back, but it was best if he thought she hadn't heard him.

NATE LET THE determined woman in front of him *almost* steal the ball before he deftly hooked it with his foot and passed it to his pint-size teammate. When Josh rushed at her, Jenna squeaked and kicked it to Molly.

Backing into the goal, Josh watched the ball with the same eagle eye he did during games. No way he was going to be humiliated by his sister or another *girl*.

Anna deserted Nate to race toward Molly.

"Kick it in!" Nate called. "Or back to me or Jenna."

Jenna had a killer instinct, but he was afraid Molly might be too timid for the game. She definitely hadn't liked the ball flying at her when she tried playing goalie.

Alarm more than expertise explained a kick that sent the ball right in front of him instead of at the goal—and gave him the perfect opportunity to tap it into the corner.

Josh groaned theatrically and flopped on the ground. "Three against two isn't fair. I have to play guard *and* goalie."

Nate laughed. "You don't think you're the equal of two girls who've never played the game?"

"'Course I am!" He sprang to his feet. "I'm going to score on *you* now."

"You can try."

When Nate had suggested earlier they all go to the elementary school to kick the ball around, he'd expected Anna to make an excuse not to come. But she was looking at Josh and then Molly when she'd agreed.

They voted that Josh couldn't wear shin guards or soccer shoes since no one else had them. Anna had appeared in jeans, a blue T-shirt and athletic shoes, her golden hair in a ponytail.

During the drive to the field, he'd asked, "Have you ever played soccer?"

"In high school, I was on my school team. Not good enough to get recruited by colleges, but it was fun." She sneaked a look over her shoulder. The kids seemed fully engaged in arguing over whether it would be better to have a dog or a horse. "I…haven't made a big deal out of it." Fleeting sadness crossed her face. "He and Kyle had fun together developing his skills."

In other words, she'd let her husband enjoy her kid's adulation, whether he knew anything about the sport or not.

Instinct told him to keep it light. "So you're telling me I recruited a ringer for the other team," Nate said.

She didn't look at him, but he saw her smile. "Maybe."

So it had proved. She was superbly athletic. From the first drop of the ball, he'd been blown away by her speed and grace. Some women with such spectacularly long legs were coltish, even gawky, but not Anna. Her footwork was so deft she could have been dancing.

The result was she and Josh were formidable opponents. They'd all had fun, even Josh occasionally going easy on his sister so she could have some success.

This time, Nate left Jenna in the goal and came out to meet Josh and Anna, who passed the ball down the field as if they'd done it a thousand times. He and Molly tried without success to steal it. He launched himself forward to block Anna's pass and crashed into her. She went down, and he toppled with her.

He tried to catch some of his weight on his shoulder, but he heard her hard exhalation of air when he landed on her. Dazed for a moment, he couldn't move. Finally, he lifted his head.

"You okay?"

She squeezed her eyes shut, then opened them again. Her eyes were a little glassy. "I...think so."

"Damn, I'm sorry."

"It was just as much my fault."

Now was when he should move, get to his feet. Help her up. No, he should have already done that, before his body had a chance to notice he was lying on top of a woman who was soft in all the right places.

Too late.

He felt mesmerized, unable to look away from her face. Her mouth was tantalizingly close. If he dipped his head a few inches, he'd be kissing her. Her lips parted, and he forced his gaze upward to find startled awareness in her eyes. For an instant, they were in a bubble separated from the rest of the world. He heard the kids' voices, but as if muffled by distance. He saw only Anna, her eyes a wide, stunning shade of deep blue, her lips soft, her cheeks pink.

Then he gave his head a shake and awkwardly lifted himself off so he didn't do more damage. That's when the kids came back into focus. Looking worried, Jenna crouched next to Anna. Josh stood above her. Even Molly hovered anxiously. Nate checked to be sure his shirt hung low enough to hide his erection.

"Mommy? You're not hurt, are you?"

Anna laughed, the strain something he was apparently alone in hearing.

"No, I'm resting. Your dad is *heavy*," she told Molly, who produced a shy smile. Then she looked at Josh. "Did we score?"

He grinned. "Of course, we did."

Laughing more naturally, she took Nate's hand and let him hoist her to her feet. "Ha!" she said saucily. "Tackling me didn't work."

"You really okay?" he asked. "I took you down hard."

Anna rolled her shoulders, then bent to touch her toes. "I really am. So what's the score?"

He had no idea and couldn't care less.

"We're tied fifteen-fifteen," Josh said. "You're not supposed to have scores that high in soccer."

"The way we bent the rules made it inevitable," Nate suggested. "Shall we play a sudden-death overtime, or go have pizza?"

"Pizza!" two of the kids cheered.

Molly looked worried again. "What's sudden death?"

Josh bounced the ball on his head most of the way back while Nate tried to explain why the sporting world equated losing with death. He was grateful that Anna lagged behind with Jenna so he wasn't compelled to watch the sway of her hips or her pale nape, revealed every time her ponytail swung. He had time to cool off and reinforce his thinking that taking Anna into his bed was a bad idea on so many levels there was no reason even to enumerate them. What he ought to do was look around at other women… except he couldn't remember the last time he'd met one who interested him.

Except, of course, for Anna Grainger.

WHAT HAD BECOME a weekly pizza outing was challenging Anna's determination to keep her and her children's lives neatly separate from Nate's and Molly's.

Molly…well, including her fully when her father wasn't around seemed natural. Anna was glad Josh especially was willing, or their hours at Molly's house would have been awkward. Jenna would never be a problem; she liked everybody. Josh, however, had been getting to an age when he preferred to ignore the existence of girls. She doubted that compassion explained his generous friendship. Molly's Xbox and wealth of other toys and DVDs was a more likely explanation. At school he probably pretended he didn't know her.

Anna wished she could think of a way to limit the time the two families spent together once Molly's dad came home to assume responsibility for her, but she knew how strange it would look to the kids if she insisted on an instant departure every day as soon as Nate walked in.

She gave an almost soundless sigh as he devoured the last piece of pizza. "Not worth taking home with us," he'd declared with a grin that had an electric effect on her.

All *she* wanted was to take *herself* home where she could think about those few stunned minutes when intense arousal had come out of nowhere. Yes, it was the first time since Kyle's death—since probably a month before his death, really—that she'd had a man's body lying atop hers. When she'd felt the growing bulge pressed almost where it felt best, she'd clenched inside in involuntary, intense reaction. She had come so close to letting her thighs part and arching up to meet him. Right there on the mowed field in front of their kids.

Now she'd reverted to the numbness that was her usual protection. It allowed her to carry on a conversation during the drive home, and nobody except possibly Nate knew anything was wrong. He did send a couple odd glances her way. There'd been that moment when their eyes met, when she thought he might kiss her. He knew his body wasn't alone in reacting to their proximity.

That's all it had been, she assured herself. After all, she'd been conscious of him all along as an attractive man. What woman wouldn't be? But Anna knew she was a very long way from being ready to start a relationship with any man. From trusting a man. Even if that time came, how could it be Nate Kendrick?

It can't, she told herself firmly and desolately. If nothing else, she and the kids wouldn't be here past Christmas break at the latest. Surely before then, Sonja would understand that she could lose her daughter for good if she didn't fight her alcoholism. If she didn't try, if she failed...

Nate would have to find a permanent live-in housekeeper/child-minder. Anna was sure he'd have no trouble at all doing that.

CHAPTER ELEVEN

ANNA TAPPED HER fingers on the steering wheel as the line of cars edged forward slowly. There was no reason to stew; she'd allowed plenty of time. Three days a week, she picked up Josh and Molly after school so they could make it to soccer practice in time. When she'd reminded them this morning as she walked them to the bus stop, Molly had sighed heavily and begged, "Can't we miss *one* practice?"

Before Josh could jump in, Anna had said, "Josh made a commitment, and that means I did, too. Besides, he enjoys playing. I'll tell you what, though. Maybe Friday we can arrange for you to go home with Arianna until practice is over."

Molly had brightened at that.

They inched forward two more car lengths. Anna could finally see the stretch in front of the elementary school where kids were waiting. In the back seat, Jenna nibbled fastidiously on a molasses cookie.

The line moved again. Anna was sure she saw Molly and Josh, mostly because Molly's hair was so distinctive. Although they stood side by side, they didn't seem to be talking. In the car, they'd start squabbling like brother and sister, but she'd been right that they were more like reluctant acquaintances in front of their friends.

Suddenly unable to stand one more round of *Sesame Street Silly Songs*, Anna ejected the CD.

"Mommy!" Jenna complained.

But Anna hardly heard her, because Josh was running all out toward her car. Molly...where was Molly? Not where she'd been standing.

Gasping, he wrenched open the passenger door. "Molly's mother is here, Mom! She's trying to make Molly go with her."

"Stay here with Jenna." Anna leaped out, uncaring that her car would block the single lane, and sprinted for the pickup area. Her head turned as she looked desperately for that red hair.

There Molly was, hesitating—no, resisting—as Sonja urged her toward the passenger seat of the sleek Jaguar Anna recognized.

"Stop!" Anna yelled. Children and adults all stared at her. Sonja flashed a single glance her way before lifting Molly and thrusting her into the car. She slammed the passenger door and raced around the front bumper to the driver side. She was hemmed in enough not to be able to pull out quickly. Anna didn't hesitate to jump in front of the Jaguar, any more than she had when she'd caught the private investigator filming her.

She slammed her palms down on the hood and yelled, "Help! She's not allowed to take this child!"

Two adults—teachers?—hurried forward, while a third herded the cluster of waiting children farther from the curb.

Both recognized Anna immediately.

The older woman said, "Molly told us this is her mother."

"She is, but she's allowed only supervised visitation right now. She can't take Molly on her own, and especially not in a car. She has a drinking problem."

Sonja had opened her door and heard her. Over the roof, she glared at Anna. "I have primary custody of my daughter. This…woman has no say in whether or not I take her."

"I'm sorry." The teacher—fourth grade, Anna thought—stepped forward and opened the passenger door. "Honey, you need to get out."

Molly appeared relieved and had started to comply until her mother snapped, "You stay where you are." Confused, Molly froze partway.

Anna hustled around. "It's okay," she said quietly to Molly, holding out a hand. "You know I'm supposed to pick you up today."

Face pinched, Molly gave a small nod and joined Anna on the sidewalk just in time for

Sonja to reach them and grab her daughter's arm and try to yank her away. Expression furious, she said, "Why don't you tell the teachers what relationship *you* have to my daughter. Or, oh! Would that be none?"

"I'm taking care of Molly right now, and you know it." Much as she hated the idea of using a child as the rope in a tug-of-war, Anna held tight to Molly's hand. Looking over her head to the teacher, she said, "I think we need to take this to the principal's office. We're blocking all the other parents waiting to pick up their children."

"Yes, that's exactly what we need to do." The teacher smiled at Molly. "You come with me right now and we'll all sit down with Mrs. Bailey." She leveled a look at Sonja. "Mrs. Kendrick, please circle around and park your car in the lot."

"This scene is completely ridiculous!" Sonja stormed. "Neither of you have any business keeping my daughter from me."

Anna finally noticed the teacher's name tag. It was Mrs. Olivares who said, "I apologize for the inconvenience, but in a case of conflict like this, I have no choice. Once again, I have to ask you to move your car."

Sonja made a furious sound, whirled and got back into her Jaguar. Since she was no longer blocked in, she accelerated fast.

Anna released a breath of pure relief. "Thank

you, Mrs. Olivares. I'll go rescue my kids and see you in the office. Just…please hold on to Molly until I get there."

The teacher smiled reassurance. "Of course I will. Come on, honey. I bet I can find you some juice and a snack when we get in there."

Ignoring their audience, Anna jogged to her car. She waved an apology to the drivers behind her, hastily put the car in gear and started forward.

Josh leaned forward. "Mom? How come Molly didn't come with you?"

"We have to go to the principal's office to straighten this out. Mrs. Olivares will make sure Molly's mom can't take her."

A minute later, she parked close to the main entrance of the school, took out her cell phone and called Nate.

"We need you," she told him, and explained.

"I'm on my way." The last thing she heard was him swearing.

NATE WAS GRATEFUL to the aide who took all three kids to a break room. He wouldn't have wanted any of them, but especially Molly, to hear what had to be said.

"No," he explained to the school principal, "I did not remove her mother's name from the list of people permitted to take Molly. That's my mistake. I wasn't sure I could do that without a court order."

"You couldn't!" Sonja said triumphantly. "You see? I have every right to pick up my own child."

Mrs. Bailey's pleasant composure never faltered. "Mr. Kendrick?"

"I trusted Sonja to comply with our agreement," he said grimly, grateful for Anna's calming presence in the chair beside him. "Some weeks ago, Molly called to tell me she couldn't wake her mommy up. She thought she was dead. I found Sonja in an alcoholic stupor. She spent the night in the hospital and agreed the next day to complete a thirty-day, in-house, alcohol treatment program before she could have Molly at home with her again."

"I never agreed—"

He ignored her. "Unfortunately, she chose to walk out of the treatment center at barely the halfway point. I checked on her to make sure she was all right, and found her drinking and emotionally volatile. I offered to pay for treatment when she is willing to resume it. Molly needs her mother, too."

"Too?" Sonja exclaimed. "You mean, she needs her mother, *period.*"

"So Molly has been living with you, Mr. Kendrick?" the principal said.

"That's correct. Mrs. Grainger—" he gave

a slight nod and smile at Anna, knowing he couldn't afford to betray how much he felt for this woman "—has been caring for her when I have to be at work. Molly already knew Mrs. Grainger and liked her. In fact, you may recall that Molly is in the same class with Josh Grainger."

"That's right." Mrs. Bailey smiled briefly. Then, sounding troubled, she said, "I sympathize with your stance, but do we have a legal right to keep Mrs. Kendrick from taking Molly?"

Out of the corner of his eye, he saw Anna move as if to protest.

Fighting to maintain his calm, he said, "Sonja did not have the courtesy to inform any of us that she intended to pick up Molly. Mrs. Grainger would have had every reason to be terrified if she'd arrived to find Molly had inexplicably disappeared. I would certainly have called the police at that point, if you hadn't already."

Mrs. Bailey bent her head in acknowledgment, but also some reservation.

He met Sonja's bitter, angry gaze. "If we ask a Bellevue police officer to do it, would you be willing to submit to a Breathalyzer test?"

She leaped to her feet. "You're accusing me of being *drunk*?"

She gave off such a strong smell of mint, it had to be camouflage. His certainty gave him the confidence to say, "I think it very likely that you've had enough to drink that you shouldn't be driving. Especially with a child in the car."

"How dare you!"

"Do you deny any part of what I just told Mrs. Bailey?"

"Yes! I reacted because I mixed a medication with a drink. You turned that into a crime."

He couldn't be merciful. "The paramedics saw an alcohol overdose. They checked the kitchen trash, finding it half full with liquor bottles."

"That's such an intrusion—"

"They described you as hypothermic," he continued, relentless. "Your breathing was irregular and too slow. If I hadn't called for an ambulance, you could have died. On top of that, it was pure luck you landed from the couch on your side so that you didn't choke on your own vomit. You and I both know I've been concerned for some time about your drinking. I think if a blood test had revealed a medication that might be partly responsible for your condition, you'd have thrown it in my face. Now, I'll ask again. Will you submit to a Breathalyzer test?"

Her face twisted. "Because *you* asked? No, I won't. But I'll see you in court, you *bastard*." She yanked the door open, lurched into the jamb on one side and rushed out.

The three people remaining sat in silence for

a minute, hearing the rap of her high heels receding. Nate felt the gentle brush of Anna's hand against his. It couldn't be by chance.

He was able to blow out a breath. "I'm sorry I put you in this position, Mrs. Bailey, or made you listen to more than you ever wanted to know about Molly's mother or our relationship."

"Mr. Kendrick, it might astonish you to know how intimately acquainted I am with the family circumstances of a great number of our students. I do need to ask what you intend to do now."

"File for full custody. I spoke to my attorney during the drive. He has no doubt my petition will be granted unless Sonja left here to check herself back into treatment. I doubt that's what was on her mind."

He saw her relief. "No, I don't think so. I encourage you to try to hasten the process, so we don't have to go through this again tomorrow."

Nate rose and rested a hand on Anna's back when she stood, too. He wouldn't have been able to keep it together nearly as well had she not been here. Touching her now...settled him.

"Can you prevent her from taking Molly the next couple of days, or do I need to keep her home from school?"

"I believe I can justify that, knowing you've filed for custody and why. And that Mrs. Kendrick didn't argue the fact that Molly is currently living with you and cared for by Mrs. Grainger."

At last, they were able to claim the three kids and walk out to the cars. Molly seemed to have shrunk in size, her shoulders and arms squeezed tight to her body, her eyes fixed on her feet. She'd seized fiercely on to both Anna's and his hands. He looked down and saw how crooked the part in her hair was. She was seven years old. He should know by now how to part her hair. Guilt struck even as her silent misery infuriated him. *Damn* Sonja.

His eyes met Anna's. "Can you still get Josh to his practice?"

"Oh…" Anna broke the connection to check the time on her phone. "Maybe half of it."

He was embarrassed by how much he wished she'd said no. A little gruffly, he said, "While you do that, why don't I take Jenna and Molly home?"

She laid her hand on her daughter's head. "What do you think, sweetie?"

Jenna nodded eagerly. "I can play with Molly."

"That okay?" Nate asked.

Molly's posture didn't loosen, but she said, "Uh-huh."

They parted ways at the parking lot, Nate shifting Jenna's booster seat to the back of his Lexus and helping her buckle up while surreptitiously watching as Anna drove away.

Damn it, focus. Molly was what mattered right now. Was bringing Jenna along a mistake?

It meant he and Molly couldn't have the necessary talk yet—but he thought she needed a dose of normalcy first.

Starting the car a minute later, he glanced over his shoulder. "Did you two get a snack?"

"Mrs. Stockley gave us peanut-butter-and-chocolate bars. They were okay, but they weren't as good as Mommy's cookies. Were they, Molly?"

"No," his daughter said softly.

"I'm thinking we might be able to find something tastier if we search the kitchen. What do you say, girls?"

Molly's "Yeah" was a little quieter than Jenna's, but satisfied him.

"Then let's go home." And it was home and not just a house, thanks to Anna.

Who wouldn't be in his life a few months from now if she stuck to her plan. And, yeah, for a take-charge guy like him, he hated knowing there was only so much he could do to affect her decisions.

THAT EVENING, NATE stopped Josh with a hand on his shoulder. Anna had already opened the door to the staircase leading to the apartment. She was carrying Jenna, whose eyelids were drooping. This was Nate's first opportunity to talk to Josh out of Molly's earshot.

"Thank you for running to get your mother

today," he said gravely. "If you hadn't done that, Molly's mother would have gotten away with her."

"She looked kinda scared," the boy said, shifting uneasily. "But…her mom wouldn't have *hurt* her, would she?"

"Do you know what it means when we say someone is drunk?"

His forehead wrinkled. "Uh…kind of. Like, falling down and stuff?"

"Right. If the police pull over a driver because they suspect he or she is intoxicated—drunk—they ask that person to show that they can walk in a straight line. Often, they can't."

His face cleared. "So they can't drive straight, either."

"Exactly. Molly's mother has a problem. I think she might have had too much alcohol today to be able to drive safely. So Molly *could* have been hurt if they'd gotten in a car accident. Today, you were her hero, and mine."

"Oh." He squared his shoulders. "Molly and me are friends, and I could tell she didn't want to go with her mom."

"You acted without hesitating. That makes you special."

Anna reached out a hand to Josh and gave Nate a tremulous smile just before she closed the door behind her small family, leaving him alone.

Nate scrubbed his fingers through his hair. He'd thought his job was stressful. The months before Sonja moved out were difficult. Seeing Molly leave with her mother had been one of the worst moments of his life.

Nothing like discovering he'd been playing in the minor leagues. Having your kid at risk, *that* was bad. A financial deal falling through? That was nothing.

There was a certain irony in him remembering what Sonja had said to him the day he'd told her he couldn't join her and Molly for the field trip.

Some of us want an actual life.

She was right. His priorities had been skewed, although she was never willing to understand why he couldn't take time off whenever he felt like it.

"You own the company!" she'd complained.

Where she'd been dead wrong was in declaring that she and Molly would be fine without him. They hadn't been fine that day, and they'd become even less fine since.

Nate had come to despise the woman he'd humiliated today in the principal's office, but he felt shitty about what he'd done to her, too. Not so long ago, he'd loved Sonja or at least convinced himself he did. Liked her, anyway. Enjoyed her in bed. She'd always been over-the-top emotional, but happy as often as she was sad. She was a smart, funny person. Alcohol had altered her entire personality. Or had he helped the change along?

No news there, he thought wearily, but now he was left to try to contain the ongoing damage to Molly. He didn't know what to say and felt so damned alone. He'd have given a lot to have Anna with him right now.

Yeah, and how many times a day did he think the same thing?

He trudged upstairs anyway, hearing the sound of running water in the bathroom. Funny, he'd almost been sorry when Molly didn't need help brushing her teeth anymore. He'd been responsible for her getting-ready-for-bed routine in general. Tucking her in had given him joy. It was to Sonja's credit that she'd understood he and Molly needed that father/daughter time.

He went into her room and sat on the bed while he waited. A minute later, the bathroom door opened and Molly appeared, already wearing her Wonder Woman pajamas. She hesitated, as if surprised or dismayed to see him.

He smiled and patted the bed. "I came to say good-night."

Her expression serious, she climbed in under the covers, although she stayed sitting upright.

"Daddy? Is Mommy in trouble because of… you know?"

He swiveled to face her. "No, but I'm mad at her. Do you understand why?"

She concentrated on pleating her sheet. "Um…kind of."

He did his best to put into terms she'd understand his feeling that Sonja had broken faith with him after making an agreement. He talked about how scared and upset Anna and he would have been if Molly had seemingly been snatched from school instead of being where she was supposed to be when Anna got there.

He finished by saying, "I'm not going to give up on your mom, and you shouldn't either. She loves you a whole lot, and she was a great mother until she started needing the next drink of alcohol more than anything. Quitting drinking is really hard. We just have to be patient until she can do that. In the meantime, I love you. Keeping you safe is the most important thing in the world to me. Do you understand?"

Her head bobbed. He waited and was about to say good-night when Molly suddenly dove forward into the arms he managed to open to receive her. Tears streamed down her cheeks.

"I love you, Daddy! And…and I didn't *like* Mommy today! I almost wish—"

With his cheek pressed to the top of her head, he prompted her. "You wish…?"

"That I didn't have to see her anymore. And that Anna was my mommy. Except I love *my* mommy, too."

All he could do was hug his little girl, rock her and somehow convince her that this tumult of feelings was understandable. That she didn't need to feel guilty, even though he knew she would, anyway.

Even though he, too, was guilty of wishing Anna could be her mommy.

CHAPTER TWELVE

MONDAY THE FOLLOWING WEEK, Anna was called for the first time to sub as a paraeducator. Confident she'd be staying longer with Nate and Molly, she had finally registered with two school districts, trying to improve her odds of working regularly. This job was at Rush Elementary in the Lake Washington district, north of Bellevue.

Jenna was happy to go to Mrs. Schaub's and spend the day with her friends. Anna assisted in a second-grade classroom, leading reading groups, helping students with projects, gently guiding kids at a distractible age to keep their attention on their work. By the time she left, the aide she was replacing had called to let them know she'd be out another day, and Anna was asked to come back. She felt positively triumphant by the time she raced out to her car.

The trick was getting back to Bellevue in time to pick up Molly and Josh, which she barely managed. Fortunately, this was the next-to-last week of practice. Only two more games.

She was pleased when Nate asked right away

after getting home how the day had gone—and then she got a good look at his face.

The lid to the saucepan she'd just picked up dropped to the counter. "What happened?"

"Nothing." The creases on his face didn't smooth out, but he shook his head. "It's just this Sonja thing getting to me. We have a hearing scheduled for Wednesday."

"Wow, that's fast."

"Thank God." He rolled his shoulders. "I don't trust her for a minute."

"No." What if Sonja had gotten to the school ahead of her today? She wouldn't have been there to intervene. "Maybe I shouldn't work until it's resolved."

"No." He reached over the breakfast bar to lay his hand on hers. "I'm keeping Mrs. Bailey up-to-date. She's alerted the teachers and aides to be on the lookout."

Anna started at his touch, but didn't immediately move her hand even though she knew she should. For that instant, there was a warm, tingling connection between them.

"Molly and Josh were standing right next to an adult when I pulled up this afternoon," she said, striving for composure. "I didn't think about it, but I'll bet it wasn't by accident."

"No." He sighed, taking his hand back as if unconsciously. "Sonja called me at work today to deliver a drunken tirade. Stupid, because I recorded her."

"Wait, isn't that illegal?"

"I checked. In Washington State, it's okay if you inform the other party they're being recorded. The informing part has to be on the recording. I have to admit, after the scene at the school, I set up Google Voice, just in case. I warned her right away that I was recording, but she didn't let that stop her."

"Does she really think she has any chance of retaining custody?"

"I doubt it. What I'm afraid is that she'll try to grab Molly again, anyway. Her behavior isn't exactly rational right now."

"That's a scary possibility." And a fear Anna shared.

A sizzling sound made her jump. Water boiling over onto the burner. "Oh, heavens. Dinner is ready."

He made an obvious effort to smile. "You are staying to eat?"

Embarrassed, she said, "If you don't mind. I'm not as organized as usual tonight."

"Please," he said simply, and went to call the kids to the table.

Even Molly, the pickiest of the three kids, seemed to like the beef Stroganoff. Anna had learned that peas were also on her okay-vegetables list.

Nate asked again about her day. Since they'd already covered how each of the kids' days had gone, Anna chatted about the fun projects students had done in her classroom. "I really enjoyed leading the reading groups. It's great seeing even a tiny breakthrough for a child who's having difficulties."

She looked up from her plate to see two incredulous stares: Molly's and Josh's. "What?"

Her son said, "But...*we're* in second grade."

"Yes?"

In almost the same tone, Molly said, "*We* do the same stuff."

"I know. I'd love to volunteer to help out in your room, like I did last year in Josh's. If neither of you mind, I'll talk to Mrs. Tate."

They exchanged a glance and seemed to come to a silent consensus. "That's okay, I guess," Josh said without a lot of enthusiasm. "But it's not that much fun."

She laughed. "Moms and dads—*and* teachers —see it differently."

Their identical dubious expressions made her laugh again. Nate's grin gave her another burst of pleasure, if only because she had someone else with whom to share these moments.

Diverting Anna from her pang of guilt because Nate was taking Kyle's place, Jenna proceeded to tell them all that *she* thought it sounded like fun, and she already knew her letters and how to spell a bunch of words.

"Like *bat*. And *cat* and *fat*."

"Big whoopee," Josh mumbled. "Those words are all the same except one letter."

Anna smiled at her. "That is excellent for a four-year-old. Just don't start reading too well, or you won't need to go to school at all."

Josh rolled his eyes and looked disturbingly like a teenager for a minute, while Jenna did a little flounce in her seat and stuck out her tongue at her brother.

Nate chuckled.

"What?" Anna asked.

He kept smiling, his earlier grimness mostly gone. "You just reminded me how much I hated eating alone."

Only Anna knew what he was talking about.

ON WEDNESDAY, NATE walked beside his attorney out of the brick building where the hearing had been held. Relief made him feel as if he'd lost a hundred pounds.

"Her visits with Molly do need to be supervised, but not necessarily by you," his attorney said. "We can set up—"

Nate lifted his hand. "Give me a minute, Keith."

He changed paths to cross Sonja's. It hurt to see her face, bone white, eyes dark with pain and highlighted by the bruised skin in half circles beneath them. At the same time, anger still simmered—anger that had made him willing to crush her if that's what it took to protect his child. He might know alcoholism was a disease, but it was a struggle to summon compassion.

"You have to lick this, Sonja," he said as gently as he could.

"You really are a son of a bitch." Her voice shook. Her hands did, too, he couldn't help noticing. "You have no evidence I have *ever* been careless with Molly."

Maybe lying to herself was her only protection, but those lies also kept her from taking responsibility. And damned if he'd let her get away with that.

"We both know that's not true." No more gentle; now, he sounded harsh even to his own ears. "Anytime you're drunk, you're useless if something bad happens. What if there was a fire or Molly got really sick in the middle of the night, and you're passed out in bed? When you drank yourself into a stupor in front of her, you didn't give a thought to how she'd feel. Molly was scared to death, Sonja. She'd been scared for a while. You just don't want to see that."

"This from the man who failed her over and over again." She glared at him. "All you're doing is playing at being a real daddy. Let me know when you're tired of it." Then she strode away, arms crossed tightly.

Hugging herself. Or trying to hide the tremor in her hands. The hearing had been held at two in the afternoon. Disturbed by the indication of withdrawal, he wondered whether she'd been boozing from the minute she got up in the morning ever since she'd escaped his watchful eye post-divorce. Or had her problem worsened after Molly's near-drowning and Kyle Grainger's death? Was she anesthetizing herself?

Hell, he could diagnose her all day, but in the end, what it came down to was that she couldn't be trusted with Molly.

What he needed to think about was what he'd do if Sonja did complete treatment and succeed in staying sober, whether a few months down the line or a few years. Was he willing to hand over Molly and go back to being an every-other-weekend father? Could he and Sonja figure out a better arrangement?

Or was he being seduced by Anna Grainger into thinking family life was fabulous? Would he be as eager to go home every day after work once she and her kids were gone?

The answer didn't help his mood.

ANNA WORKED TUESDAY in the same classroom, and Friday in a special-education class at another elementary school in the Lake Washington district. Both pleased and a little alarmed, she wondered whether she'd be working full-time before she knew it. Financially, it would be great, allowing her to save for the uncertain future.

In other ways… She worried about the new issues because that was her way. What would the impact be on Jenna? She had fun spending a few hours here and there at Mrs. Schaub's, but what if that changed to her being there all day, five days a week? Looking into more formal preschools was an option…but then again, as long as Jenna was happy, maybe Anna should leave well enough alone.

And then there was the fact that her first obligation was to Nate and Molly. On working days, she was a lot more frazzled by the time she got the kids home. Had Nate even noticed the difference?

She really should talk to him. Which was easy to think—and even easier to put off.

Saturday morning, he rapped on the apartment door to say that he'd like to join her to watch Josh's soccer game. As she'd discovered other weeks, that meant him assuming he'd drive. Did he ever let *anyone* else drive? On the other hand, the kids weren't as squished in the back seat of his car as they were in hers, which cut down on the bickering.

Roomy as the Lexus was, she felt too close

to Nate in the front seat. Too conscious of his body, his every movement, the way the fabric in his chinos pulled taut over the long muscles in his thigh. When they reached the soccer fields, Anna all but leaped out of the car even if she immediately felt the cold drizzle on her face.

They'd all brought raincoats, of course, and she had an umbrella. She'd noticed before that the fathers on the sidelines all pretended to be impervious to cold, sleet or pouring rain. Nate turned out to be no different, scoffing at the idea of using one.

Today was her turn to provide snacks for the whole team. With the big cooler resting on his shoulder, Nate fell into step with her. As usual, Josh raced ahead as soon as he saw two teammates, one carrying a big net bag full of balls. The two girls lagged, but Anna could hear their voices.

Nate touched Anna's arm. "Once Molly and Jenna get distracted, can we talk?"

Her pulse picked up speed. He might intend to ask her to stay longer…but what if, instead, he'd started looking for a permanent housekeeper willing to provide child care, too? What if he'd *found* someone and wanted to let her know when she needed to move out? The reminder of her vulnerability stung. She'd felt good about working three days this week, but she couldn't support herself and the kids on the money she'd earned.

She wanted to be a coward and put him off, but then she'd only worry more. So she said, "Sure," as if his request was no big deal.

By the time they reached the sideline, Josh was already warming up with his teammates. Molly and Jenna latched on to their usual crowd of girls and a few younger boys.

Anna watched them start a game of tag, before suddenly realizing Nate still stood beside her, watching, too.

For no good reason, she said aloud what she was thinking. "Most of those kids are older than Jenna. So why is she taking charge?"

His mouth quirked. "She usually does. Are you just noticing?"

"No." Anna made a face. "I have a bossy daughter."

"And I have one who hangs back." Of course he sounded rueful; a man so obviously accustomed to being in charge might well be dismayed to have a kid who was a follower, instead.

"Molly's not herself right now, not with everything going on," she suggested.

"She's retreated a little, but..." Furrows formed on his forehead, as they often did when they talked about Molly. He paused, maybe searching for the right words. "She's always tended to be shy. Happy playing by herself."

"There's nothing wrong with that. Anyway, she's reconnecting with friends from last year." Molly had gone home with Arianna after school one day this week, saving her from Wednesday's soccer practice, and then to another girl's house on Thursday. Josh had actually seemed disappointed that she wasn't home to hang out with.

"That's true." Nate seemed to shake off his concern, turning to face her. "Walk with me?"

Evidently, he didn't want nearby parents to hear what he had to say. Anna nodded mutely, ditching her umbrella, and fell into step as he strolled along the sideline. Once again, she found herself painfully conscious of him. The light rain had turned his hair almost black and as slick as a seal's coat. Looking down, she focused on his hand, inches from brushing hers. So much broader than hers, the fingers long, his wrist thick. Male, like his bared forearms with strong muscles and the visible tendons. Her skin prickled at the memory of how his hands felt touching her.

Damn. She forced herself to glance toward the field even though it was empty except for a couple referees chatting toward the middle. Both teams huddled with their coaches on the sidelines.

"It's looking a lot like Molly will be staying

with me permanently," Nate said abruptly. "For the foreseeable future, anyway."

Anna braced herself, but still didn't say anything.

"You probably know where I'm going with this."

He stopped suddenly, and she realized they'd reached the end of the field. *She*'d probably have kept walking until she smacked into the wall of the cinder-block building that housed the restrooms. They turned in concert, but he didn't start walking, so she didn't, either.

She did her best to sound...curious. "You've found someone permanent?"

"No." His keen gray eyes met hers. "This is me asking whether you'd continue the arrangement we have at least for this school year. I think it's going well for all of us. You staying would give Molly the stability she needs. You'd give me peace of mind."

Peace? she thought semi-hysterically. He stirred her into a state that was far from peaceful. Obviously, that wasn't mutual, even if he had felt momentary lust for her the one time.

"You'd have the opportunity to save some money," he continued, "boost your résumé and have plenty of time to make plans for the future."

She couldn't seem to look away from him even though she was peripherally aware that the teams had taken the field and were clustered in the middle, ready for the drop. And…why did she have the feeling that his pleasantly persuasive tone was a front for an emotion a whole lot more intense?

Because his eyes said something different.

"I… You don't mind me working? Even though that gives me less time for the kids?"

His subtle relaxation didn't escape her. It also confirmed what her instinct was telling her. "Of course not."

"Are you sure about this? I don't think Sonja likes having me taking care of Molly."

His jaw tightened. "The decision isn't hers. Anyway, why would she object? *You* were the one hurt by my absence or Sonja's carelessness, or just because shit happens."

"Seeing me reminds her." Of course it did. "She might be able to let her guilt go if I wasn't here as a glowing neon reminder."

Scowling, Nate said, "She should be glad I'm offering some recompense."

Anna flinched from the blow and took a step back. "So much for the idea that I could hold on to any dignity while I worked for you. You just found a sneaky way to relieve your own blasted guilt. I can't believe I fell for it." Shaking her head, she whirled and hurried toward the cluster of parents.

How had she not seen that she was deceiving herself? No, she wouldn't take blood money from Nate Kendrick—but an apartment? Hey, sure. Not the same thing at all.

"Anna." His voice came from right behind her. "Stop."

"No."

"Please."

Despite her burn of humiliation, the raw tone reached her in a way the command hadn't. She slowed, stopped, closed her eyes. Finally, she turned around, because what else could she do? Tell him to go to hell and call for a taxi to get them home after the game? Home being *his* house.

What she didn't expect was to see anguish on his face.

"What I told you at the beginning was the truth. Our arrangement isn't about my share of the guilt. I'd met you, Molly talked about you, and yeah, I took advantage of knowing you needed a refuge. But I offered it because I needed someone I could trust. I do trust you, Anna. You have to know that."

She swallowed and gave a jerky nod. Seeing him so unguarded was a shock.

"Having you and your kids has made everything better for me," he said hoarsely. "For Molly." His big hands had curled into fists, but he opened them and flexed his fingers with what appeared to be an effort. "If I thought you had a great opportunity, somewhere good to go, I wouldn't let myself be selfish. I'm not that much of a son of a bitch." His mouth twisted. "Sonja's opinion to the contrary."

They stared at each other until he said, "Say something. Are you going to pack up and leave?"

After a moment, she shook her head. He'd stripped himself bare in front of her, and she didn't know how she felt about that. If it turned out this was all a lie, that he was playing her… she'd deal with it then. Pride had held her together when nothing else could, but using it to justify a decision that would be bad for Josh and Jenna wasn't acceptable.

Not for her, either.

"No," she said softly. "You're right. The arrangement has worked out well. Josh is happy in school, and I don't want Molly to feel abandoned. If you're sure this is what you want, we'll stay until school lets out."

He bowed his head suddenly, as if he didn't want her to see his expression. His chest rose and fell with a couple of deep breaths before he lifted his head again. "It's what I want," he said in a low, gruff voice.

"Then…then we'll go on the way we have been."

"Thank you."

"You're welcome."

What a stupid thing to say! If anybody should

be saying thank-you, it was her. Because she could only lie to herself so long.

When he'd extended her a lifeline, she had grabbed right on, her fingers clamping around it. She'd have to let go eventually…but not yet.

CHAPTER THIRTEEN

EVEN THOUGH THEY'D been home for a good ten minutes, Anna's toes still hurt. Thawing out always did. How could she have forgotten how miserable November could be in the Northwest?

The rain that fell during Josh's practice today had felt perilously like sleet. Molly and Jenna and their little crowd had kept themselves warm by running nonstop, stomping rubber boots in soggy patches of grass and shrieking when the splatter soaked their jeans. Anna had worried about Josh stuck waiting in the goal, but when the ball was on the other end of the field, he jogged in place and did jumping jacks. When it came his way, he went into action—including a headlong dive into the muddy pig wallow in front of the goal.

The parents were the ones who'd suffered. Anna had stood up from time to time and walked, sometimes with another mother, or just stamped her feet, but that hadn't been enough to warm her. Clearly, she needed to double up on the socks and visit storage to find her ski gloves. Everyday fleece ones didn't cut it.

Or drop off Josh at practice and come back for him at the end. But she was reluctant to consider that. Maybe when he was older.

Grateful to be mostly warm again, she opened the oven to pop in two loaves of banana bread. For a moment, she spread her hands close to the heat before she made herself close the oven door.

The house phone rang. She might have called for one of the kids to answer it, except she hadn't needed to bother. There wasn't a second ring. Either Molly or Josh had grabbed it.

That phone was ringing more and more often. Molly and her small group of friends didn't think they had enough time to talk during the school day. They made up for it with lengthy conversations once they got home. Teenage years, here we come.

Since Josh was also in the big house until dinnertime if not later every day, his friends had this number, too. His conversations, at least, tended to be brief.

Surprised to hear silence instead of voices, she wiped the counter and then walked toward the family room. Jenna was hardly ever quiet, and if the call had been for Molly, Anna would have expected her to bring the phone out to the living room in search of privacy. Increasingly puzzled, she stepped into the wide doorway to the family room.

In profile to her, Josh held the phone to his

ear. He stood very still, his expression reminding her of how he'd received the news that his father was dead. Molly and Jenna both stared at him.

"Who is Josh talking to?" Anna asked, trying to keep her voice down.

At almost the same instant, he thrust the phone at Molly. "She wants to talk to you." At that moment, Josh saw Anna. Face stricken, he bumped her as he ran from the room.

She spun, but couldn't see him. Not hearing any door opening or closing, Anna guessed he'd flung himself down on a sofa in the living room.

After a desperate glance at Anna, Molly clutched the phone. Her huddled posture suggested she'd rather be doing anything else in the world but listening to the caller.

Sonja.

Furious, Anna crossed the room and took the phone out of Molly's hand. "Sonja?"

"I was talking to my daughter." Except every word was slurred. "What do *you* want?"

"I want you not to call when Nate isn't home. You're in no condition to be speaking to Molly. From now on, they won't be answering the phone. *I* will be." She pushed End, then set the phone down with more force than she intended.

She crouched and wrapped an arm around Molly's narrow shoulders. "Are you okay, honey?"

Molly shrugged.

"Who was that?" Jenna burst out.

Anna kept her attention on Molly. "Do you know what she said to Josh?"

Molly shook her head, but didn't meet her eyes.

Anna kissed the top of her head. "From now on, when your dad isn't home, let me answer the phone. Okay?"

She nodded.

Anna hugged her and said, "I should track down Josh. *And* put dinner on."

"But, Mommy, why won't you tell me…?"

She gave a gentle tug on Jenna's ponytail. "Because you're being nosy."

"But I wanna know!"

Anna laughed even though she didn't feel like it.

She found Josh huddled at one end of a leather sofa that faced the view of the lake through the two sets of French doors. His face had a stony set that didn't change when she sat down next to him.

"Are you going to talk to me?" she asked after a minute.

Lips compressed, he turned a burning stare on her. "*She* said it's Nate's fault that Dad died."

Her ribs felt as if they were about to crack. Fury at that hateful woman mixed with guilt and her own confusion; yet, somehow she kept her voice almost tranquil. "You know he wasn't even there, so how could it be his fault?"

"Because he was *supposed* to be there!" he shouted.

Anna looked away from his enraged face for a minute, gathering her thoughts. She'd hoped he would never hear about Sonja's accusations; she should have known better.

"We've talked about this before. Several things went wrong, leading to your dad's death."

He kept glaring.

"If Nate had been able to make it that day, the chances are good that Molly wouldn't have slipped away without anyone noticing."

"So it's true!"

"I wasn't done," she said, injecting some steel into her voice. "Nate has a really demanding job. It's why he makes enough money for an amazing house like this. When there's a crisis, he can't say, 'Gosh, sorry, I can't meet with you, I need to take a picnic lunch to a park today.' Molly and her mom were both used to him telling them the same thing he told you. He'd make it if he could, but if a problem at his office came up, he might have to cancel."

"Mommy?" Jenna had somehow sneaked up on them. "What are you talking about?"

Josh jumped up and snarled, "Butt out!"

Anna laid a hand on his shoulder, but instead of lecturing him, she turned enough to see her daughter. "You don't have to know everything. I thought I'd made it clear that I needed to talk to Josh alone."

Her lower lip poked out. "It's not fair." Still, she obediently returned to the family room.

Not until she'd disappeared did Josh throw himself back onto the couch. "Isn't *Molly* as important as some stupid job?"

Surprised at his comeback, Anna said, "Of course she is. You've seen them together." She risked pulling him into a quick hug, letting go before he could protest. "The thing is, that field trip *wasn't* important."

"It was! 'Cuz Dad—" Josh choked.

"But how could Nate have guessed Molly would almost drown? You know how careful Melissa is. There were plenty of chaperones. Nate canceling *would* have been bad if Molly's mom wasn't already going. If he'd promised to be there for three kids who wouldn't have anyone if he didn't show up. But Melissa hadn't assigned any kids to him, maybe because Sonja had told her that he might not be able to make it. Three kids and Molly were assigned to her mother, just as I was responsible for three besides you. Your dad decided to join us only the night before. That made him a…a spare. And that's what Nate would have been, too."

Josh's expression crumpled with confusion. "Then…why did she say that?"

"I think—" Anna took his hand in hers "—because Mrs. Kendrick feels guilty. Somehow—" because she'd been fiddling on her phone "—she didn't notice that Molly had wandered out of sight."

"So it's *her* fault," Josh said with a viciousness that took Anna aback.

"In a way." Right now, the last thing she wanted was to be fair to Sonja Kendrick, but her conscience wouldn't allow her to be anything else. "We talked about this, too, though. Parents get distracted. We're not perfect, you know."

His snort reassured her.

She explained again that Molly vanishing at the same moment her mother was briefly distracted was chance. "And if I'd gone looking for her instead of your dad, I might have made it out."

"Because you *can* swim."

"Right. But I also might not have been strong enough to throw Molly out of the current."

He opened his mouth, then closed it.

"Tragedies happen, Josh. It's why parents worry so much about their kids. *You* might have prevented one when you ran for help that day at the school. And it's true that, sometimes, there *is* one person we can blame when something awful happens. A drunk driver. A man who is committing a crime and doesn't care who gets hurt as long as it isn't him. A parent who isn't paying any attention to her kids at all. But I know Sonja was, because I saw her. If Nate had been there…well, what if whatever distracted Sonja distracted him, too? Or if he'd decided to play soccer with you boys? His presence that day might have made all the difference, but it might not have, too." She paused, able to see Josh's struggle. "Do you see?"

He finally nodded, but his reluctance was apparent. "Yes, but…why did we have to come and stay *here*? Why didn't you get a job with someone else?"

Anna knew how crooked her smile had to be. "Because no one else offered me one. Because this one was so perfect. And—" she held up a hand to squelch the interruption she saw coming "—because I already knew and liked Molly. I thought I could help us and her at the same time."

Josh burst out, "But it's mostly *her*—" When he clamped his mouth shut before finishing the sentence, Anna hugged him again.

"What good does it do to make accusations? Haven't you seen how sad Molly is? She's struggling with what happened because of *her* mistake, just like her mother is. I think Nate is doing the same, even though it's not reasonable to blame him at all. Stuff happens."

Josh gave her a sly glance. "You mean, sh—"

Laughing, Anna clapped a hand over his mouth in time.

When she let him go, he rolled his eyes. "I see it on bumper sticks all the time. And people say it on TV. So why can't I—"

"Because," she said firmly. "Now, I need to start dinner."

"Do I have to play with *them* again?"

"Nope. You can sit at the table and do your homework, or go get a book to read."

He actually did like to read, though mostly at bedtime. So she wasn't surprised when, shortly after she went to the kitchen, she saw him returning to the family room.

Then she put the frying pan on the burner as she cut several chicken breasts into thin slices as a first step to making tacos, a favorite for all the kids. Her hands worked independently of her thoughts, however. She'd disturbed herself with what she'd said to Josh.

They'd all become enmeshed in guilt and blame. She hadn't told Josh anything she hadn't said or thought before, but this time she truly believed every word.

She felt...adrift, as if blame had been her anchor. Or maybe it was more like the walls of a fort she could huddle behind. Now she was left with a life altered by random circumstances; yet, she'd become tangled with the very people impacted by those same circumstances.

So they could torture each other?

It might have been better for both her and Josh if she'd made a different choice—cut all contact with Nate, Molly and her mother. Except, then she might have clung to her anger, her determination to blame someone for Kyle's death, long past any point where those feelings were reasonable. As it was, she drew in a deep breath, free of the constriction that had been there whether she noticed it or not. And Josh—he'd matured as he dealt with his pain instead of burying it. Ditto for her.

Or, who knew, maybe she'd just donned a pair of rose-colored glasses.

SOMETHING WAS UP, Nate realized within minutes of sitting down at the dinner table. Josh and Molly both were subdued, and Josh kept stealing odd looks at Nate. Molly? She had the art of withdrawal licked.

When he came in the door, Nate had been happy to see the dining table set for five people. Anna and her kids stayed to eat with him and Molly more often than she had earlier in their arrangement, but three or four days a week, she hustled her kids out and left him and Molly to stare at each other across the table. Some of her decision, he'd long since realized, had to do with the menu. Because it was a meal designed for each person to assemble, tacos would have meant her taking about a dozen small containers of food. That would be a hassle.

On the other hand, maybe the menu wasn't the only reason she'd hung around tonight. He had a feeling they'd be having a post-dinner conversation.

He did his best to help her keep a conversation going without any contributions from either of the older kids. Jenna...well, she was her usual motormouth, until she said, "Mom and Josh were mean when they wouldn't tell me what they were talking about."

"Shut up!" her brother snapped.

"We don't talk to each other that way." Icicles all but hung from Anna's voice. "Please apologize."

After producing a mumbled, "Sorry," Josh sank into sullen silence.

The four-year-old decided to sulk, too.

Nate glanced around the table. "We're all cheerful tonight."

Nobody argued. But now that he was focusing on Anna instead of the too-quiet kids, he had the intriguing realization that something was different about her. Damn, she was beautiful when she wasn't trying to close herself off.

"Nobody cheerful here," she said with a hint of humor. "Why don't you tell us how *your* day went?"

He laughed, a lot of his day's stresses melting away. She did that for him, even if she also threw him into a state of sexual frustration all too often.

"Along with some routine meetings and phone calls, I met with two guys who think they have an idea for a snowboard that will kick butt— their words—in freestyle competitions. In case you didn't know, snowboarding is big business these days. One concern is that I couldn't decide whether they've chosen not to think about the recreational snowboarder or whether they know that's too crowded a market already. Are competitive snowboards a large enough niche to interest us? I made some calls and decided this is worth pursuing for the moment. So we'll be doing more serious research on their idea and the potential, not to mention the two guys' backgrounds and ability to get beyond design to building a moneymaking business."

Nate liked how intently Anna listened. "You must get to be an expert on a lot of strange things," she commented.

"Yeah, I do. That challenge and the variety are two of the reasons I love my job."

"And how many people can say that?"

As they kept talking, Nate became close to forgetting the kids were also at the table. He couldn't quite, not when his daughter sat quietly beside him, unhappiness clinging to her like a heavy scent. But he couldn't ask her what the latest problem was, not in front of the others, and he had a feeling Anna knew, anyway.

Finally, she said, "Kids' turn to clear the table."

Surprised at the lack of protest, Nate tried to ask a question with his eyes. Anna shook her head slightly. "I'll put on coffee," she said.

"Why don't you let me?" He rose and went to the kitchen, deliberately crossing paths with Molly. He gently tugged her sagging ponytail. "Hcy, sweetie," he said softly.

She wrapped her arms around him and gave him a fierce hug that he had no chance to reciprocate before she rushed back to the table to wad up napkins and gather the place mats to throw in the laundry.

Even more disturbed, Nate located the coffee in the refrigerator and scooped some with only half his attention. What in hell had happened today?

Anna let the kids return to whatever they'd been doing earlier, and, by unspoken consent, she and Nate carried their cups to a corner of the living room where they wouldn't be overheard.

Plunking down at one end of the sofa, Anna kicked off her shoes and tucked one leg under her. He chose the other end rather than the nearby chair.

Lifting his coffee cup to her, he said, "Seems

like we're always sneaking away to put our heads together."

Her nose crinkled. "It does, doesn't it? We wouldn't have to if we were—" She not only stopped in her tracks, but she also looked horrified. And...was she blushing?

Nate reran what she'd said, and where she'd broken off. His mind slotted in a possible answer. *If we were really a family. We'd talk in bed at the end of the day.* Was that what she'd been close to saying?

An image of them lying in his big bed appeared instantly, her head nestled on his shoulder, her hand resting right above his heart. He'd hold her close even though that meant tipping his head so that he could see her expressions. It was too easy to know how content he'd be with this quiet time, this catching up that was essential, because the minute everything important had been said, he could tug her to sprawl on him or roll her under him. Either way, he'd slide his fingers into that silky blond hair, cup the back of her head and draw her into a kiss. A prelude.

And, shit, this wasn't a smart thing to be thinking. His body was reacting in a way she wouldn't be able to help noticing—and she might have been thinking something completely different.

He took a gulp of coffee and gave himself an order. *Redirect.* "Okay. What was going on?"

Cheeks still pink, she wasn't quite looking at him. "Sonja called."

His fantasy vanished with a poof at the mention of his ex's name. "And?"

She told him. His fury made it hard to sit still.

His jaw muscles hurt when he had to unclench his teeth to say, "She has no goddamn sense at all. And even less consideration for Molly's feelings."

"Who has any sense when they're drunk?" Anna hesitated. "I admit to being a little surprised that she was so far gone at four in the afternoon."

He swore and bounced his head on the cushioned back of the sofa. "I've had a suspicion. At the hearing, she was cold-stone sober but suffering from obvious withdrawal. I wonder if most days she isn't having her first drink as soon as she gets up."

"So you really think she was impaired when she tried to take Molly after school."

"Oh, yeah." Nate groaned and straightened. "Damn. Do you think the kids will stick to your new rule and let you answer the phone whenever it rings?"

"I'll make sure they do. But…maybe you should talk to her again, too. I told her she needed to call only when you're home. You could reinforce that."

"Yeah." He cleared his throat. "I'll do that."

Neither of them said anything for a minute. He could faintly hear the sound of the television.

"Does Josh hate me now?" Nate finally asked.

For the first time in the conversation, her gaze slid away from his. "We had a talk. I think he understands."

Nate set down his coffee cup. "What does he understand?"

She had a little speech prepared, summing up everything she'd apparently told her son. It seemed he'd been pretty well absolved of guilt. Again, a hint of color stained her cheeks.

What he couldn't tell was whether she believed herself or was only saying the right thing for Josh's benefit. And, damn, he might be sorry if he asked, but his memory of the one, shocked stare that day at the hospital remained like a rock in his gut. Indigestible.

His voice came out gravelly as he challenged her. "What about you, Anna? Do *you* still blame me?"

CHAPTER FOURTEEN

ANNA'S THROAT CLOSED at a question that had hovered over them all along even as they developed a cooperative relationship, one that sometimes felt so smooth she'd almost blurted something stupid a few minutes ago.

She hadn't foreseen that they might start functioning as a unit: parents who wanted the best for all the kids and watched out for each other, too. Unit? No, they felt like a family. Not all the time, but too often. Without consciously realizing it, she liked being someone he could come to, as she turned to him. The constant sizzle of sexual awareness...that she did her best to bury down deep.

His question... She had to be honest.

"The part of me that's rational doesn't blame you." Anna tapped her temple. "I *saw* Sonja. I know why Molly was able to slip away."

He leaned forward. "What—"

"That doesn't matter to this." *Us.* "I never should have blamed you. Like I told Josh, you weren't even there."

He visibly reined in his impatience, clearly knowing that she wasn't done.

"In my heart," she said quietly, "it's not so easy. I'm...pretty mixed up still."

"You don't blame yourself." He sounded incredulous.

"No. But I have a lot of complicated feelings about Kyle." Why was she telling this man about her marriage? Yet she continued. "We had problems, and I felt so angry after he died—"

His gaze had somehow sharpened. "Because he left you and the kids without any financial cushion."

"That's...only part of it. The rest is private." She had to establish *some* boundaries. "But I know I've been moody, and you must wonder why."

"Do you think I haven't guessed?" he said after a minute, with an undertone of temper. "Or do you assume I'm satisfied if you take care of my daughter and don't really see you as a person?"

"I—"

"Well, you're wrong." Muscles spasmed in his jaw even as dark gray, troubled eyes never looked away from her. "You're on my mind a whole hell of a lot more than I find comfortable. And if you don't know why that is, you're not as observant as I think you are."

In shock, she quit breathing as she stared at

him. He was implying—no, he was *saying*—
that she hadn't just been imagining he was attracted to her. And...that he knew his feelings
were reciprocated?

She shot to her feet. "I won't talk about this.
I *work* for you."

Still watchful, he rose more slowly. "That
doesn't make it any less true."

Anna shook her head and kept shaking it.
"No. It can't be. *I* can't..."

"Can't you?" One stride, and he was inches
from her. This close, she couldn't look away
from a lean, rough-hewn face that fascinated
her. Unwittingly frozen, she took in the shadow
of his evening beard, the way his eyes had darkened to charcoal.

Heated by a horrible mix of panic and the
same intense awareness she'd felt when his body
had covered hers that day on the soccer field,
Anna tried to shuffle back.

He lifted a hand and cupped her cheek, his
thumb tapping her lips. Only once, but they tingled as if he'd kissed her.

"No," she whispered. The temptation was
there, to lean into that warm hand. In fact...
had she swayed toward him? Her second "No"
was aimed as much at herself as him.

Familiar creases formed on his forehead. "Is
it so bad if we acknowledge—"

This time she cried, "Yes!"

His hand dropped to his side. She slid back a couple more steps, until she was no longer trapped between the sofa and the coffee table.

"My husband died not even five months ago. *Five.* We may have had our problems, but how can you think I'd be ready to happily move on that fast? And especially with—" Oh, dear God. She hadn't said that. But, seeing his shock and quickly hidden hurt, she knew she had.

"Guess I shouldn't have bothered asking that question," he said, his face now wiped of expression. The chill in his voice conveyed enough on its own.

"I didn't mean that. I told you—"

"You did." He turned to go around the other end of the sofa. "I'll finish cleaning the kitchen, if you want to get Josh started on his homework."

Back at the apartment, he meant. Feeling sick, she nodded but felt compelled to say, "I'm sorry. I told you I'm a mess."

"I understand." He started for the kitchen to do *her* job.

To his back, Anna said, "If you want us to leave…"

He barely paused. "No. I was an idiot. Like we've agreed before, this arrangement has worked out well. If you don't feel the same, I'd appreciate some notice."

"Yes." She felt as if she was being strangled. "Of course."

One nod, then Nate turned on the water to start rinsing dishes. To all appearances, he considered himself to be entirely alone.

The irony was, she, too, felt alone in a way she hadn't since she accepted Nate's offer of a refuge that allowed her to keep her dignity.

IF NATE COULD have kicked his own butt, he would have. Instead, he stared up at the dark ceiling of his bedroom and tried to understand why he'd been so stupid.

Anna had provisionally let him off the hook as far as her husband's death went, and what had he done? Come on to her. Four and a half months after said death. And right after she'd told him she still had mixed feelings, that her rational belief that he wasn't to blame hadn't convinced her emotional self.

What if he'd screwed this up so bad she did decide to take her kids and leave? He might have to hire the damn PI again so he'd know where she'd gone and that she was okay. Then if she found out, she'd be mad again.

She'd been magnificent when she stormed into his office to tell him off. For a long time, Nate had convinced himself that his need to help her was driven solely by guilt, but now he thought that he'd toppled that day. He wasn't close to putting a label on what he felt for her, but his anguish bit deeper than it had since he and Sonja parted ways—and then he'd hurt because he was losing his daughter, not because of Sonja.

He slapped his pillow over his face, mumbled some obscenities into it, then yanked it off.

He'd apologize to Anna. Grovel. Talk her into staying.

If she agreed…then came the hard part. He'd have to quit with the lust, be pleasant, collegial, friendly at the most. He'd be whatever she wanted him to be. Give her the time she shouldn't have had to ask for.

And then they'd see.

THE CONVERSATION WAS every bit as difficult as Nate had feared.

He'd barely crossed the threshold after work the next day then she was hustling her kids out the back. Seeing Molly's bewilderment, Nate felt even more like a shit.

My fault.

He said, "Anna, can we talk for a minute?"

She went still, her back to him, then bent and spoke quietly to her kids. Accepting a casserole dish from her, Josh ushered his obviously reluctant sister out of sight and presumably upstairs to the apartment.

Nate hugged his daughter and said, "Can you give us a minute, punkin?"

Perplexity showed on her small, freckled face as she said with her worrisome docility, "Yes, Daddy."

Stripping off his tie, he walked to the kitchen, where Anna waited. She must have subbed at one of the schools today, he realized, seeing that she wore black slacks and a thin three-quarter-sleeve, formfitting cotton cardigan with tiny buttons that served to emphasis the curve of her breasts.

Damn it. He had to suppress that kind of awareness. There he went, despite his resolve of last night. Yeah, this wasn't going to be easy. The fact that he hadn't had sex in, what, eight months or more didn't help. In fact, he'd quit assessing women as possibilities even longer ago than he'd thought. Say, from the minute Anna had confronted him in his office.

She nervously brushed her hair behind her ear. "Yes?"

Nate stopped this side of the breakfast bar, sensing that he couldn't afford to crowd her. "I owe you an apology."

"No, you—"

"I do." He cut her off without compunction. "Please don't decide you have to leave. I trust you. I'd…miss you and your kids, both. Losing you, too, might break Molly's heart." Using his daughter was low, but he also thought he'd spoken the truth. Molly was unbelievably fragile right now. "I trust you to keep her safe."

"How can it help but be awkward if I stay?"

"Because you can trust me, too." He expected the tiled countertop to crack any minute beneath his flattened hands, but she didn't have to know how much pressure he was putting on it. "I was out of line. We can be friends, co-parents, just like we have been. And that's it." He wanted to add, *Unless or until you signal me that you're ready for more*, but knew he couldn't. Then she'd feel like a mouse with a cat watching, waiting.

He couldn't tell what Anna was thinking, but she looked away for a minute. She'd knotted her hands in front of her.

Her eyes met his again. "All right. The kids are really happy here, and I have to admit I'd really miss Molly." Her smile was so brief he wouldn't have seen it if he'd blinked at the wrong time. "She did a lot of the work tonight on dinner. Be sure to rave about it. I think she really enjoys cooking."

He nodded.

"Despite Josh's current…uncertainty, he's thrived with the attention you've given him. That wasn't part of our deal, but I appreciate it."

"I like him." He had to swallow to loosen his throat. "Jenna, too."

Anna dipped her head. "So…we can go on the way we have been. If you change your mind, though, all you have to do is tell me."

"I won't," he said roughly.

Her eyes searched his for the briefest of moments. "Then, good night." This time her nod was as awkward as she undoubtedly felt. She turned and was out of sight in seconds. He heard the door open and softly close.

Nate's shoulders sagged. He'd ached to ask if she wouldn't miss him, too, but somehow had kept his mouth shut. He only had—*God*—seven months and a few weeks of restraint to go until the end of the school year…and the anniversary of Kyle Grainger's death.

KNOWING THE KIDS had a project that was more time-consuming than usual due this week, Anna had sat them down at the table with their packs not long after dinner. As Jenna got bored, she'd taken to distracting the others. Anna had just decided to put in a movie for her when Nate walked in.

The week since the scene with him had been really hard. To start with, all three kids were clearly disturbed by the new stiff courtesy between them. Anna didn't know how Nate felt about it, but she was bothered, too, felt as if she'd lost something she might never find again.

In self-defense, she'd ensured the time they spent together was extremely limited.

Her biggest struggle was with her increased awareness of Nate—his every move, breath, flicker of expression. She couldn't seem to block it out anymore. When she felt the hot coal low in her belly, guilt stabbed, sharp and unstoppable. How could she be attracted to another man so soon after Kyle's death?

No, things hadn't been right between them in several years, but she *had* made the decision to stay with him. To accept his flaws because of all the qualities that made him a good man and father. What horrified Anna now was wondering what would have happened if she'd met Nate Kendrick while she was still married. Would she have responded as helplessly to a casual touch? To a steady regard from his gray eyes, or the sight of his bare throat and a hint of dark, curling chest hair when he undid the top buttons of his dress shirt soon after getting home after work?

It wasn't as if she hadn't admired men while she was married. She'd seen Kyle's eyes tracking sexy women now and again. But that was just nature, and very different from the *need* she felt for one particular man anytime her guard slipped.

But…they'd gone on. And just today, before dinner, she'd been playing Chutes and Ladders with Jenna when she heard Molly's indignant, "Jo-shu-a! You bring that back!"

Anna sat cross-legged on the floor in front of the coffee table in the living room, Jenna on her knees across from her. Suddenly, Josh burst out of the family room and zigzagged through the dining and living rooms, tauntingly waving something above his head, laughing like crazy. Molly tore after him. Astonishingly, she was giggling the whole way.

Anna had a feeling her mouth had dropped open.

Now she wanted to tell Nate. To be able to talk the way they had before he'd bluntly put into words something she already knew and feared.

At that moment his gaze flicked to her as if he'd sensed what she was thinking. Their eyes held for a minute too long, enough to make her heart pound.

Grabbing for her defenses, she said, "Molly, tell your dad about the Thanksgiving celebration."

Molly wrinkled her nose. "I like having a feast, but I *hate* having to be in a play. What if Mrs. Tate makes me *say* something?"

Nate smothered a chuckle. "I'm sure you'll do fine."

"Molly is supposed to be a girl Pilgrim," Josh informed them. "*I* get to be the turkey."

Had he thought about the dying part? Anna

worried. Another quick glance from Nate suggested he'd read her mind again.

"I want to trade so I can be a pumpkin," Molly whispered. "'Cuz that's what Daddy calls me. And I can just sit there."

"Did Mrs. Tate assign parts?"

She bobbed her head.

"You could talk to her," he said. "On the other hand, if she's given you a speaking role, it's probably because she has confidence you can handle it."

Surprise widened Molly's eyes. "Oh."

Anna prepared to kick Josh in the shin if he said a single denigrating word. When he kept quiet, she smiled at him.

Instead of gathering her kids to go back to the apartment, the way she had every other evening this week the minute Nate walked in the door, she stepped away from the table. When he turned, she said, "Do you have a minute to talk?"

"We should catch up on how the week has gone." Agreeable, pleasant, remote.

That hurt even though it was what she wanted.

When she emerged from the family room after putting in a DVD for Jenna, she saw that Nate had poured coffee and carried two cups out onto the covered terrace.

At least it was clear tonight, though undoubtedly cold. She took a red cashmere throw from the back of a chair and wrapped it around herself before following him out.

"This is sinfully soft," were the first words out of her mouth.

There was a pause. "Soft shouldn't be sinful."

"I'll have to be careful not to spill on it."

He shrugged and turned too-discerning gray eyes to a sailboat gliding in to dock a couple houses away.

Anna took a deep breath. "It's this Thanksgiving event, which isn't far away. I was thinking you could invite Sonja."

He thought about it and then gusted out a sigh. "Can we trust her to come semi-sober and behave herself?"

We. He was including her as if they were a team. Despite everything, that gave her a warm glow. "I don't know," she said, "but she's Molly's mother."

"You think she should be there for Molly's sake."

"Sonja's, too. It might be, I don't know, a lure. A normal, happy event for parents."

"I'll think about it."

She nodded. After a minute, she told him about Molly's delight in the great chase, and about the project the two older kids were currently working on. He talked about another meeting with the two twenty-five-year-old guys with the "awesome" idea for an improved snowboard. Finally, he said, "Can we have Thanksgiving together? All of us?"

"What about Sonja?"

He groaned.

Anna laughed.

Just like that, they were looking deeply, searchingly at each other. Happiness tangled painfully with guilt and a deep but less identifiable fear, inciting panic.

She should run away. Snatch her kids and never come back. How on earth had she ever thought she could work for Nate and keep her distance?

He was the one to stand up. "My fault," he said huskily, and went into the house, leaving her to huddle in her cashmere throw and calm herself.

CHAPTER FIFTEEN

AFTER SONJA ARRIVED at the house on Thanks-giving Day, she handed an unopened bottle of wine to Nate without saying a word, drew Molly into a hug that lasted too long, then said hello to "John" and "Jennie." She strolled over to the breakfast bar and swept Anna with a disdainful expression. "You've certainly made yourself at home in my kitchen, haven't you?"

Anna's vision of them having a warm, com-fortable, blended-family holiday crashed. Straightening from the hot oven, she did battle with her temper. Despite the smells of turkey and stuffing and the pies that had come out of the second oven only minutes ago, she'd swear the odor of alcohol wafted her way from Sonja. She hadn't bothered with breath mints today. On the other hand, she wasn't staggering, which was something.

Anna said pleasantly, "I'm so glad you could come, Sonja. Happy Thanksgiving."

"It's so sweet of Nate—" she glanced over her shoulder at him "—to include the housekeeper and her children."

"Knock it off, Sonja." Nate walked into the kitchen and set the wine bottle on the counter. "Anna and her kids *are* family these days."

Anger flashed on his ex-wife's face. If he'd intended to pacify her, that wasn't the right tack to take.

Either oblivious or not caring, he continued, "Having Josh and Jenna here at home to play with has been really good for Molly."

"Better than having her mother?" Sonja asked sharply.

The three kids stood not far away, certainly within earshot. Molly had red splashes of humiliation on her cheeks, and she looked as if she wanted to be anywhere but there.

Anna opened her mouth, but Nate spoke first.

"We're glad to share our holiday with you, Sonja, but you need to adjust your attitude, if only for the kids' sake." His voice was hard, one Anna wasn't sure she'd ever heard. "Is that clear?"

His ex didn't like being chastised. Her lips thinned and her nostrils flared, but then she dipped her head. "Have you no sense of humor?"

"Apparently not," he said coolly. He raised his voice. "Molly, what happened to the olives and veggies and dip? Your mom might like some."

Anna dumped milk in with the potatoes and picked up the masher. "Dinner is just about ready to go on the table. Give me five minutes."

Sonja did have the grace to say, "Is there anything I can do?"

Anna couldn't quite make herself smile, but she did say, "Thank you, but I have everything in hand. Besides, your dress is so beautiful I'd feel awful if anything splashed on it."

Body-forming, a rich russet color that suited her coloring, it was spectacular, as were the enormous diamonds in her earrings and a pendant that settled just above her generous cleavage. Four-inch heels gave her walk a sultry sway as she sauntered toward the living room.

"Do open the wine, Nate," she called over her shoulder.

Anna glanced at the kids, who still hadn't moved. "Time to wash hands," she told them briskly. "Then you can help carry some of this to the table."

They dashed away like antelope running from a water hole visited by a lioness. Who could blame them?

Nate was closer than Anna had realized, because she could feel the warmth of his breath when he murmured, "Can I run away, too?"

Anna choked on a laugh. "Not a chance. But you can go supervise the hand-washing, if you want."

He made a sound in his throat. "How about if I accidentally-on-purpose drop the damn bottle and it shatters?"

Just as softly, Anna said, "Something tells me this lovely holiday gathering is in danger of descending into disaster."

He opened a drawer and located the corkscrew. Out of the side of his mouth, he murmured, "As if it isn't already on its way."

ANNA WAS THE one to insist that they give Sonja another chance at Christmas. The few times they'd seen her since Thanksgiving, she'd been subdued and making an obvious effort to be pleasant. Anna was convinced she was ashamed of herself. Nate was still angry at Sonja's nasty jabs, at Anna in particular, and took a more cynical attitude. He agreed they didn't have much choice, however, what with the holiday spirit and all.

Besides, Sonja had no other family in the area...and she would always be Molly's mother. What's more, she'd mended fences with Molly during recent visits, making an effort to appear semi-sober, and even remembered Josh's and Jenna's names.

Christmas Eve, the kids were as ramped up as if they'd eaten nothing but sugar all day long. Nate glanced up from his newspaper when he heard Jenna ask her mom in a distinctly whiny tone, "When can we...?"

"After dinner. And remember, two presents tonight, the rest in the morning."

He admired Anna's patience. Personally, he was finding the kids' excitement to be contagious.

Last year, since his parents spent the holiday with Adam and his family, Nate had joined Sonja and Molly for Christmas Eve, then had Christmas dinner with John and his family. He'd been grateful for both occasions, but it was hard not to be aware he was on the outside looking in. Negotiating the celebration of Christmas in this new world had been interesting. To his secret satisfaction, the plotting had brought him and Anna together like nothing else could. And, damn, he'd been scrupulous in not taking advantage of all those private conversations.

Regular dinner on Christmas Eve, they'd agreed—cheeseburgers, baked beans, peas and the cookies the kids had helped her cut out and decorate. The kids would be able to open two gifts—parents' choice.

Christmas morning, the deluge. Plus, Anna was cooking a turkey with all the trimmings, since it had been such a hit at Thanksgiving. Sonja was to join them as early in the day as she felt inclined.

He'd made the decision not to invite her for Christmas Eve or to spend the night. He wanted some stress-free fun time for Molly—and himself. Anna, Josh and Jenna did feel like family to him, and he thought they deserved the chance to celebrate as one. Needless to say, all he'd told Anna was that he wanted Molly to enjoy Christmas Eve without the tension her mother was bound to introduce.

Now Jenna circled out of the kitchen to clamber onto a stool next to Nate, whose offer to help with dinner had been politely rebuffed.

After kicking her heels against the legs of the stool for about two minutes, she took another stab at hurrying things along. "Mommy, can't we eat *now*?"

Nate laughed and gave her a squeeze. "Give it up, honey. We'll eat when your mom is done cooking, and not a minute before." He nodded toward the truly enormous tree filling about a quarter of the living room. "While you're waiting, why don't you go admire your presents?"

"I can pick out what I want to open!" she said excitedly, stumbling as she jumped down.

He swung around to steady her. "Nope."

"Oh, pooh!"

Anna laughed. "Fortunately, dinner will be ready in about five minutes."

Nate was careful that she not see him watching her over the top of the newspaper while she did five things at once in the kitchen. With that long, sleek body, she kept making him think of a dancer more than a runner. He indulged himself momentarily, picturing those incredible legs wrapped around his hips. Given how long he'd been fantasizing about her, it was hard to believe he'd never kissed that pretty mouth, cupped her breasts in his hands, tangled his fingers in her honey-blond hair.

Oh, hell. He gave the newspaper a little shake and did his damnedest to focus on the article about the mayoral race in Seattle. He knew two of the candidates and *should* be interested.

Fortunately, his erection had subsided by the time Anna asked him to ferry serving dishes to the table and call the kids. Politics had a way of doing that.

Molly and Josh bounded down the stairs in a headlong rush, bodychecking each other in their attempt to reach the table first.

Even as Nate suggested they slow down, he quietly rejoiced in behavior his subdued little girl wouldn't have considered much over a month ago. Having a "brother" and competitor was proving to be good for her. He only hoped her mother didn't try to squelch the budding changes in Molly's personality out of resentment that Anna and her children had something to do with them.

Yeah, always a new worry to add to the old one: that Sonja would show up hammered. Nate had already resolved that, if she was too far gone, he'd call a cab and send her home. With unopened gifts. He still regretted not doing exactly that five minutes after she'd shown up here on Thanksgiving.

The kids gobbled, then congregated in front of the heap of presents beneath the tree while Anna and Nate finished their meals in a more leisurely fashion.

"How about a cup of coffee?" he suggested, dropping his napkin on his plate.

He loved her laugh, bubbly and a little husky. "That's just cruel. You're lucky they didn't hear you."

Nate chuckled, too. "I think we should forget the Santa thing. There's already enough under the tree."

She glanced fondly toward the three, huddled with noses together as Josh rattled one of his presents. "I got carried away."

"Me, too. Having Molly home…" He had to stop for a moment. "And, you know, Sonja always did the buying and wrapping. She let me hang the ornaments out of her reach and put the star on top. Otherwise, I just showed up and smiled when it came time to open presents."

Anna studied him, a couple tiny lines on her forehead. "Surely you had some to open, too."

He shook himself, shedding the chill of memories. "Of course I did. My fault if I didn't get more involved."

"Kyle—" Her gaze shied away as she hesitated. He guessed she thought she might offend him by introducing the subject of her husband. And, yeah, he had mixed feelings about the guy, but he wasn't about to tell her that. "Kyle?" Nate prompted.

"Oh, I was just going to say that he loved to shop for presents. The ones he bought weren't always the most practical, and he spent too much—" She frowned. "He was like another kid where holidays were concerned."

"Um…are you mad at me for buying the remote-controlled speedboat for Josh?" Good thing she'd never know how close he'd come to buying her a new car instead of the modest-sized diamond earrings that were wrapped under the tree.

She laughed. "No, because I know *somebody* will be playing with it, even if it isn't Josh."

"Guilty."

"Josh will love it."

"You know," Nate said slowly, "I feel more like a kid this year than I have since I *was* a kid."

Her smile dawned and her eyes sparkled. "I'm glad. What say we start?"

He grinned back. "I'm ready."

When they pushed back their chairs and stood, the kids cheered.

"I know which one I want to open first," Jenna insisted.

"Can I open the big one?" Josh begged. "Can I?"

Her face glowing beneath the multicolored lights that wound around the ten-foot-tall noble fir, Molly said, "I don't know which one to open."

Nate took a seat at one end of the sofa while Anna went to her knees beside the tree. She reached for a sizable gift and handed it to Jenna.

"Youngest first."

Nate leaned forward, but it wasn't the big-eyed girl tearing at the paper he watched. No, it was the tenderness on Anna's face that captivated him.

THE DOORBELL DIDN'T ring until eleven in the morning. Anna had seen how edgy Nate was and how Molly's head turned at every sound from outside.

She leaped up from where she and Josh had been building a spaceship with Lego.

"Mommy's here!"

Anna's eyes met Nate's as he rose to go to the door. Molly beat him there, but Nate had a hand on her shoulder when she let her mother in.

Moment of truth.

Anna's children quit what they were doing, too, and watched in silence as Sonja walked in, smiling and carrying a big bag. Even from a distance, Anna could see that it bulged with wrapped gifts. Was there a bottle of wine in there?

Sonja set the bag down and crouched to sweep Molly into a hug. Molly held on tight to her

mom. The sight of the two heads so close together, their hair the exact same vivid red, gave
Anna a pang. When Sonja finally rose, Anna
thought she was blinking back tears.

"Nate." She gave him a hug, too, and he kissed
her cheek. Then she said, "It smells wonderful
in here. Anna must be responsible for that."

Anna came out to accept the obligatory hug.
The smell of mint was strong, but Sonja's eyes
looked clear. "Molly's been watching the door
all morning."

Sonja surveyed the wreck in the living room.
"Well, it certainly isn't because there was a
shortage of presents."

Anna laughed. "No, it isn't."

Sonja lifted her bag. "Just in case…"

Expression avid, Jenna left her own construc-
tion project and came to investigate. Uh-oh.
Anna hoped the other woman had thought to
buy modest gifts for Josh and Jenna. But, bless
Sonja's heart, when she laid out the presents
on the coffee table, they seemed to be almost
evenly distributed between the three children.

Nate stood beside Anna, close enough their
shoulders brushed and she smelled a hint of his
aftershave and the something more that was
him.

The kids chattered about what they'd already
gotten as they tore paper. The gifts were all well-
chosen: a Stomp Rocket for Josh; a dry-erase,

light-up board for Molly; and a kit to build play forts like simple tents to hide in throughout the house for Jenna.

And no booze.

Actually liking Sonja for the first time, Anna relaxed and returned to the kitchen to peel potatoes. Nate glanced after her, but finally sat on the arm of the sofa and joined the conversation in a relaxed way. He'd dressed down today, in jeans worn enough to hug every muscle in his long legs, athletic shoes and an aged sweatshirt that said Stanford on the front. Of course, he'd pushed up the sleeves. His forearms had become more of a weakness than she wanted to admit.

For some reason—possibly because of Sonja's proximity to Nate—Anna was sharply aware of what a beautiful woman his ex-wife was. Slim, almost delicate, except for breasts that had to be a C cup, at least. Anna suddenly felt like a flagpole in comparison. The deep V-neck of Sonja's emerald-green sweater showed plenty of creamy flesh and cleavage. Given that he was sitting higher than Sonja, Nate must have quite a view. Had he paid for those breasts?

Anna wanted to slap herself. Way to demonstrate Christmas spirit. The woman was being nice. She was trying hard, making Molly happy today. Jealousy had no place here.

Too bad peeling potatoes wasn't the kind of task that fully engaged Anna's attention. It left her free to notice when Sonja scooted over on the couch to be closer to Nate so she could tell him something, and he bent with a hand braced just above her bright head. At that moment, Anna sliced her finger with the peeler. Since she fully deserved to shed blood, she stifled her gasp, ran cold water over her hand and bandaged herself without anyone noticing.

NATE COULDN'T HELP getting an eyeful of Sonja's cleavage. Given his state of sexual deprivation, he was surprised not to feel even reminiscent pleasure at the sight. He glanced, dismissed.

Maybe because of he'd had the example of his parents' marriage, seeing both love and the spark he hadn't acknowledged as sexual attraction until he was an adult, he'd never been a man who was happy to take a woman he didn't at least like to bed. Sonja had certainly killed everything he'd felt for her long ago. Now, it seemed, he didn't even appreciate her body. Possibly because he'd become addicted to slim and graceful, breasts the right size to fit his palms with no waste.

For a minute, the kids' excited chatter flew right by him, as did whatever Sonja was trying to tell him. He wanted Anna with every fiber of his being, in every way he could have her. If he'd been a more religious man, he'd think God was punishing him. Out of all the women in the world, why had he become obsessed with this one? Sometimes he was afraid there was something really twisted about it, but then she'd smile at him and—

"Daddy!" Her tone reproving, Molly stood in front of him with her hands on her hips. "Didn't you even *hear* me?"

He smiled at her. "Sorry, kiddo. My mind was wandering." To Anna Grainger, currently slaving in the kitchen while the rest of them sat around the Christmas tree.

"I want *you* to put these butterflies in my hair." She picked up a package of sparkly butterflies attached to bobby pins that her mother had given her.

Sonja reached for them. "Sweetie, I doubt your father is any better at doing your hair than he ever was."

Molly shifted away, still clutching the package. "He is! You'll see."

Hurt crossed his ex-wife's face. Nate would've felt the same. But about all he could do was take the package, tear it open and try to figure out what to do with pins that didn't seem to have any functional purpose. The moment was awkward, and right after they'd been doing so well with the spirit of joy and goodwill.

Maybe Molly was trying to make him feel better because she'd asked this morning for French braids, and he'd had to admit they weren't in his repertoire. She'd settled on a single, ordinary braid.

"Okay." He slid a bobby pin in so a purple butterfly sparkled above her left ear. Another went above her right ear. But butterflies flitted; they didn't line up precisely like Canada geese with their V in the sky. And, hey, there were eight of these. He started poking them in all over, and she giggled.

When he was done, she raced for the bathroom to see herself and came back delighted. "I can hardly *wait* to wear them to school." After the tiniest pause, she said, "Thank you, Mommy."

Sonja did smile. "You're very welcome. They look beautiful, don't they, Jenna?"

Anna's daughter had been watching. "I wish *I* had some."

Molly giggled and went back to Jenna's new game, which she was obviously playing out of the kindness of what Nate had come to realize was a very generous heart.

"I actually am getting better with the hair thing," he said in a low voice to Sonja. "But this morning I had to admit I don't have the slightest idea how to do French braids."

"And that's one of her favorite ways to wear her hair," she said smugly.

He'd give her the jab, but he excused himself to go help Anna. Fortunately, she was to the point where she needed someone to dig the stuffing out of the turkey and carve it while she mashed potatoes and simultaneously stirred the gravy she'd just started.

Wielding the butcher knife, he caught sight of a large bandage on her finger. "What happened?"

"Oh, a careless moment." She lifted it ruefully. "The darn thing keeps bleeding. Can you stir while I change the bandage?"

"Sure."

She was back in about a minute to take over.

"This smells fantastic." His stomach growled, and she laughed.

"It does, doesn't it? I think this is my absolute favorite meal. Except…" Lines formed between her eyebrows.

"Except?" He added another slice of moist white meat to the platter.

"Maybe pizza."

He looked up and met her eyes. They had one of those out-of-time-and-space moments when suddenly no one else existed, when he couldn't have looked away if he'd tried.

But the intensity faded, thank God, and animated voices intruded.

"Yeah," he said hoarsely. "I really like pizza, too." He wasn't sure he'd ever enjoy it again without her and her kids.

When they all gathered around the table a

few minutes later and bowed their heads to say grace, Nate thought he'd be completely happy if only this family wasn't temporary.

CHAPTER SIXTEEN

IT HAD TO be some supersensitive mother instinct, because Anna couldn't possibly have heard the crack of breaking bone from so far away. Whatever she'd heard or didn't hear, she found herself running onto the soccer field even while the skirmish in front of Josh's goal was still going on. Bewildered boys stumbled out of her way. A few were exchanging high fives because the ball had gone into the goal, while others clustered around Josh, who hadn't gotten up after his attempted save.

Wide-eyed, they stepped back to let her drop to her knees beside his son, who was curled into a pained ball on the damp grass, his desperate gaze fixed on her. At least he was conscious. This wasn't a head injury.

"Where do you hurt?" She started touching him, testing.

"Arm," he whispered.

"Josh?" It was the coach, who'd persuaded most of the boys on his team to sign up for the spring soccer league sponsored by the Boys & Girls Club. This was the very first practice.

When she got up this morning, Anna had been very conscious of the date: March 27. Nine months to the day since Kyle's death. She'd almost refused to let Josh come today, but she had been so certain that was silly. And now see what had happened.

She persuaded him to uncurl enough to let them look at the arm he cradled with his other hand. He was thin enough that it didn't take a doctor to see that his forearm was no longer straight. Unless it was her imagination, it had already started to swell.

"Do you hurt anywhere else?" the coach asked.

Josh shook his head. His face was white, his mouth pinched closed. How could he be so stoic as the coach helped him sit up?

"Ambulance?" the coach asked.

"No!" Josh burst out. "I can walk."

"I can drive him to the ER," Anna said, sounding steadier than she felt.

Fortunately, they were practicing on the field closest to the parking lot. Shocked and silent, his teammates stood solemnly by as she escorted him off. Anna looked around automatically, and found another mother had summoned Molly and Jenna and folded Anna's lawn chair. She followed with the chair, talking quietly to the girls, who scrambled in. For once, Anna let Josh sit in front, where she could keep a better eye on him as she drove.

She thanked Jaden's mother with a weak smile, closed Josh's door and hurried around to get in herself.

Halfway there, she realized her stomach churned in part because they were on their way to Overlake Hospital. It was the same hospital where she'd given birth, twice, but now all she could remember was driving there as fast as she could go that June day after leaving her kids with another parent. Knowing the news wouldn't be good, but nonetheless refusing to believe the worst until she was led to a small room off the ER, where a doctor waited for her. Just his face had told her. She hardly remembered what he'd said.

"We'll be there any minute," she said unnecessarily, since the hospital was now visible above lower buildings. Since Josh was able to walk, she turned into the parking garage. By the time they hustled into an elevator, his arm was discolored and hugely swollen. He'd been stricken pale and silent, the sight of him scaring the girls enough to keep them quiet, too.

The receptionist in the emergency room told them to take a seat, but that the wait should be brief. The minute they sat down, Anna with an arm around Josh, she took out her phone. She was listening to the ringing even before she had justified the call in her own mind.

No, she needed to let him know that they wouldn't make it home when she'd said they would. After all, she did have his daughter with her.

He answered on the second ring. "Anna?"

"We're at Overlake," she told him.

"What?" His alarm was apparent.

"It's Josh, not Molly. I'm sorry, I should have said that first. I'm…rattled." She kissed the top of Josh's head. "He made a spectacular dive to stop a kick and broke his arm."

"You know that for sure?"

"It's…obvious."

"I'm on my way. You're at the ER?"

"Yes, but you don't have to—"

"Of course I do." And he was gone.

Relief out of all proportion flooded her. Bothered by her reaction, she tucked her phone away. "Nate's coming."

Josh gave a tiny sniff and burrowed his face into her. He had to hurt terribly to let his mom cuddle him in public.

"Mommy?" Jenna whispered. "Will they fix Josh?"

"Of course they will. He'll probably end up with a cast."

He lifted his head. "I can't play goalie then!"

"You can't play soccer," she had to tell him.

"But…"

A nurse in a colorful smock emerged from the back. "Josh Grainger."

Anna rose and ushered her flock across the waiting room. "I'm Anna Grainger."

The nurse smiled. "At least he has company."

It seemed only minutes later that Nate joined them in the cubicle, his sheer size instantly shrinking the space. He laid a hand on her shoulder, silently sympathetic. Anna reacted with both warmth and tension. Somehow, she hadn't become immune to even his most casual touches.

"Has he been seen yet?"

"The doctor just left to order an X-ray."

Stepping close to the bed, he studied Josh's arm. "Yeah, that looks broken, all right. How are you, kiddo?"

Her son visibly girded himself. He'd hate knowing he had a few tear tracks on his cheeks. "It hurts, but…you know."

Nate squeezed Josh's foot. "I do know. I broke my arm when I was only a little older than you. Left one, too. I was bummed because it didn't get me out of schoolwork."

Josh groaned. "I should've landed on my right side."

Anna rolled her eyes. Catching her, Nate grinned. "Bet your mom never broke *her* arm."

"That's sexist. And you'd be wrong."

"It was sexist," he admitted. "Now you have to tell us when you broke a bone."

"It wasn't doing anything fun. My grandfather was getting shaky on his feet. I tried to keep him from falling and we both went down. I'm the only one who got hurt. He felt so bad." Had she ever told Nate that her grandfather had died when she was a teenager? It wasn't all that much later. Six months?

His eyes narrowed slightly, but he only gave an acknowledging nod. Turning the mood light again, he said, "So, you broke your arm being noble. Josh because he's an aggressive athlete. Me because I was an idiot."

Molly piped up, "Daddy climbed a tree after his parents told him not to, and then he fell."

"An idiot. What did I tell you?"

An orderly arrived to take Josh for the X-ray. Once he was gone, Nate dug into the pockets of his windbreaker and handed out crumbled cookies from a sandwich bag.

"I hurried and baked these just for you guys."

Jenna stared at him indignantly. "Mommy baked these!"

He grinned and ruffled her hair. "I know she did. I've never baked cookies in my life. I'm pretty sure if I tried, they wouldn't be this good."

"Uh-uh," she agreed, around a big bite.

Even Anna gobbled her first one gratefully,

although why she was so hungry she couldn't have said. A glance at the clock on the wall surprised her. Soccer practice would still be going on. Even if Josh hadn't gotten injured, she and the kids wouldn't be sitting down to lunch at home yet. When she finished the cookie, she saw Nate's amusement.

"You really didn't have to come," she said. "I thought... I don't know."

His expression changed. "You'd rather I hadn't come?"

"I..." She couldn't make herself lie. "Of course not. I feel guilty, that's all. You were working."

"I'd have been insulted if you hadn't called."

Anna opened her mouth to say something, but couldn't think what she *should* say. *You're not Josh's father? I'm afraid I'm becoming too dependent on you? I never considered* not *calling you?* Instead, she took a page out of his book and nodded.

And then, because his face remained expressionless, she reached for him. The hard line of his mouth softened, and he enclosed her hand in a warm grip.

"I'd like to find out how bad the break is and what they're going to do, but then I can take the girls home if that would help more than having us all keep hanging around."

"Thank you." Her eyes stung. The adrenaline

she'd been running on had drained away and left her shaky. "Let's see what the doctor says before we decide, okay?"

Josh was wheeled back in only a few minutes later, followed by the doctor. Seeing Nate, Dr. Sloane introduced herself and seemed to assume he was Josh's father. She showed them the X-rays, which made Anna wince. Both bones in the forearm had buckled and looked torn halfway through.

Nate wrapped an arm around her.

"This is what we call a greenstick fracture," Dr. Sloane explained. "They're most common with kids, because their bones are softer and more flexible than adults'."

She planned to make sure the bones were aligned and then splint his arm as a temporary measure. "We can't cast it until the swelling goes down, which may be as much as a week."

"How long will the cast be on?"

"Likely at least six weeks. We'll probably do repeat X-rays to see how Josh's arm is healing. Rarely, we need to keep the bones immobilized for as long as twelve weeks." She patted Josh's good arm. "No spring sports for you, I'm afraid."

He struggled to sit up. "But if I don't play, someone else will take over as goalie!"

"You know that won't happen," Anna began.

"It will!" he said furiously.

"You're too talented a player for that to happen," Nate said firmly. "What's more, you have plenty of years of soccer ahead of you if you keep playing. You'll make up a couple of missed months in no time. It happens to every good athlete."

"That's true," the doctor assured him. "A couple of days ago, I treated a Mariner baseball player with a lot more serious break than this. He had to have surgery, and he won't be able to rejoin the team until June or July. He isn't happy, but he's taking it in stride."

"Oh." Josh subsided. "I guess I can still run and stuff."

If *stuff* meant skateboarding, no, he wouldn't be. But Anna didn't see any reason to say that now.

"Not for a few days," Dr. Sloane said with a smile. "So, we're ready to splint that arm. Your mom or dad can come with you."

"I'll come," Anna said quickly.

"Then I'll take the girls home, if you're okay."

She nodded. He spoke a few quiet words to Josh, then ushered the girls out. All Anna's worries stayed intact, but she was glad she'd called him, anyway. And she couldn't take her eyes off his tall form until he went through the doors at the end of the hall, a reassuring hand on each girl's head.

THE NEXT SATURDAY, Nate concentrated on the financial information displayed on his laptop. Instead of going into the office, he had stayed home. He'd been doing that a lot more than had been his habit, even on days like this when Anna was available to watch the kids. His attention span might not be as long, but he could take breaks and go downstairs to talk to her, tease Molly or hit a Nerf baseball with Josh. He liked the trade-off and felt no hankering to escape.

Last weekend, Nate had counted another month off on his mental calendar. Nine months since Kyle Grainger died saving Molly's life. He didn't feel guilty anymore; at least, he didn't think he did. Still, there was a twinge in his chest because, yeah, his absence that day had had profound consequences.

That made his impatience for Anna to get the grieving done even worse. More inexcusable.

And when in his life had he waited for any woman or girl like he was for her?

Anna's voice pulled him from his momentary brood. He looked up from his laptop to see her standing in the door. Her timing was impeccable. Even in jeans and a sweater knit out of nubby, thick yarns that should hide her figure, she looked good enough to make him want to shove the computer aside and pull her onto his lap.

"I'm sorry to interrupt," she began tentatively.

He blanked on what he'd been working on before his thoughts wandered. Oh, yeah. He'd been studying the pro formas—the financial projections—for a start-up he was as yet undecided on.

"No problem," he said.

She still eyed him in a way that made him wonder what she saw on his face, but then she drew a deep breath. "I hate to ask when I know you're working, but is there any chance I can leave the kids here while I grocery shop?"

He frowned. "Sure, but I could go to the store for you."

It turned out she liked to select her own produce and didn't totally rely on her list, either.

"I can work downstairs while the kids are playing," he said.

"They're hyper. If only it weren't raining."

"What? You'd throw them out the door?"

She laughed. "Something like that. Okay, I'll get ready to go."

Ten minutes later, she was gone. He sat on a stool at the breakfast bar, laptop in front of him again, but before he could become engrossed, his mother called.

"Are those happy shrieks I hear?" she said cheerfully.

Nate smiled, watching as the trio raced past. He cringed when Josh bounced off the back of the sofa but stayed on his feet, uninjured. "Yes, it is. I'm in charge while Anna grocery shops."

"She's been a blessing, hasn't she?"

A mixed one, he couldn't help thinking. Happiness and torment, all in one. "Yeah," he said. "How's Dad?"

"He had another crisis last night." She no longer sounded cheerful, and Nate realized he'd heard the underlying strain from the beginning. "They kept him in the ER for several hours, but they're confident he's just having panic attacks."

"He doesn't believe it." This had been going on for months.

"I think he does until the next time he has chest pain. They won't even give him nitroglycerin, because he doesn't need it."

"Maybe they should give him sugar pills," he suggested, half-serious.

His father had suffered a major heart attack last May. He'd had a five-way bypass and a month later insisted he was as good as new. But his subconscious wasn't as convinced, it appeared. The next apparent heart attack came in September. Nate hadn't even made it to the hospital before his mother called to say it was a false alarm.

They'd left earlier for Arizona than they had the year before because Mom was convinced he just needed to get away, to relax. Nate could have told her his dad didn't know how. The driven personality he and Adam shared had come from their father. He'd pushed them hard as they grew up, but Nate suspected some of it was genetic.

"I'm sorry," he said now. "Dad's too stubborn to believe any damn doctor."

She sighed. "Especially one he's sure can't be of drinking age. I know any cardiologist has to be well into his thirties, at least, but this one did have one of those boyish faces."

Nate laughed out loud.

They were planning to return to Seattle in just a few weeks so his father could see his own cardiologist. As if that would help.

They talked for a few more minutes before he called Molly to say hi to her grandma and grandpa, after which Nate got back on to talk to his father.

"There's something going on they're just not seeing," he insisted. "Telling *me* I'm having a panic attack? I'll have the last laugh."

"When they do the autopsy, you mean?"

"There's no call for you to get morbid," his father grumbled.

"Dad, are you taking the antidepressants Dr. Richards prescribed?"

Silence.

"Take them." Nate made sure his father knew he meant what he was saying. "You're wearing

Mom down. For her, you need to try to overcome this."

"Yeah, yeah." His father sighed deeply. "I'll do that. At least then I'll die happy."

Nate was still laughing when he set his phone down and focused on the open laptop. Now what had he been doing?

Just as he began to focus, he realized he was hearing dance music and wild giggles coming from the family room. Surfacing, he thought, *Wait. Where's Josh?*

He had a panicky minute—speaking of panic—before he found the boy in the formerly empty room designed to be a home office. Josh sat on the floor, leaning against a wall, despondency in every line of his body.

Nate hoped his heart rate settled back into a normal range soon. He didn't chew the kid out, though. Instead, he asked, "Bored?"

Josh shrugged. "All they want to do is dance. Who wants to dance?"

"Not me," Nate said truthfully.

"I wish it wasn't raining," the boy said discontentedly. "Then I could have taken my boat out or skateboarded or *something*."

Not skateboarded—his mother had nixed that until the cast was off, and he knew it.

"Maybe you could go to a friend's house." Nate immediately wished he'd bitten his tongue. Saturday equaled soccer.

"Most of my friends are on the team," he said disconsolately. "Besides, they don't want to sit around just 'cuz *I* have to."

"I could play Soccer Challenge with you," he suggested. Screw work.

The electronic goal, a present for Josh's eighth birthday in February, hung on the wall in here so he could play anytime. The player earned points by hitting the board with the kicked ball. Different parts of the board earned more points than others, encouraging pinpoint control. Nate had had fun with it, too.

"It's not like really playing."

"I guess not," Nate said, after a minute. He lowered himself to sit next to the boy on the floor, back to the wall. Unlike Josh, he stretched out his legs. "Got another idea?"

Talking to his knees, Josh said, "Mom says it's not your fault that…you know. Dad died."

Oh, crap. So much for this having been laid to rest.

Yeah? Who did you think you were kidding?

With the next breath, Nate discovered how much he hated thinking of what questions had been eating away at this boy in all the months since his father's funeral. "Ask me anything, Josh. Anything at all, and I'll answer."

CHAPTER SEVENTEEN

IT WASN'T THAT she didn't trust Nate. Checking on the kids the minute she walked in the door was second nature, that's all.

Anna set several bags of groceries on the counter, then followed the shrieks to find the two girls dancing and spinning to the sound of a silly pop tune until they had to be dizzy. Neither noticed her, so, smiling, she withdrew and went looking for Josh.

Nate's laptop sat open on the breakfast bar, so the two were presumably together. He and Josh weren't out on the covered terrace or down on the dock. Since it was still pouring outside, that wasn't a surprise. Down a short hall, she saw the bathroom door open, as was the door to the recently converted playroom. She heard the low rumble of a man's voice and went that way to rescue Nate.

"Well…" Her son's voice was low, tentative. "Do *you* think it was your fault?"

Oh, heavens. Josh had to be referring to Kyle's death. What on earth could have brought this up again?

During the long pause, she stopped in the hall, not sure whether she should interrupt or not. She couldn't see them, which meant they didn't know she was within earshot, either. Normally, she didn't approve of eavesdropping…but this was her son.

"No," Nate said gruffly. "I don't believe it was my fault. I almost said no when Sonja asked me in the first place. Would anyone have considered the accident my fault if I'd never been expected to come on the field trip?"

Another silence. Anna eased herself to where she could see two sets of jean-clad knees. From the position, they must be sitting on the floor with their backs to the wall. Josh's hand plucked at a tear in his jeans as he thought.

"I guess not," he said finally.

"I don't think so, either. I'll tell you this, though. I'd give just about anything to have been there that day, to have seen Molly trying to sneak away." Nate's voice thickened, and he stopped to clear his throat. "Since I've gotten to know you and Jenna and your Mom, come to care so much about you all, I've wished even more I could go back, make a different decision, so your dad was still here for you."

"I wish he was, too." Josh was crying now. "Except…then we wouldn't even know you, would we?"

"No." Was it possible *Nate* was crying, too?

Or at least on the verge? "But you don't miss what you don't know."

Anna realized suddenly that her view of the two sets of knees had blurred. She touched her face to find it wet. Oh, no. Her heart hurt as she imagined never having really known Nate Kendrick. *You don't miss what you don't know.* But, somehow, she felt sure she would have, that she'd have carried a hollow place inside for the rest of her life.

No, that was ridiculous. She'd have gone on, trying to love a good yet undependable, frustrating man. Maybe someday the balance would have tipped enough for her to have left him, but maybe not. From the state of their finances after his death, she knew they'd have had to sell their house soon, anyway, moved to where living costs weren't so high.

Where she would never again have so much as set eyes on Nate or Molly.

Anna pressed her hand to her breast to quell the ache. Leaving Molly and her dad was going to be inexpressibly awful. Shuddering, she knew she should have moved on long ago. Even if Nate asked them to stay—and she knew he wanted her—how could she? All she'd be doing was trading her dependence on one man for the same kind of relationship. She'd be safe but feel inadequate. So far, she thought, the trade had been fair, but if she married him…no, the weight they carried wouldn't be close to equal.

"It's confusing," Josh confessed. "Sometimes, I feel guilty when I'm happy. You know?"

She knew. Oh, yes.

Unable to handle any more, Anna backed away, turning to hurry toward the kitchen. At the foot of the stairs, she decided to detour to use the bathroom up there. Wash away the tears so Josh and Nate would never know she'd heard them talking.

Especially, never let Josh wonder how his father, in the same position, would have handled his questions. Because she knew. Kyle would have jollied Josh into a better mood without ever admitting to any doubt, any emotional punch. The awful thing was that she wasn't sure whether Kyle didn't like delving deep—or whether he didn't have any depths.

And…how had she not noticed that when she fell in love with him, married him? Was young love that blind? Or would his lack of real depth, of the ability to consider his own behavior, never have really mattered if only he had been financially responsible? She had to remind herself again that he'd had some great qualities.

I didn't know I needed to look below the surface, she thought sadly. She'd been so hungry for a family, to belong.

The answer was pretty much irrelevant now,

anyway. She wasn't the same woman she'd been during their marriage, far less at the beginning of it. She wanted to think she was stronger now...but was this terror at the idea of really trusting anyone again strength? Or was it cowardice?

ANNA WAS UNUSUALLY quiet at dinner that evening. Nate decided to be glad she hadn't divvied up the casserole and taken her two kids up to the apartment to eat separately. In all the months that had passed, they'd evolved to eating as a family most days. But a couple times a week, she'd decide she needed some distance, or that he and Molly deserved to spend time alone. It was just often enough to keep him on edge every day when he came home from work. Will she or won't she?

It served another purpose, too, certainly for him and likely for her, as well: she was reminding them that the days and evenings they hung out together were an illusion.

And, man, he hated it every time she did that.

Were her eyes a little puffy? Why would she have been crying? Surely, after nine months, she'd quit crying over her husband. By the time she served blueberry pie and offered him coffee, Nate was sure she'd cried, and he needed to know why.

The kids, with their smaller servings of pie,

gobbled and bolted. Saturday night, no home-work or at least none that couldn't wait until to-morrow. Nate watched them go, perplexed by Josh's exuberance. Was the kid bipolar?

"What's that expression about?" Anna asked, after taking a sip of coffee.

"Josh was depressed earlier." He hadn't meant to tell her, but really she should know how hard he was taking his inactivity.

"I...heard a little of what the two of you said."

Ah. Not the part of the conversation he'd been thinking about. "I hope I didn't say anything wrong."

"No," she said softly. "I'm glad about what I heard."

Wary now, he set down his cup. "Why?"

She nibbled on her lip for a moment as she studied him. "I liked that you were really open with him and let him see your emotions. A lot of men prefer to uphold their tough-guy image."

"That wouldn't have sent such a great mes-sage to Josh, given what we were talking about."

"No, it wouldn't." She hesitated. "I'm sur-prised the subject came up. He hasn't said any-thing to me in ages."

"About his dad?"

"No, he talks about Kyle once in a while. Some-times I wish he would more often, but..." She shook her head. "I meant about the day he died."

"He was feeling down to start with. He's having a hard time without any outlets for his energy."

She made a face. "I know. But what can I do? Join a health club so I can put him on a treadmill?"

"Maybe we could buy a really big hamster wheel," Nate suggested.

She chuckled, the warm, sexy sound that flowed over him like damp kisses. Damn it. He took a hasty bite of his pie.

"He'd be sure to run too fast and end up taking a tumble," she said.

"Yeah. There's got to be something he *can* do."

"Baseball's out. He meant to play Little League until he found out about the spring soccer."

Nate nodded.

"Kayaking? Sailing?"

"Bowling. We could go tomorrow. Has he ever tried it?"

"I don't think so." Her nose crinkled. "Could Jenna bowl, do you think?"

"Ah…we could help her."

"Well, that actually sounds like fun, but doesn't solve the problem."

"No." He frowned. "Maybe the five of us could hit the soccer field again tomorrow. If we banned Josh from playing goalie…"

"There's too much chance it would get physical, anyway. Remember how, um, we collided."

Oh, he remembered. He broke out in a sweat just thinking about it. Was she blushing? Her eyes had darkened to navy. Neither of them reached for a cup or did anything but look at the other.

Nine months, he reminded himself.

He fumbled for something to say, then remembered the phone call he'd taken just before Molly called him down to dinner. After his earlier talk with Josh, it had almost seemed anticlimactic.

"Sonja let me know she's entering treatment again."

Probably relieved because he'd reduced the tension, Anna asked, "Today?"

"That's what she said. I'll call Monday to find out when Molly can see her, but I assume, like last time, it'll be ten days, at least."

"Do you know what inspired this?"

"It almost has to be Molly, doesn't it?" He'd wondered, though. What if Sonja had been picking up DUIs? Or waking up after blackouts? "She has to be humiliated to be able to see Molly only here, with me present." He'd refused to put Anna in the awkward position of supervising visits.

She was quiet for a minute. "You'll have some decisions to make if she succeeds."

"Yeah." He rubbed the back of his neck. "I won't be in any hurry to make them, though. Finishing a one-month program is no guarantee she won't backslide. From what I hear, the craving may never go away."

"No." Anna tipped her head, looking at him. "I don't think I've ever seen you drink."

"I do when I meet a business contact for drinks, or at the kind of dinner where it would be noticeable if I turned down a glass of wine. But I sip. I've never been attracted to booze." Even as a teenager, he'd known why. "I like to have a clear head. Working, I don't want to let something slip I didn't mean to. I hate the fuzzy feeling as the intoxication wears off."

"I don't, either. Plus, I don't like beer, and cheap wines aren't so great, either. Maybe I could develop a taste for expensive ones, but why would I?"

He chuckled. "I'm the wrong one to ask." Reflective again, he said, "Sonja always had a bottle of wine going. She liked a mixed drink before dinner. I figured that was normal. Trouble was, I never paid attention to how long a particular bottle lasted. Maybe, with no job or volunteer activities, she was bored."

"I was happy staying home when the kids were little. They *are* a full-time job."

He grimaced. "Not if you have a nanny, even if she was part-time."

"You did? Really?"

"Really. I hardly knew the woman. She came evenings sometimes when we were going out, but otherwise, having her here meant Sonja could meet friends for lunch or go shopping." She'd done a lot of shopping. The woman must have fifty pairs of shoes, and their huge walk-in closet had been full to the point she'd taken over a closet in another room for her off-season garments. *If it made her happy*, he'd tell himself. In the end, it hadn't, and he felt some guilt knowing he'd given her free use of the credit cards instead of his time and attention. Maybe his marriage would have lasted if he'd changed his ways for her, as he had for Molly's sake—and for Anna.

Yeah, but he had a bad feeling he hadn't because, once past the first infatuation with Sonja's beauty, she'd bored him. He couldn't imagine Anna ever would.

"I wouldn't have wanted a nanny," Anna said, hauling him back from his wandering thoughts, "but I have to admit I was looking forward to Jenna starting school so I could get a job. A second income would have been good, plus I like people. Other mothers at playgroups weren't enough to satisfy my curiosity about the big world out there."

"Are kids at school any improvement?"

Her laugh lit her face. "Well, they're variations on a theme. Anyway, now I'm suffering from teacher envy. I keep thinking about how much better *I* could do it if I were in charge."

He grinned. "Envy? Sounds more like hubris. A sin I know all too well."

Her smile faded and she cocked her head. "You mean that, don't you?"

"About myself? Yeah. Arrogance is a useful quality, but it can also act like blinders."

"That makes sense. Except—" her searching gaze had him wondering what she saw "—I haven't seen that in you. Well...not since our first meeting."

He moved uncomfortably. "I wanted to fix everything by writing a check."

"Have you gotten over that?"

If she'd marry him, the issue would never arise. No answer he could give leaped to mind.

"What are you thinking?" she asked, sounding suspicious at his lack of response.

"You have to understand," he heard himself say. "I'm wealthy. Money I could replace by picking the next great start-up would make your life so much easier. Yours and the kids. So, no. I haven't gotten over it."

Her eyebrows rose, but she said lightly, "Thanks for the warning. I'll keep myself armored against temptation."

"We can have a knock-down, drag-out when the time comes."

Anna laughed as if he'd been kidding. Standing, she reached for her empty coffee cup. "I know it's Saturday night, but I'll bet you didn't get much work done today. I'll grab the kids and reduce the racket by two-thirds."

"Not two-thirds. A hundred percent. Molly is quiet as a mouse once Jenna and Josh leave."

Concern changed her expression. "I'd hoped that had changed."

"It hasn't. Anna." He swallowed. "Don't go yet."

Her hesitation reminded him of a bird on the verge of flight. Afraid he'd spook her, Nate didn't move, although given his mood, he doubted he looked harmless.

Finally, she asked, "Would you like another cup of coffee?"

No, but he'd take it. "Sure. Thanks."

She carried away his cup, too, and returned a few minutes later.

In hopes of easing back the throttle, he asked how she was liking the job. Just last week, the Bellevue School District had hired her as a full-time paraeducator at Eastgate Elementary to replace a woman having a difficult pregnancy.

Anna relaxed noticeably. "It's good. In a way, I enjoyed the variety of working with different ages and abilities, not to mention different teachers, but I really like having the chance to get to know everyone. Kids, teachers, eventually parents. I don't have to guess when I respond to a problem. I know what's going on with the families, what issues the kids are already struggling with. And the teacher I'm working with is great. I hit the jackpot."

"Good. Have you put in an application for fall?"

"For a teaching position, you mean?" She shook her head. "Living expenses are so high around here. First-year teacher salaries are fine, but as the sole income for a family? I don't think so. Although it's true I need to start applying for jobs."

Nate thought he heard a molar crack, as hard as he was clenching his teeth. *Stay.* Too soon to say that…but if he didn't, she might find the perfect job in Cheyenne, Wyoming or Winnemucca, Nevada. Who knew where she'd be willing to go?

His frustration deepened, adding some gravel to his voice. "Apply for jobs locally."

Her eyes widened. "What?"

"You heard me."

"But…"

He shot a hunted look toward the family room. He and she were alone—but that could change in a split second.

To hell with it. He pushed back his chair and stood, taking a chance, holding out his hand.

Anna stared at his hand, then warily at his face.

"Please."

"This isn't a good idea."

"Take a chance."

Her pulse beat fast in her throat. Her eyes were big, shimmering pools of anxiety. Pushing her might be a mistake, but Nate envisioned her finding a job, planning her move, while he stood aside and kept silent.

Her hand resting on the table balled into a tight fist, then loosened. Slowly, so slowly, she lifted it and reached for him. Relief punched hard. He had to make an effort to tug her up gently, give her time to withdraw.

But she was gutsy enough not to. She rose, her fingers returning his clasp, her gaze never leaving his. Nate kept pulling, until mere inches separated them. And then he lifted his free hand and touched her face.

She had baby-fine skin, her cheek a softness his own lacked. He rubbed her lips with his thumb, feeling the moistness of her breath when they parted slightly. Damn, his heart was about to pound its way out of his chest. You could want something too much.

He freed her hand and cupped her face, savoring the chance to study her closely. All her worries were in her eyes, but so was temptation. Wanting. Nate bent his head slowly, bumped her nose with his deliberately before, smiling, he brushed his mouth over hers.

She made a little sound. Suddenly, the distance between them had been erased. One or both of them had moved, swayed forward. He groaned, gripped her nape and kissed her with all the passion he'd buried for six damn months.

CHAPTER EIGHTEEN

IN FAR TOO many waking *and* sleeping dreams, Anna had kissed Nate. Now that it was actually happening, she couldn't seem to think. All she could do was soak up sensation—and kiss him back with a desperate desire she hadn't known she had in her.

Her arms found their way around his neck even as one of his big hands gripped her buttock, lifting and pulling her tight against him. When he all but consumed her with teeth, tongue and lips, she gave back the same. Need, coiled low in her belly, was almost pain. Her fingers tangled in his hair, and she rubbed her breasts against his broad chest.

"Mo-ommy!" The outraged, tearful screech was just about the only thing that could have snapped her back from this mindless physical hunger. She knew her children's voices even in a gym crowded with other kids. Those voices were a deeply embedded trigger.

With a gasp, Anna wrenched herself back. The heated gleam in Nate's eyes told her how aroused he was, even if she hadn't already been so aware of other evidence.

At her retreat, he gave his head a bewildered shake. "What…?"

The thunder of feet gave him an answer before she could.

"Josh is *mean*!" Jenna cast herself at her mother, wrapping her arms around Anna's leg. "He hit me!"

"I did not!" Josh was there to glare at his sister. Eyes wide, Molly hovered behind him. "It was an accident."

Anna's brain didn't want to work. She tried to pull herself together, but felt as if she was swimming through molasses, thick and sticky. Still, she looked down at her youngest, weeping against her hip.

"Where do you hurt?"

"My head," Jenna said through hitched breaths. Shielding herself behind her mother, she lifted a hand. "I have a bump!"

"Oh, no." Anna knelt, praying she didn't have red burns on her face from Nate's evening stubble. And what did her hair look like? She'd felt his fingers in it. Surely the kids were too young to guess what mommy had been doing. She said, "Let me see," and cradled Jenna's face in her hands.

"She's just being a baby!" Josh yelled.

A bump was definitely rising above Jenna's temple.

"Ice," Anna said.

"I'll get it." Nate's deep voice. Out of the corner of her eye, she saw him rest a hand on Josh's shoulder. "You need to back off. Your mother will hear your side in a minute. Come on, sit down. You, too, Molly."

These sibling disputes were everyday reality. Having someone else to step in, that was something she hadn't had in a long time. Maybe ever. Kyle would have rushed for the ice, but he also would have tried to make everyone laugh. She missed his laughter and good humor, but his refusal to take anything seriously had been at the root of most of their troubles.

Anna picked up Jenna and sat, cuddling her in an easy chair in the living room, facing her mutinous son and Nate's anxious daughter. When he handed her an ice pack wrapped in a dish towel, she laid it gently against the bump. Jenna squealed and jumped.

He crouched in front of them, smiling at Jenna. "Cold, huh?"

"Yes!"

Then his eyes, still heavy lidded, met Anna's. "Do we need to make an ER run?"

His lips were fuller than usual, too, she saw, which meant hers also were. Josh *was* staring at her, but she thought mostly he was mad.

"Let's wait and see," she said to Nate. She peeked beneath the ice. "They've both had major goose eggs before. This doesn't look that bad so far."

"Okay." He rose and went to sit on the couch between Josh and Molly. Molly immediately scooted over to lean against him, and his arm went around her. But he also ruffled Josh's hair.

The small act seemed to relieve some of Josh's quivering tension.

"Okay," she said. "Josh, you go first. What happened?" When Jenna protested, Anna shook her head. "You go next."

"We were playing, that's all!" he burst out. "I was swinging my Nerf baseball bat. Just to hit wadded-up paper balls. Jenna jumped up on the couch behind me and—I don't know what she was doing. But I hit her on the backswing, and she fell off the couch and bumped her head on the coffee table. It wasn't my fault."

It was true that, able to use only one hand on the bat, Josh's swings were likely to be wilder.

"Jenna? Is that how it went?"

Her daughter's lower lip stuck out. Way out, which usually meant a guilty conscience. She gave a sniff for good measure. "Kind of. Except he was hogging the bat! It was *my* turn."

He glared at her. "It wasn't! It was Molly's turn next."

Nate didn't smile, but the crinkling beside

his gray eyes told her he was suppressing one. "Molly?" he said.

She squirmed, but finally mumbled, "He said it was his bat and he didn't want to give anyone else a turn—"

"I would have!"

"But he didn't mean to hurt Jenna," she finished in a rush.

"Jenna, you should know better than to be that close to someone swinging *any* kind of bat." The lower lip didn't retreat, but Jenna also didn't protest. "Josh, you were being selfish. If you're playing with someone else, they should be having a good time, too. I'll bet you could tell Jenna and Molly weren't."

He hung his head. "I was just teasing them. I would have let them have turns if they weren't being so whiny."

"Well, I'm going to call the end of playtime tonight." Grateful for an excuse to run away herself, she kept her eyes on her son. "You need to go get ready for bed. You can read, but that's all."

He jumped up and stormed out.

Molly wriggled closer yet to Nate.

Anna lifted the ice again and verified that the swelling hadn't increased. "I think you'll survive, sweetie." She kissed the top of her daughter's head. "Let's go get you ready for bed, too."

"Okay."

Anna left the now-soggy ice pack in the sink and took the dish towel to drop in the laundry basket when they passed the utility room. She stole one look at Nate, who had risen to his feet and watched her unreadably.

"Good night. We'll see you tomorrow."

"Right." His voice hit an even lower register than usual. "Don't forget our outing."

"Our—oh." Bowling. It was a good idea. So she told herself as she endured Jenna's demands to know whether they were going to a water park or a trampoline park or… All the way upstairs.

THESE PAST MONTHS had taught Nate a lot about having a family. He didn't regret most of it. He'd surprised himself by the fun he'd had with the kids. However much he had loved Molly from the moment she was handed, squalling, into his arms, he hadn't believed he'd be patient enough to spend a lot of time playing games geared to five-year-olds or kicking a soccer ball gently enough for younger children—or refereeing childish disputes. On his job, patience was a real challenge for him. His mind moved at high-speed, and he didn't relish waiting for others to catch up.

Turned out he'd been wrong, though. If he hadn't been so frustrated sexually, he would have said he'd never been as happy in his life as these past six months.

In all that time, though, he'd never once asked himself how he planned to separate Anna from the kids. All the kids. Especially now that she was working full-time, too, albeit not the extra hours he did. Even a date wouldn't solve the problem, unless they wanted to find a deserted road and give the Lexus a workout. Unless and until Anna was willing to move into his house, kids and all, they'd have to *plan* sex. Take Jenna to day care. He boggled at the obstacles.

Of course, that was assuming Anna was ready to jump into bed with him at all. Having her avoid his gaze and flee with her kids told him one passionate kiss qualified as a foot in the door, but that's all. And she might well back off, insist it had been a mistake.

Would he be able to get her away from the kids tomorrow long enough to have a necessary talk? He gave a grunt that wasn't quite a laugh. They talked all the time. That wasn't what he had in mind.

Thoughts of Anna weren't all that ate at him while he supervised Molly's bedtime routine and tucked her in. He needed to talk to her about her mother, too.

Before he could launch in, Molly asked whether *he* had been a brat like Josh when he was eight, and he had to admit he definitely had been.

Smiling, he said, "Your uncle Adam and I

didn't have a sister, but we did a lot of damage to each other. When I climbed that tree? It was his idea."

"Did you tell on him?"

"Nope. We kept each other's secrets." Sobering, he said, "Your mom called right before dinner with good news. She's going back into treatment for her drinking problem."

Molly tugged her covers higher. In a small voice, she said, "I didn't like visiting her there."

"I know." He shifted on the bed so he could smooth her hair back from her face. "Quitting drinking made your mom sick."

"She was *mad*, too." This was almost a whisper.

"Yeah, that too. But this time *she* chose to go into treatment, instead of me making her. I hope it'll be different."

She nodded, not saying anything. Nate waited.

Suddenly, she lunged toward him. He got his arms around her and lifted her onto his lap. "What is it, punkin?"

Molly raised a wet face to him. "I was *scared* when she got drunk. Every night, I was scared."

His own eyes burned. "I wish you could have told me."

"I wanted to!" she wailed. "But…but…"

"She's your mom," he whispered.

Still crying, she nodded. "I didn't know I could live with you."

His fault. "It's hard to figure out what to do when someone you love and trust changes like that. I wish I'd told you that anytime you needed me, I'd be there."

She rubbed her cheek against his chest, dampening his T-shirt. "You did come."

"Yeah. Always." He smiled crookedly. "Even when you're fifty years old and I'm white-haired and use a cane, I'll come hobbling to your rescue if you need me. Cross my heart."

Her giggle was soggy.

"Molly, something I've been wondering." Maybe this wasn't the right thing to do, but it had been eating at him. "The day you sneaked away to go down to the river by yourself."

She went completely still, becoming a small statue in his arms.

"Was your mom drinking? Is that why she didn't see where you went?"

Molly sagged a little, as if in relief. "Nuh-uh. She was doing something on her phone. Like it was really important."

Not boozing. He closed his eyes momentarily. Thank God. "Talking?"

Seeming to ponder, Molly shook her head. "Maybe texting?"

Hearing her uncertainty, he gave her a big squeeze. "Stuff on the phone does seem awfully important to grown-ups, even when it really isn't."

She sniffed.

"Are you okay?" he asked.

A nod. "Do I have to visit her at that place?"

"Yes, I think so. She'll be really lonely, and thinking about you. We need to support her when she's doing something that hard."

He watched as she thought about it. She gave a solemn little nod. "Okay. Only…does this mean she won't ever get like that again?"

"Drunk?" Seeing that's what she meant, Nate could only say, "I hope so."

They talked a little more before, with another kiss, he left her, the door cracked open and the hall light on until he went to bed.

Then he went downstairs, where he failed to settle to work or a book. He was too antsy. He walked out onto the terrace for a few minutes, but unless he wanted to get wet, that was as far as he could go. And, damn, it was chilly.

What was Anna doing? Contentedly curled up on her sofa reading a good book? Watching TV with the sound low? Baking, if she felt restless? He wanted to tell her about his talk with Molly.

Suddenly resolved, he went in, propping open the door at the foot of the stairs to the apartment before mounting them. He couldn't hear a sound from inside. What if she'd gone to bed, too?

But he couldn't imagine that. It wasn't even

nine o'clock. After the briefest hesitation, he rapped lightly on her door.

It opened quickly, Anna appearing in the opening, still dressed. "Is something wrong?"

Trust her to leap to the conclusion Molly was bleeding to death.

"No. I mean, Molly and I had a talk." He shrugged awkwardly, feeling like a gawky sixteen-year-old. "I always want to tell you things."

"Oh," she said softly. "Well, I guess you could come in, but we'd have to be quiet. Josh sleeps like a log, but Jenna wakes up if there's any noise."

She meant talking. Wasn't that what he wanted? But maybe not, because Nate was thinking that making out, done right, wasn't a silent activity, either.

"Why don't you block open the door and join me in the kitchen?" he suggested. "Even Jenna is old enough to come looking for you."

She thought about it for long enough to make him think she was going to say no. Obviously cautious, she nodded at last. "I'll have to find something to hold it open."

Several minutes later, she returned with a bright blue baking pan—he thought—that seemed to be flexible. Folded, it squeezed beneath the door and held firm. What the hell?

"Silicone," she said, voice still hushed. "You don't have to grease a bread pan like this."

Strange.

He descended first, hearing her soft footsteps behind him.

SILICONE? REALLY? HE'D chased her up the stairs to find out what kind of bread pans she used?

Embarrassed, Anna stopped in the kitchen a safe distance from him, hands clasped in front of her. Ms. Sophisticated, whose cheeks were warm and who was breathing fast because they were alone. "I take it you want to talk?"

"I think maybe I lied," he said raggedly. His eyes were a charcoal so dark they were almost black. "I was thinking about this."

The distance wasn't so safe after all. Nate covered it in a long stride and gathered her into his arms. Excitement thrummed to life as if she'd only been waiting for his knock on the door. She flung her arms around his neck and melted into him.

The kiss started out clumsy, her fault. Earlier, she'd reacted; this time, her brain hadn't turned off. He *was* sophisticated. How many lovers had he had? Why would he want her, anyway?

Anna wasn't so sure she knew how to do this.

But their tongues slid together, tangled in an urgency that made her strain against him. It was as if every cell in her body had found due north.

She had the fleeting thought that if she couldn't merge her body with his, she might die.

His hips rocked, and somehow he'd squeezed a hand between them to cover her breast. He momentarily lifted his head. Even as she gasped for air, she prayed he wasn't stopping. No, his lips covered hers again, and this time his tongue established a driving rhythm. She hooked a leg around his, instinct telling her to climb him.

Abruptly his body became rigid and he lifted his head again. What? Why? Then she heard the sound, too, but not from upstairs. It was the faint growl of a car engine, a neighbor returning home.

Her head cleared just enough. What if it hadn't been a car? What if the sound had been footsteps on the stairs?

Nate relaxed and bent his head again, but she pulled her arms from around his neck and planted her hands on his broad chest.

"We can't do this." She sounded like a die-away Gothic heroine and felt shaky. Weak. Not something she wanted to be. She stepped back.

The sight of him was enough to make her melt again. His dark hair stuck up in unruly chunks—because her fingers had raked through it. Her hands tingled with the memory of the texture, like coarse silk. A muscle jumped in his jaw, and his dark eyes were lit with a fire somewhere inside. His mouth…

No, no. Anna backed up a couple more steps. "Any of the kids could walk in without us hearing them coming."

"Molly doesn't come downstairs at night." He didn't sound like himself, any more than she did.

"I told you. Jenna sleeps lightly, and she has a headache. I gave her some acetaminophen, but that doesn't mean she won't feel miserable and come looking for me. And you can't tell me Molly never has nightmares."

Nate groaned. "She's woken me up a few times."

"What if one of them *saw* us?"

He narrowed his eyes, obviously not liking her panic. "Would it be that bad?"

"Yes!"

He stiffened, his expression becoming guarded.

Hugging herself, she tried to explain. "It might give them expectations."

His jaw hardened, if that was possible. "I repeat—would that be so bad?"

"It's too fast." And...when she said expectations, was their thinking the same?

He stared at her for what had to be thirty seconds. Then he mumbled what she felt sure was an obscenity and let his head fall forward. He scrubbed his hand over his head, mussing his hair worse than she had. "Okay," he said finally. "Can we sit down and talk?"

Was she ready for that? But maybe he meant

talk talk, not *the* talk. Decompressing would make it more possible for them to go on the way they had been. "I have to absorb what's happened."

He nodded. "Would you like some coffee?"

"It would keep me awake."

He walked into the living room and sank into an easy chair facing one of the sofas. His message was clear—he'd keep his distance.

"We always seem to get interrupted when the kids are around," he said gruffly.

"Here I was thinking how well they entertain themselves."

She settled at one end of the sofa, curling her bare feet under her. When she looked up, it was to see his gaze lingering on her feet.

He surprised her by not starting right in on their relationship. Instead, he sounded thoughtful when he said, "I never realized how lonely Molly must have been. Being an only kid is tough. When Sonja's drinking got bad, Molly was so scared, but she still thought her mom was all she had. My fault."

They argued about that for a minute, before he said, "I wonder if she's really a shy introvert or whether she had to learn to be self-sufficient."

"She's not very shy with my two," Anna agreed. Talking to him like this relaxed her. They'd done it so often it felt comfortable. Okay, and intimate, too, especially with the house dark around them.

"No. Until there's conflict. That upsets her."

She smiled. "Give her another couple of months. Dealing with Jenna and Josh will cure her of that."

Nate laughed. "They do act like siblings."

She tried to hide her retreat, but suspected she'd failed.

Nate rolled his shoulders. "I'm staying over here, Anna." His knuckles showed white as he gripped the arms of the chair. "It's been killing me to keep my distance."

"I thought…" She moistened her lips. "That our arrangement—" her intonation echoed his when he used the phrase "—was working so well we shouldn't mess with it."

"I never thought that. I was respecting your wishes. You needed time to mourn."

Her "oh" was almost soundless.

"I meant to give you longer. But I want you, Anna. You have to know that."

She gave a small nod.

"You've made it clear the feeling is mutual."

A denial would be pointless. "This is…a big leap. Can't we take it slower?"

"With more family dinners?"

"We do have time to ourselves." She knew she was begging. "We don't always have to talk about the kids."

His face softened. "Don't get me wrong. I like it when we talk about them."

Her smile felt tremulous. "Me, too."

Nate let out a long breath. "Okay. I let myself get impatient. I'll try to rein it in."

Anna ached to ask whether he'd been waiting all this time for sex, or more. Did she want more? Had the complications really dissipated? She couldn't be sure, but already knew that new ones had sprung up like weeds in spring. She had to think about his motives, and her own.

"I need to go to bed."

"I won't argue." But he did stand when she did and walked her to the foot of the stairs. And when he said, "May I kiss you good-night?" she nodded.

This kiss was fleeting and so tender her eyes stung as she climbed the stairs without letting herself look back.

CHAPTER NINETEEN

SONJA SMILED WHEN Nate and Molly appeared in the doorway of the small visitors' room at the rehab center. "Thanks for bringing her, Nate."

"I'm glad to," he said, which wasn't completely true. He was beat tonight after a stressful day. He would have given a lot to stay home, starting with a lingering cup or two of coffee with Anna that led to a kiss when the kids were out of sight. On the other hand, he was genuinely glad that Sonja had only days left to complete the monthlong program. For her sake, and for Molly's. "Sounds like the Mariners are on." He nodded down the hall toward the rec room. "You'll know where to find me."

Sonja smiled brightly, while Molly gave him an apprehensive look before dutifully going to her mother. Nate retreated, wondering if Sonja had a clue how much ground she had to make up with Molly.

He nodded at the few patients who glanced his way when he stepped into the recreation room. The Mariners were playing the Rangers and were down two runs in the fourth inning.

He watched Major League baseball only occasionally, mostly glancing at scores on the *Seattle Times* sports page. He had to be able to make small talk with potential investors.

A triple by the Mariners shortstop kept his attention for a few minutes, although even then he had multiple tracks going in his head. What were Sonja and Molly talking about? Would Anna and her kids wait at the house for them to come home, or would they have returned to the apartment? Then there were his major second thoughts about getting into the snowboard business. He'd persuaded investors to put up one hell of a lot of money, and they'd hold him responsible if they lost it. His usual confidence seemed to have gone down the toilet.

Hubris. Damn, if you lost it, could you ever get it back?

Maybe if he managed to have sex again someday, he'd bounce back. Get cocky. The intentional pun amused him.

He half watched the game, skimmed emails and texts on his phone, and counted the minutes.

Not wanting to be the bad guy, he waited until Sonja and Molly came looking for him. Sonja walked them to the entrance doors, where he gave her a quick hug and said, "Congratulations on toughing it out."

Molly and she embraced, and then he was out the door with his daughter, feeling he could finally take a deep breath. He held Molly's hand until he had to let her go to get in the Lexus.

The drive home was quieter than usual. When he asked if she'd had a good visit with her mom, she answered, "Uh-huh." Not a happy *uh-huh*, not a sad one. Just…neutral. He didn't want her to think she had to report every word said to him, which meant he couldn't push.

Sure enough, from the driveway he saw a figure moving in front of the window above the garage, and he and Molly found the house silent when they let themselves in.

"You know what?" he said. "I'm going to have another piece of that apple pie if Josh didn't polish it off. Would you like one, too?"

This "uh-huh!" was a lot more enthusiastic. No surprise, since she'd picked at her dinner. She always did when she knew she'd be visiting her mom.

He dished up, scooping ice cream onto both pieces, and carried them to the table. Damn, that pie was good, even though it might have been better if he'd thought to warm it in the microwave.

"Daddy?"

"Yeah?" He chased melting vanilla ice cream with his fork.

"Mommy said this was the last time I'd have to visit her there."

"That's true," he agreed. Unless Sonja fell off the wagon, of course.

"She said we'd be home again before I know it."

We'd? Alarm bells rang. "As in, you going back to the condo with her?"

Perplexity showed on her freckled face. "I think so."

How should he handle this?

He set down his fork. "I need to say this straight out."

She stared at him.

"You *won't* be going home with your mother for a while. She needs to prove to both of us that she won't backslide and start drinking again. I've told her what I'm telling you—you're staying here for the time being. In fact, I think you should finish the school year here no matter what. You and she will have visits. Once we're all more confident, you can have an overnight. But it has to be when *you're* ready. I know you don't want to hurt your mom's feelings, so it'll be me who's being the bad guy."

Tears sprang into her green eyes. "I like it here!"

He scooted his chair back and plucked her out of hers to set her on his lap. Holding her close, his chin on top of her head, Nate said, "I like having you here, too. No matter what happens, I don't want to go back to seeing you twice a month. I think we can figure out a way for us both to have you on a more equal basis, although I don't know how we'll arrange that. But right now, your mom still has some work to do." Did Sonja remember how to function without a mixed drink or a glass of wine in her hand? How would she handle meeting friends for lunch when they were all having a drink? What would happen the first time she had a fit of depression or just got mad? He continued, "Until you feel safe with her, you won't even be spending the night. She thinks the two of you can go right back to the way it was, but it isn't that easy."

Molly shook her head in what was more of a shiver, then whispered something he couldn't hear.

He resettled her so that he could see her face. "I didn't hear you."

Her face crumpled. "I like being with you and Anna. And Jenna, and even Josh, most of the time."

"Yeah." He had to clear his throat. "Me, too."

They cuddled for a long time, until the ice cream formed puddles on their plates.

ANNA SMILED AT the usual hoots from the family room, but she'd swear Nate was actually glaring that direction.

"What?"

"Do you know how much I'd like to get you alone?" he grumbled. "Can't we arrange for them all to spend Friday or Saturday night with friends?"

"Jenna has never spent a night away from home."

"Seriously?" He looked shocked. "She's almost five."

Anna was already planning the birthday party, even though mid-May was still a couple weeks away. Jenna wanted to invite all her friends from day care, and Molly and Josh had to be there, and she'd *really* liked this girl named Fern from Josh's soccer, so could they ask her, too?

Anna had found a place that offered pony rides, so that's where the party would start. Nate had suggested the cake and ice cream be here, thank goodness, so she didn't have to try to squeeze the crowd into the apartment or gamble the weather would be nice so they could do it in a park. May weather in the Pacific Northwest was too risky for that.

"Seriously," she told him. "Grandparents are usually a first step, and my two don't have any."

"Kyle's parents are gone, too?" He frowned. "I guess I should have realized, or you could have turned to them."

"He was adopted by an older couple. They got divorced, and he stayed with his mother. She died while he was in college, and by then he'd long since lost touch with his adoptive father. I think…maybe that was a little bit of what drew us together. Everybody else seemed to have family."

She had craved family, the lack was a bottomless hole inside her until she had her own. *Part of a family*, she thought now wistfully.

As if he'd read his mind, he said, "You'll like my parents. Did I tell you they'll be home in a few weeks?"

Her eyes widened. "No. Where do they live?"

"Vashon Island."

A short ferry ride from Seattle. "Do you see them often?"

He shrugged. "Every couple of weeks. They pop over to do errands and we have lunch. Mom and Sonja didn't have much in common, but since the divorce we get together for dinner or they spend the night fairly often. They take Molly for overnights regularly, too. She loves the beach." His expression shifted. "I'll bet they'd take the whole crowd."

Suddenly, it was a little hard to breathe. Anticipation? Panic? Probably both. There was so much she hadn't worked out—like whether she could enjoy making love with a man who hadn't offered any commitment. And if he did…she still couldn't figure out why he'd zeroed in on her.

Guilt. Okay, maybe not that. A sense of responsibility. It almost had to be, didn't it?

Besides… "Like your parents wouldn't guess what we were planning to do?"

He grinned. "Would that be so bad?"

"Yes!"

Creases formed between his eyebrows. "Why?"

Only a man would have to ask. "It would be embarrassing. I'm not sure I could ever look them in the eye again." See his frown deepen, she said, "Let me think about it, okay?"

One eyebrow twitched, but he reached for his coffee without comment.

"You haven't told me how the visit went yesterday."

That diverted him.

"Apparently, Sonja thinks Molly will cheerfully move home with her." He told her about the talk he'd had with Molly yesterday evening.

"Sonja's going to be unhappy," Anna said slowly, knowing that was a major understatement. "Feeling positive is important if she's to succeed."

"You suggesting I should hand Molly right over?"

"Of course not. But…haven't you been clear with Sonja about what would happen?"

"I have been." Sounding deeply irritated, Nate said, "She hears what she wants to hear, and nothing else." He let out an explosive sigh. "I don't think Molly wants to go back to living with Sonja."

"You know she loves her mom."

He scowled. "Your point?"

"Only that you might have a hard time dealing with it if Molly chooses her mother over you."

She could tell he hadn't thought of it that way and wasn't happy to have to confront the knowledge—or with her for suggesting he might be so selfish.

"It would be easy to influence Molly. I just hope…"

He gave a clipped nod. "I'll keep that in mind."

"Sonja doesn't want to admit that Molly doesn't feel safe with her anymore."

"Despite everything I've said, I don't think she's even admitted that possibility to herself." He rubbed a hand over his jaw, the rasping sound faint.

At least he was still talking to her. "How are you going to handle this?"

That was a really nosy question, coming right after she'd sounded as if she was sitting in judgment on him. Except…she and Nate talked over everything happening in their lives. The change from their first stiff conversations over dinner in September to wide-ranging, relaxed, often intimate talks had happened gradually. In fact, she was a little shocked to realize how real, how important, their relationship was, despite her reservations. Her pulse picked up. No wonder he was getting impatient.

Why had she doubted that he wanted a commitment? Whenever he was out evenings, he always warned her in advance and even talked about who he was having dinner with. He never sounded thrilled about what were clearly business dinners or cocktail parties. There'd never been even a hint that he was seeing another woman romantically. If he wasn't—that meant he hadn't had sex in at least the seven months since Molly had come to live with him. Maybe since Kyle died. Or even before that. She couldn't imagine he'd ever been celibate for going on a year, certainly not since his first high school girlfriend.

If he had been now…it was because of her.

She suddenly realized he'd said something—answered her question—and she hadn't heard him.

"What's wrong?" he asked.

"Nothing." She was freaking out, that's what. "I… Nothing. I feel bad for Sonja—" *lie, lie* "—but worried for Molly, too."

He reached across the table and clasped her hand. "You and me both."

Anna smiled shakily and nodded.

Now all she had to do was figure out what *her* problem was.

NATE'S HEAD CAME up when he heard an engine in the driveway. Anna and her kids had just gone out the door, but that didn't sound like her car. Sonja must have arrived early. Unfortunately, sobriety hadn't lessened her resentment of Anna. His hopes of peace and goodwill toward all had long since waned.

Instinct had him hustling to the front door to see that he was too late to prevent the two women coming face-to-face. Didn't it figure, Sonja had parked so that Anna wouldn't be able to get her car out of the garage. Not that his ex had any reason to know which bay held Anna's junker.

Sonja was eyeing Anna and her kids over the top of her car, her perfectly shaped eyebrows arched as she said in a snide tone, "I see you're right at home here."

Anna had emerged through the front door instead of from her apartment, and it was mid-morning. He knew what Sonja had read into it.

Her mouth had an unpleasant little curl when she looked at him, instead. "Is Molly ready?"

"I'll go get her." Molly had not been eagerly awaiting her mother's arrival. In fact, he suspected she was holed up in her bedroom. "If you wouldn't mind moving your car, Anna could get hers out of the garage."

"I'm not in any hurry," Anna said hurriedly.

"Of course." Sonja got back into her car.

Anna gave him a why-did-you-do-that? look, but guided her children toward the garage while pushing the remote in her hand. The door lifted.

Nate hesitated, then went into the house for his daughter.

He'd had the talk with Sonja while she was still at the treatment center so that she'd have access to a counselor, but not to alcohol, while she burned off her anger. Since going home, she'd called often, and come for a short visit here. Today was the first planned visit where she'd be taking Molly away.

"I'll think of something fun." That had been her blithe explanation for what they'd be doing.

Now, he paused at the foot of the stairs. "Molly?"

The silence lasted long enough that he had put a foot on the first step before he heard the soft sound of her bedroom door opening.

"Your mom's here," he added.

She appeared, pulling her pink day pack by one strap so that it slid on the hardwood floor in the hall and bumped down the stairs behind her.

When she stopped a couple steps above him, he kissed her head and swung her to the floor. "It's only for the day. Be nice. Your mother has to be excited."

"Why can't I stay home with you?" she begged.

Remembering when she'd tried to wriggle out

of visits with him, Nate felt sudden empathy for his ex-wife. He had to remind himself that she'd done it to herself.

Just as he had blown it with his excessive work hours.

"Nope. Go. Have fun."

Looking forlorn, she dragged her pack toward the front door.

Sonja waited on the porch. The closed garage door told Nate that Anna was gone.

"Sweetie!" She stooped to hug their daughter, then hoisted the pack. "What's all this?"

"Stuff. 'Cuz I don't know where we're going."

Oops, he thought. Should have asked. Had she brought a book or her iPod? Either would probably annoy Sonja, who'd want Molly's undivided attention.

She jingled her keys. "Well, let's be on our way. I'm sure your father is eager to get to work. Or eager for *something*."

"No digs," he said quietly.

Apparently resigned, Molly climbed into the back seat of the car and closed the door.

Sonja gave him a dirty look. "When I go back to court for custody, the judge might be interested in knowing that you've moved your lover into your house, even though your daughter is there."

"Don't be a bitch." He maintained his relaxed position leaning on the door frame.

"Anna and her children live above the garage, as you know well."

Although he damn well wished she was his lover. But they were getting there. His body had taken to vibrating whenever he saw her. Or thought about her.

"Are you bringing Molly home before dinner?"

"Of course not. I plan to treasure every possible minute, since I've had so few of them."

"Before bedtime, then."

She rolled her eyes and got into her car. He stayed where he was, lifting a hand when he saw that Molly's head turned so she could keep him in sight as long as possible.

He was left feeling out of sorts. Why hadn't he planned to go into the office? But he knew—he hadn't expected Anna and her two to be gone today, as well.

Peace and quiet, which he ought to savor. Instead, the empty house reminded him of the year and a half after his divorce, when he'd lived alone and missed Molly.

Now he didn't like Molly's unhappiness at having to go with her mother, and he was ashamed of the part of him that was gratified because she preferred him.

And he wanted Anna home, where he could at least catch glimpses of her moving around the house, humming off-key when she thought she was unheard, laughing with one of her children. This peace and quiet reminded him of what he'd have if she went through with moving out and on with her life.

He wished he understood what was holding her back.

CHAPTER TWENTY

"CAN I, MOMMY?" Jenna pleaded. "Practically everyone else is spending the night."

Who'd have thought Mrs. Schaub would offer a sleepover? It made sense, though; because her regulars kept coming to her, she hadn't taken any younger children in years. Jenna was the last to turn five, a milestone. Mrs. Schaub had decided to give them a treat, now that they were old enough—the kids laying their sleeping bags out on the living room floor, watching rented videos, eating pizza and popcorn and nothing but goodies instead of the usual healthful meals.

Anna laughed, hiding the excitement simmering below the surface. In the three weeks since that passionate kiss, Anna had plotted a dozen unlikely ways to have a night without her children. Now one had dropped into her lap.

"Of course you can go! You're a big girl, plenty old enough. Just think, you'll be in kindergarten in no time."

"Yeah! I *'specially* want Sierra and Ashley and Livy in my class. I *thought* I wanted Austin, but he's a poophead."

They had a brief discussion about why that kind of name-calling wasn't very nice, even as Anna chose not to remind her that, come fall, there was still a possibility they wouldn't be in Bellevue where her friends would be starting kindergarten.

Instead, she calculated who she could foist Josh off on Friday night. This was to be Molly's first overnight visit with her mom, so the timing was perfect.

With a gulp, she thought, *If I'm not ready now, I never will be.* Anyway, it was just sex. No promises.

Just before bedtime that evening, she stopped Josh before he went into the bathroom to brush his teeth. "Hey, did Jenna tell you about her sleepover?"

He curled his lip. "That's *all* she talks about."

"You know Molly is spending Friday and Saturday nights with her mom. This might be a good time to invite yourself to one of your friends' houses."

His expression brightened. "Or I could have one of them stay overnight *here*. He could sleep in Jenna's bed, and we could use the Xbox and—"

"No, you can't," she said firmly. "Molly's house isn't ours, even if we treat it that way most of the time. With her gone, we'll be stuck in the apartment."

"But there's nothing to *do* there," he whined.

"That's why I suggested you go to a friend's house. Besides, maybe I could have an adult outing." Like an overnight romp in bed with the sexiest man she'd ever met.

He looked at her dubiously. "Like what?"

"I do have friends, you know."

He snorted. "I'll ask Jaden. Or maybe Patrick." During the forced hiatus from soccer, Josh had become closer friends with Patrick, a budding computer nerd.

"Let me know."

The next evening, he told her he and another friend, Dylan, were both spending the night with Jaden. She hugged him. "Sounds fun."

And then she tried to decide whether to tell Nate they'd have a whole night to themselves… or surprise him. If she could persuade her kids to keep their mouths shut.

NATE APPEARED WEARY and irritable when he came in the door Friday evening at almost seven o'clock. Heart drumming, Anna closed the oven door, set the cookie sheet with sourdough biscuits on the granite counter and said, "Hi. Perfect timing."

"Really?" He yanked off his tie and tossed it with his laptop case and suit coat toward the sofa. The tie fell short, but he didn't seem to notice. "I thought I'd have to warm up my own dinner."

"Nope." She smiled. "I was about to give up on you and eat, but it so happens tonight it's just you and me."

He froze. "What?"

Maybe she should have popped out from behind the kitchen counter naked. Or wrapped herself in ribbon. Or...warned him in advance?

"Surprise." Well, that sounded weak, maybe because most of her bold decision to do this had drizzled away while she waited for Nate to come home.

He walked toward her. *Stalked* was more like it. "Where are your two?" he asked roughly.

"Mrs. Schaub decided to have a sleepover for all her kids. Since Josh wouldn't have had anyone to hang out with, he went to Jaden's."

He stopped inches from Anna, who still wore an oven mitt. "If you'd called, I'd have cut out of the office hours ago."

"I didn't get home until four thirty, and I wanted to make us a nice dinner."

The hunger in his eyes wasn't for food, but he read something on her face. Shyness? Nerves? He flicked a glance at the steaming stir-fry in a ceramic bowl and settled for stroking his knuckles over her cheek. "We could have gone out on the town."

"I'd rather stay in, with you." Her voice had gotten a little husky, too.

He backed off a step. "What can I do?"

Convince me this isn't a mistake.

No. It wasn't. It couldn't be. Whatever came of their relationship, she needed to make love with Nate. Create a memory she could hug in the future, if that's all she had.

"Not a thing. All I have to do is dish up."

She'd set only two place mats, not across the table from each other, but kitty-corner so they could easily touch. Carrying a bowl of rice to the table, she admitted, "This isn't actually a very fancy dinner. It's just something the kids would hate."

He grinned, studying the stir-fry. "You're right. All those different foods mixed together."

"Although maybe I'm wrong." She had to chatter to hide her nerves. "It does have green beans."

He looked more closely. "Molly would have had to pick out the onions and cashews—she claims not to like them—and soy sauce? Nope."

"Then I made a good choice for tonight." She added the basket of biscuits and butter. "Maybe I should light some candles."

"I like electric lights," he said huskily. "I can see you better." He moved to pull out her chair.

Flustered, she let him seat her. A soft pressure

to the top of her head let her know he'd pressed his lips there before he sat down.

They'd eaten so many meals at this table. This shouldn't feel so different, but it did. They talked, but kept their voices low; silences had a weight and intensity. He did want to know how she'd kept Jenna from telling him about the sleepover, and Anna admitted to having conned her daughter into "surprising him," with a promise that she could tell him all about it tomorrow.

"You don't think she'll chicken out in the middle of the night?"

"No, this is perfect. She knows everyone, loves Mrs. Schaub and is somewhere she's spent so much time, it must feel like home. Although I'll keep my phone close." She chuckled. "The hardest part was convincing Josh that he shouldn't take advantage of his sister's absence to host his own sleepover."

Nate's mouth curved, although his eyes remained dark and intent. "How'd you pull that off?"

"I reminded him that this is not his home, and he didn't have free run of the Xbox and your TV."

Nate's smile vanished. "I'd like your kids to feel like this *is* home."

"Are you sorry massive explosions aren't erupting from the family room right this minute?"

"No. I'm not sorry about that. The home part, though…"

"Let's not talk about that tonight."

He didn't like that, she could tell, but he nodded and applied himself to his meal.

Anna went back to picking at hers. She should be hungry—this had always been a favorite—but nerves and anticipation had knotted in her stomach.

What if making love with Nate didn't live up to her dreams? No, that wouldn't happen—she couldn't imagine he'd be a selfish lover, and she already knew that his slightest touch ignited her body.

What if she disappointed *him*? She and Kyle had had their routines, satisfying but not wildly imaginative. What if Nate asked for something that shocked her? What if…?

She yanked the reins and tried to restore herself to sanity. Maybe the dinner wasn't such a good idea. If they'd just gotten it over with…

Except, she hoped "it" would happen more than once. That a meal would be the last thing on both their minds once they got in bed together.

"You know," he said, heat in his eyes, "if you keep looking at me like that, I'll have to kiss you. And then dinner will get cold."

"Oh." Her cheeks warmed. "I'm sorry."

"There's not a thing for you to be sorry for."

THE MEAL WAS probably amazing, but he ate only because he didn't want to hurt her feelings. All he could think about was finally stripping her and exploring her body, finding out where the skin was softest, where she was most sensitive. He was achingly hard already, but tried to avoid shifting to relieve his discomfort—assuming anything short of him driving deep inside her would do that.

"You didn't look like you were in a very good mood when you first got home," she said, forcing him to wrench his thoughts back to the romantic dinner she'd planned.

"Ah…" He had to struggle to remember anything about his day before she said those magic words: *tonight it's just you and me.*

"I didn't like knowing Molly wouldn't be home." Yeah, that was it. "I wish I trusted Sonja, but I don't." In fact, her supersweet act toward Anna last weekend had made him uneasy.

Anna nodded. "I don't blame you, but I'm sure she was sober when she picked Molly up, and Molly seemed happy to see her. She did wish Jenna or one of her friends was going, too, and Sonja promised she could have a friend overnight some other weekend."

He hoped she'd hold off with that for now.

"Spent part of my day dealing with Thing One," he added. "Remember him?" He loved her laugh.

"Yes! Did he fire another CEO?"

"No, but he had a management brainstorm I had to squelch. Sales on his first game are going well, if not spectacularly, but the best we could have hoped for after the original promotional misfire. The second game is months away from launch. He's lagging on the third game, not happy with the artwork or the physics or something, so he's practicing avoidance." Nate prayed that second game took off into the stratosphere, inspiring one of the big players in the business to buy out the idiot savant and make him someone else's problem.

When he said as much, Anna laughed again.

Nate looked down to see that he'd emptied his plate, and she'd become more relaxed.

"Normally I'd beg for seconds," he said. "But all I can think about is you."

Her fork clanged to her plate. "I... Me, too. Except... I guess you can tell I'm nervous."

He didn't want her so much as thinking about Kyle, which meant it was up to him to make her forget the guy in the coming hours.

He smiled, slow and sure. "Time to get your feet wet."

Anna gulped. "I should put the food away."

Overcoming his impatience, he asked, "Will you feel better if you do?"

"I sound silly, don't I?"

The tenderness he felt for her always blindsided him. He'd never felt anything like it for another woman. It allowed him to push back his chair without a word, stand and collect dirty dishes. He could do this.

Anna scuttled to carry the leftovers to the kitchen. She set the bowl on the counter and then didn't move. "This will be soggy by morning, anyway."

Nate bent to nuzzle her neck. The butter was still on the table, but he wasn't about to point that out. Instead, he took her hand and led her from the kitchen, flicking off the lights as they went. If he kissed her now, they wouldn't make it upstairs. Another time, one of the sofas would work fine, but tonight he wanted to do this right.

With no argument, she let him draw her toward the stairs. Driven by pure need, Nate wasn't sure how much patience he could summon. They could save the exploration, the savoring, for a second time.

Yet this—walking with her, fingers twined together—was unexpectedly sweet, and he found he wanted their lovemaking to be the same. That unnerving tenderness mixed with passion. A first time should be special.

The staircase looked like Mount Rainier to a man as aroused as he was, but as he and Anna climbed the steps, side by side, he wondered if they'd still want to hold hands on their way to bed ten years from now. Forty years from now. He hoped so.

They walked down the hall, passing several open doors: Molly's bedroom, his office, a guest bedroom, a bathroom. Two other closed doors—those rooms were empty. They'd be perfect for Jenna and Josh.

Finally, he led Anna into his bedroom.

WHY HADN'T HE kissed her into mindlessness? Why was he giving her time to *think*? In the kitchen, when his mouth had moved down her neck, when he'd let her feel a graze of his teeth… But Nate had decided to contain his intensity. When she'd stolen a glance, his expression had rattled her. The raw hunger was there, but tempered with gentleness.

Because she'd admitted to being nervous. The result was that their walk upstairs had felt… solemn. A procession that carried the weight of every complicated thing she felt, and hoped or feared he felt.

Maybe Nate was acting on the knowledge she shared that there was nothing impulsive about this. Passion usually launched a relationship. In their case, because of the guilt and anger and confusion, she and Nate had both suppressed their attraction. Now…she knew him so well. He'd shared his troubles with her and listened to hers. They already had a powerful bond. And yet she'd never seen him without a shirt, never slid her hands over the strong muscles on his back without a layer of fabric covering them. It felt a little scary to know she was going to bare herself to him now, and so literally.

It would have been so much easier if he'd just swept her away.

They stepped into his room. He shut the door and snatched her into his arms.

"Finally," he said, in an unrecognizable voice. He found her mouth unerringly, but the kiss was initially clumsy. Straining upward, grabbing on to his shoulders, Anna felt awkward, ignorant, forgetting all their other kisses, wanting so much from this one.

The kiss became softer, slower, tempting instead of demanding, as it had started. And, oh, she was tempted. The meltdown began as she gripped his shirt in two fists on his back. He kissed her until she could barely stand and was all sensation—the scratch of his evening stubble, the power in the hands roving from her butt to her nape, the groan rising from deep in his chest.

She wanted to *see* that chest. Touch.

He pulled back enough to grasp the hem of her shirt and tug upward. "Let me—"

"Yes. I want—" She reached for the first button at the same time.

"Anna."

She gave up, lifting her arms until he sent the shirt flying. *Then* she attacked his buttons. The shirt fell open, exposing dark hair centered on a muscular chest, narrowing over his flat stomach to disappear beneath his trousers. "Oh," she whispered, flattening her hands on that wall of muscle. Kyle hadn't really had any chest hair, and she was surprised to find that she liked it.

Nate liked her touch, too. Muscles jumped beneath her exploring hands, and she looked up to find him watching her with heated eyes.

"My turn," he said abruptly, deftly unhooking her bra. The straps slid from her shoulders.

Her tiny bout of self-consciousness because her breasts weren't exactly bounteous—not like Sonja's—ended at the sight of his face.

"Beautiful," he murmured with that seductive gravel in his voice.

Suddenly, he lifted her, carried her to the bed and lowered her onto her back as if she were delicate instead of lean and athletic. He looked his fill, then bent to lick her nipple. Circled it with his tongue, then teased the other one. Anna heard herself whimpering and knew she was arching upward as she grabbed for him. "Please."

His mouth closed over her breast and he suckled, the rhythmic pull so exquisitely pleasurable she twined her fingers in his hair to hold him close. If she hurt him, he didn't say anything, only shifted to her other breast.

Then he rose to claim her mouth again, his weight on her everything she wanted. Her knees had fallen apart to cradle him in an instinctive act. If only they weren't still both half-dressed, shoes and all.

He took the initiative to strip her, then himself. She'd wanted to slide that zipper down herself, but…watching was good enough to complete the meltdown.

She reared up to touch and he let her, but only for a few seconds.

"I want to take this slow." His voice was guttural. "If you do that, I can't."

"Slow? I need you *now*."

He squeezed his eyes shut and backed out of her reach. "Condom."

"I'm on the pill. I…never went off."

With a harsh exclamation, Nate lowered himself onto her again, his knee nudging her thighs apart. He covered her mouth with his, his tongue thrusting as he found her entrance. Pushed. Slow, until her hips rose and he plunged the rest of the way in. It felt…amazing.

They found a perfect rhythm immediately, as if their bodies were tuned to each other. Except she wasn't going to last. Anna heard herself making sounds she didn't recognize.

She dug her fingernails into his back—and her body imploded.

He said something—her name—and followed her over the precipice. Holding him tight after his big body came down on hers, Anna felt tingling joy from the tips of her toes to the sting in her eyes…and wondered how she'd ever have the courage to leave this man.

CHAPTER TWENTY-ONE

THEY MADE LOVE three times during the night. Nate kept aiming for slow and losing it, but when he awakened to the pearly light of morning and found himself spooning Anna's long, lithe body, he felt a wash of throat-clenching emotion. He made every touch tender. He prevented her from rolling to face him, giving him control she couldn't dynamite. Instead, he entered her from behind, loved her with hands and mouth and body.

Holding her afterward, breathing in the citrus scent of her silky hair, he realized a broad grin had spread on his face. The night had been mind-blowing, and he knew it hadn't been one-sided. She had to see that they were right together.

Yeah, but when could they do this again? If he asked her right now to marry him, would she say yes? Otherwise, they'd be lucky to get rid of all three kids at the same time once every few weeks.

Nate wanted tomorrow—no, *tonight*—not some possible date in June.

He sighed and her head lifted. "What was that about?"

"Realizing two of the three kids will be home today."

A phone buzzed somewhere. Down on the floor, he thought. His was…who knew?

It buzzed again. When she sat up, he groaned and went searching, finally coming up with her chinos. He fished the phone out and handed it to her.

As she answered, Nate kissed her shoulder and was able to hear Jenna's high voice. "Mommy? Can you come get me now?"

"You've already had breakfast?"

Nate looked at the clock and discovered the pale light that suggested dawn was deceptive; it was actually 9:30 a.m. A gray day, then.

Anna's gaze followed his, and she wrinkled her nose ruefully. "Yes, okay. But I slept in and haven't taken my shower yet, so you'll have to wait." Pause. "Did you have fun?"

After ending the call, she sighed. "At least she made it through the night."

"I'll count that a blessing."

"I suppose I'd better get moving."

He pushed her hair aside to kiss her slender nape, noting the delicacy of her vertebrae. "Can we have breakfast together once you're back?"

Anna smiled over her shoulder, the hint of

shyness that had returned unintentionally seductive. "That sounds nice. Waffles."

He fell back onto his pillow, grinning at her. "With that incentive, I'll let you go."

She scrambled into her clothes a lot faster than he'd have liked, came back to the bed to kiss him and then fled.

Nate folded his hands behind his head, stared at the ceiling brooding, then finally got up to shower, too.

Once downstairs, he started the coffee, feeling guilty that he expected her to cook. He could have done something else, but waffles? Not without a mix.

Twenty minutes later, she let herself and Jenna in the front door instead of going up through the apartment. Nate took a ridiculous amount of satisfaction from that small act. She wouldn't have done that a few months ago, not when he was home. He hadn't recognized at the time how many unspoken boundaries Anna had set, but now realized that she'd relaxed most.

Including the biggest one—he'd had her in his bed.

He needed to have patience now, but had trouble finding any store of it. He'd worn out what he had in the months of waiting.

"I promised Jenna I'd make waffles," she said, as if she hadn't seen him since yesterday. "Would you like one?"

"Or two," he agreed, not liking her smile. It was for effect, not for him.

But Jenna dumped her small pink pack and rushed to where he sat on the bar stool, one foot hooked on the rung. "I went to a sleepover, just like Josh does all the time. And I wasn't scared at all!"

"Nope." He held up a hand for a high five. "You're growing up, kid."

She giggled. "Uh-huh. And I'm going to be in real school before I know it."

The phrase had come from her mother. Did five-year-olds have any conception of how long three or four months were?

"I wish Mrs. Schaub could be my teacher. Or Mommy."

"I don't think the principal would let you be in your mother's classroom." Unless she got a job in a rural district where there was only one class for each grade? No, damn it—that wasn't happening.

Already removing ingredients from cupboards, Anna said, "I'm hoping to teach older kids, anyway. Third through fifth grade, maybe."

"Josh says he'll be in third grade."

Nate laughed at her dubious tone. "What, you think he's going to flunk second grade, and they'll make him take it over again?"

"I could catch up." Gleeful, she said, "Maybe they'll *never* let him graduate from second grade."

Anna's laughing eyes met his, and he immediately felt better. He'd imagined the renewed distance. She hadn't held anything back last night. Why would she now?

But uneasiness stirred anyway as he remembered her saying, *Let's not talk about that tonight.* Anna had given herself physically, without reserve—but maybe not emotionally.

IT WAS SO hard to behave naturally this morning. Anna kept having to squeeze her thighs together to contain cramps of longing when she focused on Nate's mouth or his hands or his thighs or... At the same time, she remembered with chagrin the sounds she'd heard come from her throat. She'd never even known what the word *mewl* meant—until she'd done it.

On the way to pick up Jenna, her fingers painfully tight on the steering wheel, she'd been sure last night was a mistake. She should have waited until she was certain how she felt about him—and how he felt about her. If he loved her, wouldn't you think he'd have said so?

Now she stared blankly at the flour in the ceramic mixing bowl. Had she added the sugar or not? And what about the salt?

Wonderful. She added both. Who'd notice extra sweet or salty waffles? At least she knew she hadn't measured out the baking powder yet. Blowing out a breath, she said, "Josh called. He's going to the soccer game with Jaden."

"The cast will be off this week."

"The season will be over soon, too."

For that matter, school would be out in... Anna had to count. Three weeks. Suddenly, she felt as if she had a chunk of concrete in her stomach. Kyle had drowned on the first field trip of the summer camp. The anniversary was just over four weeks away.

And she should have been applying for more jobs. So far she'd applied for only two, and both were local. Even though she knew she couldn't afford to live in the area unless she continued to lean on Nate. And it wasn't as if they could go on the way they were if Molly ended up going to live with her mother.

"She won't be home until tomorrow, will she?"

Nate and Jenna both looked startled.

"Molly," she had to explain.

"No." His mouth tightened. "I thought about calling to say hi, but I don't suppose Sonja would appreciate that."

"How come?" Jenna asked.

At the same moment Anna said, "That's safe to say."

Explanations to Jenna occupied both Anna and Nate until they all sat down to eat the waffles. The two adults had a scoop of blueberries atop theirs, as well as blueberry syrup. Jenna liked only butter.

"More blueberries for the rest of us," Nate said.

After breakfast, he worked for a couple hours while Anna looked again at job openings and Jenna managed to entertain herself.

Anna produced sandwiches and a fruit salad for lunch, after which all three played Chinese checkers, both adults subtly helping Jenna. Despite their best efforts, Jenna's delight at having Nate and Anna's undivided attention had waned and become boredom by midafternoon, when Jaden's dad dropped off Josh.

When Anna asked, he said, "Yeah, my team won." He sounded deeply gloomy. "The guys all claimed they want me back, but I don't know."

Nate gave him a friendly whack between the shoulder blades, said, "Of course they meant it. You're good," and excused himself to catch up on emails.

Watching him go, Anna felt a helpless longing that sharpened her worry. These were her children; the three of them were a family without Nate. Was she really this dependent on his presence, his approval, his sense of humor, his support? Or, God forbid, his money? And it wasn't only her, was it? Jenna and Josh both had come to count on Nate. He'd become their father in all but name, and she didn't know how she felt about that.

Running away seemed safest.

The kids weren't happy when she announced that they needed to return to the apartment, but they knew when arguing wouldn't get them anywhere.

"I have things I need to do on my computer," she said firmly. Like apply for more jobs. "And Nate needs to work. You two can entertain yourself with your own stuff."

Of course, what they did was squabble once they were all stuck together in the confines of the small apartment, but Jenna was noticeably flagging, and finally fell asleep. Disgusted, Josh flopped onto his bed and began to play a hand-held electronic game. Since Jenna didn't stir, Anna left him to it.

She sat down with her laptop and began to scan listed openings for elementary school-teachers. Towns that were too small—no. She rejected some communities on the grounds that they didn't look all that appealing to live. Too dry. Too hot. Too isolated.

Gee, had she maybe become a little too picky?

Living for a year in a waterfront home on Lake Washington had spoiled her rotten, she thought ruefully.

She returned to her search, finding that, while some districts listed specific openings, others only accepted general applications. They might or might not have a suitable opening. Each required a different route to apply.

She ignored her conflicted feelings. She could turn down a job she didn't want. But leaving herself with no options at all…that wasn't smart.

She set to work.

SUNDAY EVENING, MOLLY dashed from her mother's car to fling herself into Nate's arms with a desperation that instantly raised red flags for him. Sonja stayed on the far side of the car, looking over the roof.

"Safe and sound," she said sarcastically before getting behind the wheel. What should have been a three-point turnaround in her car was more like five-point.

Erasing his frown, he bent to Molly. Was that mint he smelled?

"Have you had dinner?"

She shook her head then said, "Kind of."

"What's that mean?"

"Mommy ordered Chinese food. She got mad that I didn't like it."

All those foods mixed together. What was Sonja thinking?

Resting a hand on her shoulder, he said, "We have leftover spaghetti. I'll warm some up for you. Leave your bag there, and we'll take it up when it's time for bed."

"Isn't Anna here? And Josh and Jenna?"

"No, they went to the apartment after dinner. Josh had homework waiting." He glanced at her. "What about you?"

"I guess."

Nate laughed. "Don't sound so downtrodden. What'll it take you? Twenty minutes?"

Eating improved her mood, but she didn't want to talk about the weekend. They didn't really do anything that fun. Mom rented movies, but Molly had seen most of them already.

It was like tiptoeing through a minefield. He didn't like the idea of Sonja grilling Molly about every minute she spent with him, and Sonja didn't have an obligation to dazzle her daughter with fun activities every second, either. Maybe she'd wanted to enjoy the feeling of having Molly home again.

And maybe she was drinking.

He'd bide his time…except what if she'd had a couple of martinis before driving Molly home tonight? The wondering became a jarring buzz.

Of course, what he wanted urgently was to talk to Anna, but would she welcome a backstairs visit after the kids were all asleep? Otherwise, he'd have to wait until tomorrow night. Tomorrow, he decided, disturbed by how needy he felt.

He barely saw Anna in the morning. In the office, he pored over due-diligence reports on two maybe/maybe-not start-ups, then wandered down the hall to talk his decisions over with John, who'd reached about the same place on a plea for money to launch yet another social media site. Their discussion continued through lunch at Andaluca in the Mayflower Park Hotel, walking distance from their office.

That afternoon, he said a kind no on one project and a provisional *yes, let's talk more* on the other. Emails, texts and returning phone calls killed the rest of the afternoon. Even so, more came in during his drive to the Eastside. Think how much more he'd get done if he accidentally-on-purpose lost his phone.

He came in the door at home to catch a harried-looking Anna gazing into the refrigerator. The house wasn't redolent with the scent of dinner cooking.

When she heard him, she closed the refrigerator. "I'm sorry. Josh doesn't feel good and I'm way behind."

That explained the quiet. "Where is he?"

"In his room. I left both doors open." She sighed. "Since Molly is in the same classroom, I'm sure she's already been exposed to whatever bug he has, and, well…"

"Jenna already has been, too. How about if I go pick up a pizza?"

"Would you?" She looked grateful. "I could make a vegetable to go with it."

He smiled, making it into the kitchen to cup her face in his hands and press his lips to her forehead. "Or we could forget it."

She gave a funny, choked laugh. "That wouldn't break my heart."

"Okay. You call in our usual order, I'll head out right now to pick it up."

"Bless you."

He did pause to say hi to the two girls playing a remarkably silly game, then went back out.

His talk with Anna didn't happen that evening. She dashed between apartment and house half-a-dozen times during dinner and cleanup, reporting that poor Josh couldn't keep anything down, even the ginger ale she'd picked up on the way home.

Jenna scrunched up her face. "Do I hafta sleep in the bedroom with *him*?"

Molly offered to share her bed, and Anna gave her permission. Once she'd brought Jenna her toothbrush, nightgown and clothes for the morning, she offered a distracted good-night and disappeared upstairs.

Family life did have its drawbacks. Even if they shared a bed, she'd have been leaping up on a regular basis to check on Josh.

He saw her only long enough in the morning to be able to tell that she hadn't gotten much sleep. She'd called in to the district office to let them know she couldn't work today. Since no kid was in sight, he slipped his arms around her and let her lean on him for a precious few minutes.

Wednesday morning, Molly woke up puking.

After Nate had changed her bed and cleaned her up, he sat beside her, smoothing her hair back from her damp forehead.

"Are you going to take me to Mommy's?" she asked in a small voice. "Or can I stay with Anna?"

"Do you want to go to your mom's?"

"No," she whispered.

"Then I'm staying home with you, unless Josh is still sick and Anna has already called in to let the school know she won't be coming. Okay?"

"Really?" She searched his eyes. "You will?"

"I will."

"Oh." She swallowed. "Daddy, I need—"

He barely got the bowl in front of her in time.

She was feeling mostly better by Friday morning, but Nate decided to let her stay home another day. He'd given up on his week, so when Anna appeared to announce that Jenna was sick now, he said, "If she's okay with me as caretaker, why don't you go to work?"

"You mean it?" Her obvious disbelief annoyed him. Did she still buy the crap Sonja had sold her about his unreliability?

"Of course I mean it."

Nate suggested Jenna recuperate on the sofa

in the living room. Molly mostly played by herself since Jenna either slept or was feverish and sick to her stomach.

He grilled hamburgers that evening and let Anna make a side dish. Watching Anna's gentleness with her daughter and her patience with Molly and Josh, Nate wondered if he'd ever get her alone again.

And, yeah, he was being an idiot. The bug ran its course within forty-eight hours. They were almost done with it—unless he or Anna got sick next.

When Sonja called that evening after Molly's bedtime, he told her about the virus.

"Well, thank goodness for Anna."

Ignoring the edge in her voice, he said, "I'm the one who stayed home the last three days."

"Why didn't you ever do that when we were married?"

Ashamed and yet defensive, he said, "I might have if you'd had a job, too."

After a brief silence, she suggested she pick Molly up after school Friday for their next weekend. "No reason for her to have to ride the bus."

"Make it here," he said without apology. "It would be a hassle for her to take her stuff to school with her."

"She still has clothes here at home. She doesn't need to bring anything."

Was this an attempt to dodge seeing either

him or Anna? Was that a little bit of a slur? Or was he hearing it because he wanted to?

Disturbed, he wondered if he was hoping she'd fail.

Once she'd reluctantly bowed to his insistence, he checked on Molly, who was sound asleep, and then made his way downstairs and back up again to the apartment. He rapped lightly on the door.

When Anna opened it, he asked, "Both asleep?"

"Temporarily." She stepped into his arms. "Molly okay?" she mumbled against his shoulder.

"Yeah." He nuzzled her temple. "It's Sonja that's worrying me."

Once again, she propped open the door, but they went only partway down the staircase since she needed to listen for Jenna. Nate sat on the step below her and circled her waist with one arm.

He confided his worst fear. "I'm afraid Sonja may be drinking again. Molly came home really withdrawn last Sunday." Even his unworthy thoughts poured out, and they talked softly.

"I'll make sure I get close enough to her to smell her breath and see whether her eyes are bloodshot before I let her take Molly on Friday," Anna promised.

"No. I should be here, not put you in the position of having to make that call." He frowned.

"Sonja's been a bitch lately, but she's not really like that. Christmas day, I saw the woman I remember."

"The withdrawal has to be awful."

Boozing hadn't done wonders for her personality, either, but he left that unsaid. Instead, he and Anna cuddled in peaceful silence. He was the one to stir. "I'd better let you go."

"It's been a fun week, hasn't it?"

"Oh, yeah." He bent his head for what he intended as a gentle kiss. But the lips that met his were slightly parted, and he couldn't resist the temptation. Within seconds, the kiss deepened. Groaning, he cupped her breast in his palm and felt her fingers clench on the back of his neck.

"Mom, Jenna is—"

The voice coming from the head of the stairs didn't penetrate Nate's consciousness fast enough.

"Mom?"

Nate turned his head to see the shock on Josh's face.

CHAPTER TWENTY-TWO

JUST BEFORE ANNA leaped to her feet, Nate murmured, "I'll talk to him with you."

She shook her head quickly, able to tell he wasn't happy to be excluded, but he conceded without a fight.

Anna still hadn't decided what to say when she joined Josh on the sofa in the apartment fifteen minutes later. She'd had to clean up Jenna, give her some liquid fever reducer and sooth her to sleep while he waited. While she was doing all that, what would Nate have said to Josh? Thank goodness she hadn't given him the chance.

Pain crawled up her neck and wrapped her head. She prayed it wasn't the first indication that she was getting sick, too.

Josh sat with his arms crossed tightly and his expression accusing. "You were *kissing* Nate!"

She discarded lying—*he was just holding me to be nice*—and admitted, "I was."

"Why?"

Somewhere, she found a laugh. "Nate's a really handsome man, you know." His appalled look made her amusement real. "We've spent a lot of time together this year. You know that. I suppose…we're exploring the possibility of becoming a real family."

"You mean, getting married?"

Anna nodded. "Neither of us has said the word *married* yet, but…yes. I do like him, and I think he likes me."

Like? She loved him. Why not be honest, if only with herself?

"But…what about *Dad*?"

Yes, what about him? For a moment, she let herself see again how much Josh looked like his father. Then she tried to explain.

"You know it's been almost a year since he died. That's the traditional period of mourning." Of course, she had to explain what she meant by that. "I loved your dad." With reservations. "But he's gone, and… Nate's a pretty amazing guy, you know." She couldn't explain how lonely and angry and frightened she'd been in the months after Kyle's death. Brutal honesty wouldn't be good for any of them. She'd made that decision within days of his death. Let Josh, especially, remember the loving father Kyle had been. Chances were, Jenna would be left with no more than fleeting memories of him.

When Josh stayed silent, Anna said, "It upset you to see me with Nate."

"It's just—" He hunched his shoulders. "I don't know."

"Unexpected."

He shrugged, but after a minute said, "If you married him, we wouldn't have to move, would we? I could stay with my friends, and my team. And…I'd still have someplace to drive my boat."

Anna's smile was probably a little twisted, since taking out the remote-controlled speedboat was an activity he only did with Nate. "I hope that isn't your biggest consideration."

"And the Xbox would be kind of mine, too, wouldn't it?" He was brightening by the moment.

She rolled her eyes. "Oh, go to bed. Except…" Anna made sure he was looking at her. "I'm asking you not to tell Jenna about seeing us kissing, or what we've talked about. Molly, either," she added hastily. "I may decide this isn't the right thing for us, so don't count on it, okay?"

"But why—"

"There's a lot to figure out, and you're still a kid. Just…trust me, okay?"

He threw himself at her and hugged her fiercely, before letting her go just as suddenly and rushing to the bedroom.

Alone, Anna sat still, closing her eyes. That had gone as well as it could have. Now if only her confused emotions would straighten themselves out—and the headache would recede.

IT FRUSTRATED NATE beyond belief to have to leave for work Saturday morning without having a chance to talk to Anna, but he felt compelled to make up for some of the time he'd stayed home this week. When he called up the stairs, "I've got to go," Josh, rather than his mother, opened the door.

"Mom says okay, and can Molly come up here."

"Does she want me to carry Jenna downstairs, instead?"

A murmured consultation, after which Josh reappeared. "No, she says she can do it."

He gritted his teeth at the message—*your help not needed*—and retreated. Molly trotted upstairs cheerfully to join them, and Nate left.

Josh hadn't looked resentful this morning. Did that mean anything?

Nate snorted as he backed out of the garage. What, was he in sixth or seventh grade, trying to read *her* feelings for him by another person's tone of voice?

Jenna wasn't bouncing back as fast as the other two, Nate discovered after getting home. The minute he appeared, Anna carried her upstairs to her own bed, accepting his offer to cook dinner. Josh took Anna a plate with a hamburger and the scalloped potatoes Nate had made from a box, returning with her thanks.

He finally went up to check on Jenna. Anna

looked startled to see him, but did say Jenna was awake.

She lay listlessly against her pillow, her cheeks still flushed and the bowl against her side.

"Hey." He sat next to her. "You don't look so good, kiddo."

Her lower lip trembled. "I don't *feel* good. I don't like being sick!"

"It stinks," he agreed, squeezing her feet beneath the blanket. "But I'll bet that by morning you're feeling better."

She sniffed. "That's what Mommy said."

"Mommies know what they're talking about."

She suddenly pushed up from the pillow. "I need to pook!"

He'd had plenty of practice at whisking the bowl in place. Anna came rushing in but saw that the worst was over. The poor kid's stomach had to be empty. Dry heaves weren't very satisfying.

"Okay, honey," he said, setting the bowl to the side. "I'll see you in the morning."

Anna stayed with her daughter, robbing him of even a brief conversation. Nate had an unsettling thought: was she, like Sonja, in avoidance mode?

What he couldn't figure out was why. They were good together. Not good, great. He liked her kids, had even come to feel…proprietary toward them. In turn, Anna treated Molly as if she were her own. He'd encouraged Anna to work, understanding her need to become solid enough financially that she could never again be left on such shaky ground.

He had to wonder if she had any idea how wealthy he was. Or maybe she did, and their lopsided financial status bothered her?

Crap. The two of them had shared so much, he'd deceived himself that he knew her as he never had Sonja or even most of his friends. This new uncertainty ate at his belief. What they *hadn't* talked about were the issues that would impact them as a couple. Deliberate on her part? Or was he the one who'd been reluctant to go there? Maybe Sonja was right, and he *was* lousy at relationships.

Nate realized how much he hated knowing he couldn't *make* Anna marry him. Hell, she wasn't even giving him a chance to persuade her. Control had always been an issue for him, as he knew it was for his brother and his father. The insight told him why Dad had refused to take the antidepressant. He'd be ceding control to a chemical.

Nate grunted. Maybe he should call his mother and ask for advice. She'd managed to live with his father all these years. To all appearances, they were even happy.

He'd be happy, if he had a ring on Anna's finger and knew she'd committed to him. He could trust that commitment. Then a new worry hit. Did she not trust *his* ability to commit? He was divorced, after all. Did this circle back to her husband's death? Nate not keeping a promise, with the consequences that followed like dominoes toppling?

Shit. He rubbed his chest, hoping this was heartburn.

THE KIDS SEEMED to conspire to help Anna avoid a serious talk with Nate, which kept him at a simmer.

Jenna still felt so-so Sunday and Monday, making meals hurried and demanding all of Anna's time.

The school held a patriotic assembly Tuesday evening. All the classes, kindergarten through second grade, did plays or speeches. Of course they all attended, Nate, Anna and Jenna sitting on folding chairs near the front.

He was studying the program when Anna leaned over Jenna to murmur, "Count your blessings that they divided the assembly."

Divided? Ah—this one included only kindergarten through second-graders. Apparently, the upper grades were to be—he flipped the program over—tomorrow night. He had a suspicion both events would be interminable, anyway.

"Could be worse," he murmured back. "What if your school was doing the same thing?"

With a glance down at Jenna, she said, "It could be fun."

Maybe, if the past week hadn't been so stressful.

Molly and Josh both had small speaking parts in their class's play. She was noticeably nervous but didn't forget her five-word line, reason to celebrate. As with the turkey at the Thanksgiving assembly, Josh said his with aplomb—and was still alive at the end.

Wednesday, Josh's spring soccer team held a pizza and awards event at a Domino's. Josh was invited even though he hadn't played in a game, and begged to attend.

Nate took the opportunity to have dinner with one of his most reliable angel investors and his wife, who'd invited him several times in the past couple weeks. Anna didn't seem to mind taking Molly along with her children to Domino's, which, she reported when their paths crossed that evening, was lucky, because Josh spent most of the evening with his friends, ignoring the two girls and his mother.

He grinned. "Gee, sorry I missed that one." Except he *was* sorry—even in the midst of a loud pizza parlor, he would have liked to be with her and the kids.

Nate realized the next day that he'd forgot-

ten to ask about that evening's plans. She'd have
let him know if he had to fend for himself, he
decided. But he couldn't ask her to marry him
while they were sipping coffee after dinner, anyway, with the kids a room away. He needed to
ask her out, just the two of them, which meant
getting a babysitter. Unfortunately, he hadn't a
clue where to find one, since he'd had no need
since the divorce and he felt sure the sixteen-
year-old neighbor girl he and Sonja had used
then had a part-time job for a lot more money, if
she worked at all now that she was on the brink
of graduating from high school.

Brooding wasn't the most productive use of
his time, so he gathered what he needed to attend a presentation being made by a woman who
thought she could hit it big with a personal shopping service. John was handling this one, but
had asked for his input.

Nate's phone buzzed before he could leave
the office. Unfamiliar number, and he almost
let it go, but decided he had time for a quick
conversation.

"Mr. Kendrick? I'm Officer Madison Whit-
burn with the Seattle Police Department. Ms.
Sonja Kendrick was just involved in a vehicle
accident, and your name is listed as her contact."

He sank back into his desk chair. "She's my
ex-wife. Is she badly injured?"

"It's…difficult to say. She's bleeding from

a gash on her head, but evaluating her further is made difficult because she appears inebriated and, er, belligerent. I'm calling against her wishes, but we felt we needed to notify family members."

"Is she being transported to the hospital?"

"Yes." She explained that they were doing a Breathalyzer test now and told him where she'd be taken.

"Was the accident her fault?" He didn't even know why he bothered asking.

"There's always an investigation." The officer hesitated. "Between you and me, I don't think there's any doubt."

He called John's PA to let her know he wouldn't be at the presentation after all. Then he glanced at the time and realized Anna would still be at work, and shut down his laptop and stowed it in the case.

His life had turned into a freaking soap opera.

Nate called at almost five o'clock to tell her about the accident and that he was still at the hospital.

"If you need to go ahead and feed the kids, that's fine. I can heat something up later."

Anna glanced toward the family room, where Molly was playing with Jenna and Josh. She dreaded telling her the latest installment in her mother's problems. No—that was for Nate to do.

"Is Sonja all right?"

"It appears so. She's sloshed enough to be feeling no pain. I suspect she'll be spending the night in jail. Do they still have drunk tanks? She punched a police officer at the scene and assaulted the other driver, who has some nasty scratches on her face."

Anna winced. Sonja had long, wicked fingernails.

"I called her attorney, but that's all I'm prepared to do for her." He sounded grim. "Now that I've seen her, I'm only waiting until he arrives. Then I'll head home."

"I take it she's not promising to go back into treatment."

"You take it right."

"I'm sorry," she said softly. "Poor Molly."

He made a sound in his throat. "I guess this confirms my suspicions."

"Yes. Except...Sonja's never done anything quite like this before, has she?"

"Not as far as I know. She's falling apart." He said even more grimly, "My fault."

"You know that's not true. Molly had to be your first priority."

"Yeah," he said gruffly. "You're right." A muffled voice came through the phone. "I've got to go," he said. "I should be home by six." He was gone without her having a chance to say goodbye.

Anna decided to wait dinner for him. The kids had already had a snack, but she prepared a plate of celery and carrot sticks with peanut butter they could use for dipping, and took it in to them.

"Aren't we having dinner?" Josh asked.

"Nate called to say he'd be late. We'll eat in an hour."

"But I'm hungry—" He stifled it after a glance at her, grabbed a celery stick and scooped peanut butter. Anna went back to the kitchen, where she stood, trying to decide what to do since dinner wasn't far from ready. She settled on having a cold drink and watching the news.

As soon as Nate arrived, she carried the ceramic baking dish with lasagna she'd kept warm in the oven to the table while the peas and garlic bread heated.

"God, that looks good," he said with a groan, and sank into his place at the table. The kids came running, and within a few minutes they were dishing up. "Anything exciting happen today?" he asked.

"Mrs. Tate says we have to do a group project," Molly grumbled. "I hate group projects. I always have to do everything, or else we get a bad grade."

"Teacher wouldn't even let us pick our own groups," Josh chimed in.

For good reason, although Anna did sympathize with Molly's complaint. She'd been that kind of student herself.

She had the impression Nate wasn't really listening. He'd just wanted to spur a conversation so he could eat in peace. Well, she corrected herself, maybe *peace* wasn't the right word.

The kids gobbled, then seized their cookies and raced back to whatever they'd been doing, leaving Anna and Nate to have after-dinner coffee together for the first time in a while.

"Bad day," she said quietly.

He rubbed his jaw. "I kept thinking she's Molly's mother. And not feeling real good about it."

"Are you—" Anna hesitated "—giving up on her?"

Bleak eyes met hers. "No. How can I? But there's nothing I can do except renew my offer to pay for treatment, as many times as it takes."

Relieved, she nodded. "I guess it's obvious I haven't said anything."

"I wouldn't expect you to." He took her hand. "I forgot to tell you that my mother called this morning. They're finally home and eager to see us. And meet you and your two." His grimace looked apologetic. "I should have asked you first, but I invited them to dinner Saturday. They usually stay the night when they're here."

"Why would you ask my permission? I'm happy to cook, if that's what you'd like. I'm sure they'll want to spend time with you and Molly, so once I've met them—"

He scowled. "No. We're family now. Haven't you noticed?"

She was suddenly breathing fast, not finding enough oxygen. "We're not. We might *act* like it, but—"

Nate set down his cup hard, sloshing coffee onto the place mat. "If you'd marry me, we would be."

CHAPTER TWENTY-THREE

"MARRY?" ANNA WHISPERED.

Oh, damn. Nate winced. This wasn't exactly how he'd planned to raise the subject. "I didn't mean to throw it at you that way."

"But you did." She seemed to remember that they were holding hands. She yanked hers free. "And if that's your idea of a proposal—"

"It's not." He softened his voice. "I meant to be a lot more romantic about it. I was trying to figure out where I could find a babysitter, so I could take you out to a nice restaurant."

She shook her head, either rejecting the plan or him. "You've had this in mind all along, haven't you?"

"From the day you started work here? No. For six months or so, yes. I haven't made any secret of it."

"You've decided to firm up our 'arrangement,' because it works so well, isn't that right?"

Holding on to his temper wasn't easy. "We've both been happy, haven't we?" And he'd be even happier with her in his bed every night.

"You'd gain a permanent housekeeper slash

cook, not to mention a solution to all future child-care dilemmas. You'd soothe any case of guilt. Oh, and have regular sex, of course, without any need to bother courting a woman."

He went still. "That's what you think?"

"Me, I'd have financial stability, and you would make a great stepfather." She cocked her head. "It doesn't worry you, that I might marry you for your money?"

"That never crossed my mind," he said tautly. "To the contrary."

"It should have. Do you have any idea how frightening it was to be on the verge of being homeless?"

"I can guess." Maybe. Empathize, anyway. "But I've seen you gaining confidence. We both know you're ready to support yourself and the kids if you have to." *Which you don't.*

She pushed back her chair and stood, her face showing so much turmoil it hurt him to see.

"I know you're…attracted to me."

He stood, too, bracing himself.

"But marriage shouldn't be a convenient solution to practical problems. It should be about love. Have you ever even thought, *I love Anna*?"

He hesitated, knowing even before he spoke that it was too late. "I do love you. I would have said so if I hadn't launched so badly into this."

"Would you?" Her smile was sad.

"Do you love me?" he asked hoarsely.

"What difference does that make right now?"

"Anna—" He reached for her, but his hand froze in midair when she shrank back. "Please don't say no. Please."

She retreated. "I have to think. Do you know what scares me?"

He shook his head dumbly.

"After Kyle died and I found out how bad things were, I made a vow I would never depend on anyone else like that again. I've already come close to violating that with you. But to marry you…" She shivered.

"I'm not Kyle. I'm not anything like him."

Her forehead crinkled, as if the concept confused her, but all she said was, "We should both think. I've been here when you needed me, and that's seductive. I love Molly, and I think she loves me. But someday she'll be a teenager who resents me, and Josh will be yelling because you don't have any right to tell *him* what to do, and I'd be lousy at entertaining the really rich people you'd invite to a party, and—"

"Enough!" Nate snapped. "If you don't love me, say so. Quit making excuses."

"If I didn't love you, this wouldn't be so hard." Eyes suddenly damp, she fled.

Standing stock-still, shocked, he heard her collecting her children.

He'd blown that, but wasn't sure the result would have been any different if he'd had candlelight before going down on bended knee with a diamond ring in his hand. He'd known she was wary, but not why. Months ago, sure, he'd understood the need to respect her grief.

His laugh was humorless. At least she didn't still blame him for her husband's death.

You so sure about that?

No, he wasn't. She might just not want to say it, but Nate found he didn't believe that.

And she'd said she loved him. He hadn't imagined that, had he?

What if he'd prefaced his really shitty proposal with the words, *I love you*? Instinct said she'd have run, anyway.

The silence suddenly penetrated and he remembered the hellish talk he had to have with Molly. Glancing at the half-cleared table, he realized Anna had left the dirty kitchen for him.

Still staggered and deeply afraid, he knew he couldn't put off telling Molly about her mother's latest disaster.

ONCE SHE WAS sure both kids were asleep, Anna sank onto one end of the sofa and drew her legs up so she could wrap her arms around them and rest her chin on her knees. The closest she could get to returning to the womb, she thought with dark humor. Floating in happy darkness, no decisions to be made.

If only Nate hadn't thrown it at her like that. If

she could have prepared herself, thought through her concerns. She'd have laughed if she hadn't been so depressed. Sure, that was what a man wanted when he asked a woman to marry him: her list of concerns.

Well, he'd deserved it tonight.

If you'd marry me, we'd be a family.

The awful thing was…she wanted that, with all her heart. She just wanted to believe that wasn't all he was offering…and that she was accepting for the right reasons.

But she'd been really hateful, hadn't she? Jumping on him because the first words out of his mouth weren't wildly romantic. Them becoming a family *was* important. They were both parents. She wouldn't marry a man who wasn't good for the kids, even if she were passionately in love with him. Nate must have the same consideration.

At least they'd run all the day-to-day tests they needed to, she thought, with what might be faint humor.

She'd been leery because she had come to count on Nate for so much. Even so, until he offered her everything, she hadn't known quite how afraid she was of giving her complete trust to another man.

Frowning, she wondered how fair her fear was to *him*. It was true that Nate wasn't like Kyle. If he'd tried to push his money at her, she'd have good reason to feel threatened. She knew what he thought of her car, and had worried he'd do something at Christmas like present her with a brand-new SUV perfect for hauling the kids around. But he hadn't, instead giving her a pretty pair of earrings that probably were real diamonds, but not such large ones as to have been horribly expensive.

Despite his personal worth, he'd been respectful of her determination to work, even if her paychecks were pitiful by his standards. He'd never belittled her job in any way, or argued when she insisted on paying for some of those Sunday pizzas for them all.

So, if her worry wasn't him…what was it?

Me. It's all me.

Even in the midst of grief after Kyle's death, humiliation and that terrible sense of inadequacy had scored her to the bone. She'd been stupid, foolish to have blindly believed in Kyle. She'd berated herself with a thousand hurtful words.

Now, separated from those dreadful days by almost a year, Anna thought, yes, she had been foolishly trusting. As an educated woman, she should have insisted on knowing everything about their finances. The man she'd loved had done really stupid things, but she hadn't known that. Except for his refusal to stick with any one job, he'd never given her reason to doubt that he handled their money fine. That day would have come soon; *he'd* seemed placid, so he must have had complete, unreasoning faith each time he made an investment that *this* one would be magic. Of course, it hadn't been, and he'd have had nowhere else to go for money. Would he have lied about why they had to sell the house?

Probably.

Which brought her back to the present. She would never again be able to give unreasoning trust, even though... Her sudden knowledge took her breath away. She trusted Nate. Aloud, she whispered, "I do."

If only she could be sure he really did want to marry *her*, not just the woman who completed his family—and the one for whom he still felt a sense of responsibility.

And if only she could be sure that she trusted *her* judgment.

She'd hurt him. Would he give her another chance? Her heart cramped at this new fear.

Still, she discovered she did have that much faith. He'd waited all these months for her. He wouldn't shrug now and decide she wasn't worth the bother.

And...would he really have stayed celibate that long and been so patient if he *didn't* love her?

THIS WASN'T THE greatest time to introduce his parents into the mix.

Nate and Anna had been tiptoeing around

each other since his ill-conceived proposal. He was a little bit encouraged because she hadn't gone back to dragging her children away the minute he arrived home each day to take charge of Molly. She'd even lingered for coffee the following day because she wanted to know how his talk with Molly had gone.

He'd had to tell her the truth: he didn't know. Molly hadn't cried or turned to him for comfort. She hadn't asked questions. All she'd done was nod solemnly when he'd explained that any visits with her mother would once again take place here, with him present. He hadn't said, *Oh, by the way, your mom may spend some time in jail before you see her again*. He didn't know the outcome of Sonja's breakdown, because she wasn't answering her phone and had requested her attorney not to tell Nate a damn thing. From the attorney's slight hesitation, he guessed the request had been phrased more profanely than that.

He'd have shrugged, believing that sometimes ignorance was bliss—except that they shared a child. What did Sonja expect him to tell Molly as time passed?

Thinking about Anna's accusations gave him some nearly sleepless nights after their confrontation. He had to be sure he had answers, if only for himself.

He couldn't deny that he loved Anna's cooking, and that having a partner was damned convenient. But Molly would grow up fast—a man didn't marry a woman when he could hire a different one to do the same job. He wouldn't, anyway. He took marriage seriously, despite the failure of his first one. Maybe even more because he'd failed the once.

Sex with Anna had been stupendous, he couldn't deny it. But that accusation made him mad. The sex had been great because of how he felt about her and—he hoped— how she felt about him. He didn't like her making it sound cheap. One woman interchangeable for another. Given how damn long it had been since he'd had sex with anyone else, claiming he just wanted easy sex had no basis in reality, and Anna had to know that.

Not having courted her…there'd been good reasons.

The one that he did brood about was whether his sense of guilt, responsibility—whatever she wanted to call it—had even subconsciously pushed him to think how neatly he could tie everything up with her as his wife. He could take care of her and her kids for a lifetime.

He made himself remember again the distraught woman at the hospital and how powerfully that brief glimpse had moved him. But that woman had been an abstract, epitomizing the tragedy. She'd made him want to write her a big check.

The Anna he'd fallen in love with was strong, proud, fiery, nurturing. Smart. Sexy. If she'd been hungry for his money and the security it would give her, he might feel differently. But then she wouldn't be the Anna he knew. And he couldn't love her without wanting to protect her, to make her happy. What kind of a man would he be if he *didn't* feel that way?

Despite his tiredness, Nate had worked extra hours this week, partly to make up for the days off, partly because the evenings weren't the un-alloyed pleasure they'd been. By the time he left his office midafternoon Saturday, he felt guilty about that. Was this how the disintegration of his marriage had started? Sonja had irritated or bored him, so he'd worked longer hours?

Yeah, he thought, it might be. Not a mistake he'd make again, not when it came to Anna. A lot of what she'd said came down to trust. He'd known in one way how badly her husband had let her down, but he hadn't really understood how crushing that would have been to her abil-ity to believe in another man. Him.

Whatever he had to do to prove himself, he'd do.

Starting, he thought ruefully, with being there when his parents showed up, instead of leaving her to handle it alone.

When he let himself in, Anna was already in the kitchen. Relief flashed across her face. "Oh. I was afraid…"

He smiled crookedly. "It occurred to me Mom might get eager and make Dad come early. Let me go change clothes, and if I can do anything to help, I will."

"I don't think…but thank you."

He took the stairs two at a time, glad to shed the suit in favor of comfortable jeans and a polo shirt. Downstairs again, he said hi to the kids, who all decided to follow him back to the kitchen.

"Mommy is making scones," Jenna said. "I don't know what they are, but she said they'd be good for breakfast."

Anna looked embarrassed. "I thought they'd be a nice alternative to toast."

He inhaled. "That's what smells so good. Lemon?"

She relaxed. "Yes. I have some icing ready to go on them. Oh, and I already baked two pies for dessert tonight."

His stomach growled, and she laughed.

"Did you have lunch?"

"Now that you mention it…"

She wanted to make him a sandwich, but he insisted on doing it himself.

"Don't kill yourself over this," he said, between bites as she iced the now-cooling scones.

"Mom and Dad are pretty relaxed. This isn't a fancy dinner party."

She eyed him. "Is that what you're going to wear?"

Nate looked down at himself. "I put on a polo shirt instead of a T-shirt in their honor."

"I was going to change clothes before they got here, but maybe I won't."

"I like what you're wearing." The huskiness in his voice probably told her how much. Today was warm, a real precursor of summer, which was why she had on chinos that ended just below her knees—capris, he decided—and a snug-fitting, soft blue T-shirt with cap sleeves and a deep neck. On her feet... He craned his neck to see over the breakfast bar. She was barefoot.

She followed his gaze and blushed. "I'll put on my sandals before I meet them."

Nate laughed. "If Mom sees you like that, she'll probably kick her own shoes off. This stretch of good weather is supposed to last, you know."

"I saw." She made a face. "Rain would make it a lot easier to keep the kids' attention in class. As it is, they're like fleas, hopping out of their seats at the slightest excuse."

"Nice image." Suddenly, they were smiling at each other. Damn, she was beautiful, her dark blue eyes sparkling, her cheeks pink, her lips soft as they curved. Best of all, he could tell she was as captivated as he was. An offer from Amazon to buy any company in his portfolio for a billion dollars couldn't have distracted him right now.

"Anna." His voice came out deep and ragged.

"Yes?" she said, barely above a whisper. He'd swear she had swayed forward.

The thunder of feet had him jerking.

"I hear a car!" Molly yelled. "I bet Grandma and Grandpa are here."

He blinked a couple times, trying to bring his brain back online. Anna gave her head a small shake. He hadn't heard an engine, but now car doors were slamming.

He had to clear his throat before he said, "I think you're right. Shall we go out and meet them?"

She bounced up and down. "Yes! Come on, Daddy."

"So much for changing clothes," Anna murmured.

Nate swept her with another hungry gaze. "They'll think you're as beautiful as I do."

Her tremulous smile made him wish his parents *weren't* here. And maybe not the kids, either, come to think of it.

He groaned and slid off the stool to follow his eager daughter to the front door.

THE SUN WAS getting low at eight that evening, but still close to an hour from setting. The two men and Josh stood at the end of the dock, Nate's father now holding the remote that controlled the small speedboat. Molly had gone with them and sat with her bare feet dangling off the dock, but seemed less entranced by the roar of the small boat skipping over the waves.

Watching them just like Anna was, Mary Kendrick laughed. "At heart, those men aren't a day older than Josh."

Anna smiled. "You know Nate gave the thing to Josh. He was so enthusiastic, I could tell he wanted to play with it, too."

"I'm surprised he hadn't already given Molly one."

"Oh, he and Josh may end up with a whole flotilla, but Molly has never shown the least interest in anything with a motor." She'd seen Josh huddled with Nate the other day as they talked about the other models of remote-controlled boats available. "Did you know there's a submarine?" she asked.

Mary chuckled again. "You'd never find that one if the remote quits on you."

Anna felt a lot more comfortable with his mother than she'd anticipated. She'd been warm and natural with Josh and Jenna, unfazed by a five-year-old's unceasing chatter. In fact, Jenna had worn herself out, for once, and presently cuddled sleepily on Anna's lap.

"My other son, Adam, has two girls," Mary said. "His wife is pregnant again, and I think Adam hopes for a boy. He's stationed at Fort Bragg, back east. I wish we saw more of them."

"I understand," Anna said softly. "I'd hate having one of my kids living on the other side of the country, or even abroad."

"It may happen."

"I know."

After a quiet interlude, Mary spoke again. "I have to tell you how glad I am that you've been here for Molly, and for Nate."

Hearing the hint of a question, Anna said, "He's been amazingly supportive of us, too. He turned overnight into a soccer dad for Josh." Hearing how that sounded, she said hastily, "I don't mean the dad part. Just that Nate had fun rooting for him at games, and it meant a lot to Josh."

Mary's lips curved. "I don't know. He looks a lot like a dad right now."

He did. Josh had regained control of the remote and was bringing the boat in, slowing it until it bumped gently against the floating dock. Nate's hand rested on his shoulder, in that way he had, as he said something that had Josh grinning at him.

"I'm sorry about all this turmoil with Sonja," Mary murmured.

"It's been so hard on Molly. Especially now, when we don't even know what's happening with Sonja…" Anna shook her head.

"Nate said the two of you haven't talked about how to handle it when she does reappear."

The two of you? When he said that, had he even been conscious that he'd automatically included her, as if they were a unit?

Why would he, when they were?

The thought staggered her. She'd been telling herself they weren't quite a family, that they were pretending, but where was the pretense? When she needed Nate, he was there. Always. When he needed her, she had never let him down. Never would. All three children had complete faith in the two adults who *were* their parents, in every way that mattered.

Her eyes focused again, to see Nate's father crouch to lift the boat from the water. Once he'd straightened, Molly accepted her grandfather's hand and scrambled to her feet. The four started toward the shore and the steps that led up to the covered terrace.

Of course, it was Nate who drew Anna's eyes, his confident stride shortened for the kids' sake, contentment on the lean face she had so often considered inscrutable in those first months. It wasn't only that she'd learned to read him—he had let her see him.

She did want this life with him, even if the sheer perfection of it scared her, too. But her throat tightened as she thought, *I do want it. I do.* What's more, it was right there in her hands. She just hadn't seen that.

Nate looked up just then, his gaze locking on her. It stayed there as he climbed the steps.

CHAPTER TWENTY-FOUR

NATE SAW HIS opportunity the next morning.

Once breakfast was over, Anna rose from the table and immediately started to stack dirty dishes.

His mother intervened. "The least I can do is clean up."

Naturally, Anna protested, but she didn't get anywhere. His mother removed the plates from her hands. "Relax."

Nate moved in on her. He was nervous but determined, and if he didn't talk to her now, she'd make plans for the entire day and evening. He took her arm and drew her toward the living room. "Come on. I want to talk to you about something."

Looking surprised but curious, she went with him. "Is it Sonja?"

"No. Until we know more, how can we make any decisions?" He hadn't heard a word about her, and right this minute he didn't give a damn. "All I know is I want to shield Molly as much as we can."

As soon as he knew he was out of earshot of

his parents, he stopped with his back to them and cleared his throat. *Just say it.* "Mom and Dad offered to stay another night to watch the kids so you and I can go out." More accurately, he'd asked them, but Anna didn't have to know that. "I…had an idea, although if you'd like to go to a good restaurant, I'd enjoy that, too."

"Is this that romantic night out?"

Was that tart or teasing? He couldn't tell. "Ah…yes." His usual certainty had deserted him. "Except I was thinking of something a little less fancy."

She eyed him. "What?"

"A picnic dinner." He smiled a little wryly. "Not that any of the parks have a better view than we do here, but I wouldn't mind some privacy."

"From our kids." Her hesitation kept his adrenaline running high. Then she smiled, actually looking a little shy. "That sounds wonderful. I'd like that. Oh. Should I—"

Hiding the effects of the crash from the release of tension, he said, "Cook? Not a chance. I'll surprise you."

TAKING A WOMAN out for a candlelit dinner at one of the highly reviewed restaurants in Seattle or Bellevue would have been easier than this, Nate decided. He'd spent a lot of time online, and finally settled on a menu from Chutneys, a favorite Indian restaurant, and ordered in time to let him pick up the food and return to the house for Anna.

Now to hope that the park wasn't jammed with kids running around yelling or sullen teenagers playing loud music. And that Anna actually would prefer his version of a picnic.

Personally, he liked the idea of being able to hold hands with her as they took a walk on the waterfront while the sun set. Find a place they truly were alone to kiss her.

His parents and the kids all lined up on the front porch to beam at them when they left. Anna laughed as he held open the car door for her. "This is embarrassing." Even so, she blew a kiss at the kids before she slid in and he closed the door.

He got in. "I gather they're all going out, too?"

"For pizza and movies. Your mother is taking Jenna to the new animated Disney movie, while your dad gets to go with Molly and Josh to something a little more sophisticated."

Heading up the driveway, Nate said, "I wonder if Dad has ever seen a kids' movie."

"He didn't take you and Adam?"

"No, he was a workaholic." Hearing himself, Nate grimaced. "My mother is a patient woman."

"I like them both."

Thank God, she hadn't said something like,

It takes one to know one. Or else, *I guess you learned at your father's knee.* Sonja wouldn't have been able to resist and add a little barb to the words.

He said simply, "I'm glad," then made a left onto Shoreland Drive.

"Where are we going?"

He laughed. "Not far." The drive didn't take five minutes. Meydenbauer Beach Park was his favorite of the nearby waterfront parks, having paved trails, a curve of sandy beach, a grassy slope and scattered picnic tables and benches.

When he turned into the park, Anna was the one to laugh. "We could have walked."

"Yeah, but then Mom and Dad would have known where we were going. Dad might have thought it would be funny for them all to pop in to be sure we were having a good time."

"Really?"

"Really. His sense of humor can be irritating."

The parking lot, he was glad to see, held only scattered vehicles. He and Anna wouldn't have any trouble finding chances to be alone.

He popped the trunk. "I hope you like Indian food."

"I love it." She inhaled with apparent pleasure. "It probably goes without saying that I haven't had it in ages."

Why hadn't he found a babysitter a lot sooner and taken Anna out to dinner, movies, the theater? But he knew—they'd been maintaining the not-so-convincing fiction that she was an employee, he the boss.

They strolled across the lawn to a picnic table close to the water's edge, and he began setting out their meal. He studied her surreptitiously, pleased that she'd dressed up a little in a sundress with a swirly skirt that would allow her to sit cross-legged on the grass. Her sandals could be easily kicked off, too, and her shiny blond hair was gathered in a messy bun with an elastic that would be easy to remove.

Nate wanted to believe she wouldn't have accepted his invitation if she wasn't prepared to accept him, too, but he couldn't be sure, not after the disaster that was his last proposal. He wanted to ask *now* but had resolved not to ruin their dinner. While they ate, he'd stay away from the subject of their future.

"Mmm, chicken tikka masala." Anna had opened the first container and was peering in.

He opened containers, identifying the rest of the items on the menu. He hoped there was enough variety. "I thought, for once, a white wine would be good."

Seeing the plastic wineglasses, Anna laughed. "You're right. This looks so good, Nate. Thank you."

They sat side by side, looking out over the lake, unusually still, shimmering instead of dancing. As they ate, his upper arm brushed hers. He told her some funny stories from work, and she did the same from her classroom. They steered clear of the topic of their kids.

Not until they were almost done did Nate ask if she'd had any response to job applications.

Anna's sidelong glance was wary. "I had a Skype interview Friday. With, um, a school district in Eugene."

In Oregon. So she'd gone ahead and applied out of the area. Was this when she told him, regretfully, that she thought it would be better for her and her kids to move away? To leave him and Molly behind?

But she went on, talking fast, "The teacher I work directly for told me she thinks I'll hear from Human Resources this week. I'll get first crack at one of the positions they have open since I'm already an employee. And teachers I worked with gave me really great recommendations."

"This is in Bellevue?"

She nodded and he could breathe again. She wouldn't have told him that if she weren't willing to stay, would she?

"There are other districts within commuting distance."

"I could look at Renton, Northshore and Issaquah."

"Why don't you do that," he said gruffly. "Let's dump our leftovers and go for a walk."

A minute later, they strolled along one of the paths, holding hands. Nate had his eye on a weeping willow ahead.

"This was nice," she said.

"It was." Except apprehension had tied up his stomach, preventing him from eating much. Come to think of it, she'd picked at her meal, too. Maybe he shouldn't have bothered spending so much time trying to choose the perfect food to present.

Her face was half-averted as she looked out over the lake. "This is such a nice night. I'm surprised more people aren't here."

There was that word again: *nice*. Good sign? Bad sign?

"It's Sunday, and a school night."

"Don't remind me," she said with humor.

"Just think how soon school lets out."

"I caught an older teacher in the break room crossing the day off on the calendar she carries in her purse. There were these rows of black x's. She asked that I not tell anyone."

"The day will come."

"I hope not. Except—" She was quiet for a minute. "I have to admit I've been dreading the end of school. Because it meant…" She didn't seem to want to finish.

He stopped and she did the same, facing him. "Leaving us."

Anna gave a funny little nod.

"Please don't do that." His begging hadn't gone so well last time, but the words jumped out, anyway. His desperate gaze found the willow tree and he started walking again, faster, towing her along.

"Where are we going? Oh," she said softly, when he brushed aside a curtain of willow leaves and led her into the shady haven within.

He took her other hand, too, so that they faced each other with not more than a foot separating them. Just as quietly, he said, "I love you, Anna. I was maybe a little afraid of putting how I felt into words, because I knew how conflicted you were about me. Then when I said something—"

"I freaked out."

A lump in his throat, Nate nodded. "If you need more time to come to trust me, I can give you that. But… I want you to marry me. Not because of the kids," he finished hoarsely. "Because I love you."

ANNA WAS TORN between happiness and tears. The happiness was so glorious she wanted to throw herself into his arms. But her vision had become wavery, and her sinuses stung, too.

His grip tightened. "Anna? You're crying."

"I don't even know why." She freed a hand to swipe at her cheeks. Then she gave up and stepped forward to lay her cheek on the soft fabric covering a reassuringly solid chest. When his arms closed around her, she indulged in tears that didn't last long but left her feeling shaky.

His hand made soothing circles on her back.

"I love you," she whispered. "So much. It's just been hard. I think… I was afraid I was looking for security, when I'd promised myself I'd take care of us."

The hand slid up to knead her nape. "It's occurred to me that your childhood must have been scary. In a way, you were abandoned over and over."

Even when she'd grieved for her mother and then her grandfather, she had felt angry, too, because they'd left her. For the first time, she understood how much that history contributed to her sense of betrayal when Kyle not only died but left her without the security he'd promised her.

She nodded against Nate's shoulder. "I wanted the perfect family, and I thought I had it, but it turned out to be a lie. And…I think I blamed myself. It wasn't you I didn't trust, it was me. My judgment. So when I caught myself feeling happy with you and the kids, I couldn't let myself believe in it."

His fingers slid into her hair and he tipped her head back. As always, emotion had darkened his eyes. "Can you believe in us?"

Her smile wobbled, but it was real. "It's taken a while, but yes. What you said, about not being like Kyle, made me think. This probably sounds weird, but I really like your determination to help Sonja."

A nerve jumped in his cheek. "I'd like to leave you with your illusions, but here's the thing. I let her down. I think, now, I shouldn't have married her. I didn't feel anything for her like I do for you. But once we did get married and had a child…I didn't put much effort into sustaining our relationship. I feel guilty about that."

"Did she?"

For a moment, his eyes appeared unfocused. "I've never thought about it like that. It didn't take her long to become unhappy. If she hadn't been pregnant…" He shook himself. "Maybe it doesn't matter anymore. I just don't want you imagining I'm perfect. I'm a long way from that. There'll be times I forget promises, break commitments. Get caught up in work and take you for granted."

A slow smile curved her lips. This one wasn't wobbly at all. "I don't have to let you."

His grin made her pulse leap. "No, you don't." He lifted his free hand to cup her cheek, bent his head to touch his forehead to hers. "Just…don't give up on me." He would hate knowing how shaky he sounded. "I need you, Anna."

"I need you, too."

The kiss started out so tender her eyes burned again. *Need* was a small word for this tangle of emotions that made her tremble. She thought his hands shook, too, though she couldn't be sure. The tenderness lasted, becoming part of the passion that blinded and deafened her. All she knew was Nate—his voracious kisses, his tongue sliding along hers, the edge of his teeth, the tight grip on her hip as he lifted and fit her against him.

She wanted to relearn everything about his body, but with her arms locked around his neck, she didn't have a hand free to slip beneath his shirt and wouldn't have wanted to separate from him enough to do that, anyway. His hips rocked, as if he couldn't help himself any more than she could.

His groan sounded more like a growl in his chest before it reached his throat. He tore his mouth from hers and strung small, biting kisses along her jaw and down her throat. Panting, she let her head fall back to expose her throat.

Nate whispered, "I want you, but we can't—"

Her mind struggled to understand why they couldn't. Their one night together had opened a door and left her hungry for his touch. Now—

A breeze off the lake made the curtain of willow leaves shiver. Park, she remembered. They weren't entirely hidden from anyone walking past. And someone would.

She forced her eyes open. "We could go home…"

They stared at each other.

"Look up the movies, see when they let out."

"Let's hurry." She grabbed his hand.

Laughing, they ran to the car.

BY THE TIME Nate and Anna heard the car outside, they were dressed again and—more or less—presentable. Evaluating Anna, he decided that her lips were noticeably swollen and her cheeks reddened from the evening stubble he should have shaved off. That was okay. Considering what he and she had just been doing, she was sure to blush the minute his parents looked at her.

He'd forgotten the ring in his pocket until after they'd made love the first time. He'd leaned over the edge of the bed, picked up the small velvet box and rolled to face Anna.

Her astonished gaze had gone to the box.

He'd had to ask, "You will marry me?"

Her head bobbed, and for the third time this evening, her eyes became damp. Her smile glowed, though, when she saw the ring. Nate had assured her they could exchange it, but she loved the diamond flanked by small sapphires the color of her eyes. That it fit perfectly—there was the scary word—had to be a good omen, right?

She was starting the coffee and he was getting mugs out of the cupboard when the front door opened.

The kids swarmed then. "The movie was *so* good," Jenna said, and started detailing the plot.

Josh talked over his sister, telling them about the movie *he*'d seen. Molly stood beside him, her gaze going from Nate's face to Anna's and back. Meanwhile, Nate was very conscious of his parents, his dad straddling a bar stool, his mother behind the kids.

"You look different," Molly said suddenly, and so loudly the other two stopped talking.

Nate's mother smiled at him. He hadn't seen delight like that on her face in a long time.

Anna faced her kids. Not even having to think about it, Nate took her right hand. Smiling, she held out her left. "Nate asked me to marry him."

All three kids stared at the ring, then at their respective parents.

"You said yes?" Josh was the first to speak up.

Her smile tremulous, she nodded.

He jumped, punched the air with his fist and yelled, "Awesome!"

"Does that mean we get to stay here?" Jenna asked.

"We do. Except, once we're married, we won't live in the apartment anymore. You'll both have bedrooms here in the house."

Nate hooked an arm around Josh's neck and pulled him into a tight embrace. He let go and then reached for Molly, bending to murmur in her ear, "Okay?"

Her head bobbed. "I wished so hard for Anna to stay."

"You get a brother and sister, too."

Josh and she made faces at each other, but Nate could tell neither of them meant them. Jenna bounced around the kitchen like a Ping-Pong ball, and he saw his father grinning.

"Lucky we came back from Arizona, since you needed a hand."

Instead of arguing, Nate said, "You're right. Thanks, Dad." He smiled at his mother. "I love you both."

"And me, too," Molly said, with a hint of worry.

He leaned over to whisper in her ear, "Always."

"So." His mother again. "When's the wedding going to be?"

Jenna tugged at Anna's hand. "Can I be a flower girl? Can I be *in* the wedding?"

"Of course you can." Anna released his hand to kneel and hug her daughter, then reach out to Molly. "And you, too."

Josh recoiled. "I don't have to be, do I?"

Anna laughed. "No, you don't. But you need to sit right up at the front—"

"With your new grandparents," Nate's mother said firmly.

Nate and Anna looked at each other. "Let's make it tomorrow," he said at the exact same moment she said, "Soon."

For an instant, it was as if they were alone. This time, she said, "July. School will be out, and…"

The anniversary of Kyle's death would have come and gone. Nate felt a punch of gratitude at the reminder of her former husband. He suspected it would never go away. Kyle Grainger had died saving Molly's life.

Nate could wait.

"July," he agreed, and saw the relief and happiness on Anna's face at the same time movement and laughter and chatter in the crowded kitchen resumed. His family.

* * * * *

If you loved IN A HEARTBEAT,
don't miss these other recent books
from Janice Kay Johnson:

BACK AGAINST THE WALL
THE HERO'S REDEMPTION
A HOMETOWN BOY
A MOTHER'S CLAIM

Available now from
Harlequin Superromance!

We hope you enjoyed this story from
Harlequin® Superromance.

Harlequin® Superromance is coming to an end soon,
but heartfelt tales of family, friendship, community
and love are around the corner with
Harlequin® Special Edition
and **Harlequin® Heartwarming**!

Romance is for life, and these stories show that
every chapter in a relationship has its challenges
and delights and that love can be
renewed with each turn of the page!

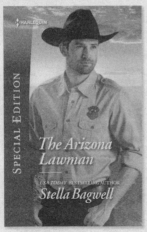

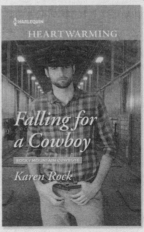

Look for six new
romances every month!

Look for four new
romances every month!

Get 2 Free Books,
Plus 2 Free Gifts -
just for trying the *Reader Service!*

STRS17R2

Get 2 Free Books,
Plus 2 Free Gifts —
just for trying the Reader Service!

READERSERVICE.COM

Manage your account online!

- Review your order history
- Manage your payments
- Update your address

We've designed the Reader Service website just for you.

Enjoy all the features!

- Discover new series available to you, and read excerpts from any series.
- Respond to mailings and special monthly offers.
- Browse the Bonus Bucks catalog and online-only exculsives.
- Share your feedback.

Visit us at:

ReaderService.com

RS16R